THE GOLDEN CITY

— THE —
GOLDEN CITY

A Story of Love, Loss and
Triumph Spanning Generations

ANTHONY COLBURN

LUMINARE PRESS

WWW.LUMINAREPRESS.COM

Luminare Press
442 Charnelton St.
Eugene, OR 97401
www.luminarepress.com

LCCN: 2021907805
ISBN: 978-1-64388-616-9

*This book is dedicated to my loving wife Claire
and my children, Avery and Elise.*

*Thank you for putting up with my many hours of working
on the computer when you wanted to use it.*

*Also, my mother, Alice (Curtis) Colburn who always
encouraged me to follow my interests, wherever they led.*

*And to my grandmother, Julia (Donohue) Curtis.
I loved the sound of her name and often romanticized
about what it must have been like for her living in such
a vibrant city like San Francisco during this time.*

*Finally, to San Francisco, the city of many
childhood memories; my favorite city.*

TABLE OF CONTENTS

INTRODUCTION

This novel is a work of historical fiction. Many of the places and people in the book are real and many of the main events described did happen, but some are fictional to support the story line. I chose to write about this time and place because of the rich history and the numerous historical figures found in the West around the turn of the twentieth century. Extensive research has been done to make the book as true to historic accounts as possible. Many of the place names, situations, people and events mentioned in Nevada and around Lake Tahoe are true. Gold bullion was transported by rail from the Assay Office in Carson City, Nevada to San Francisco in the early 1900's. The Streets, buildings, businesses, historic figures and events in San Francisco are also as accurate as I could make them but the main characters in the book are fictional. The descriptions of the earthquakes of 1906 and 1989 are also true based on eye witness accounts and news stories. My grandmother, Julia (Donohue) Curtis was born in San Francisco and was thirteen years old at the time of the earthquake of 1906. Later, she was a cashier at the 1915 Panama Pacific International Exposition, described in the book. Other people mentioned throughout the book are fictional but are representative of those who lived in the time and places mentioned in the book.

I invite you to do your own research as you read, to find out more about this very interesting place and time in history.

Ferryboat on San Francisco Bay

Chapter 1

LOOKING BACK

⸺ ⬥ ⸺

I t was one of those chilled-down-to-your-bones foggy nights along the water front of San Francisco. Early in the afternoon, a low misty curtain slowly pushed past the golden gate of the bay, silently creeping along into Cow Hollow and Harbor View. The ghostly shroud hugged the edges of the city until it finally spread out to Goat Island, heading east toward the Oakland Long Wharf. All quarters were suspended in this thick gray soup that deadened and rounded off the sounds of wagons rattling along the cobble stone and brick streets. A fetid concoction of this mist and the smoke of low-quality coal burning in the iron foundries settled upon the sleeping city.

The Union Ferry Station clock slipped past the quarter hour

THE GOLDEN CITY 3

with a swish of its enormous minute hand. Not much was going on inside the terminal. The manager of the docks sat nursing a cup of lukewarm coffee, as he glanced at his watch and put it up to his ear. One worker peered into the mist, straining to discern where the fog and water actually met. The lights did little more than cast a feeble reflection onto the softly undulating water as it lapped up against the barnacle encrusted pilings of the wharf.

"There it is!" the worker proclaimed, as if he had finally found a missing sock. At the same instant, the low loud moan of the ferry's horn cut through the soupy mist accompanied by the constant thump-thump-thump of the side paddle wheels heralding its arrival well before the sight of it.

The 'Golden City', a veteran ferry boat, gone forty-five minutes now from Oakland, eased up to the slip at pier number two with its huge single piston steam engine now thrown into reverse to slow its progress. The smoke of the coal-fired engine collided, then slowly blended with the fog to cast an eerie, almost sinister pall as it overtook the dock. As the craft met the slip, it rubbed against the pilings like a foot straining to fit into too-tight boots.

A young man, athletic and nimble, jumped to the dock and strained to wrap a large rope around the cleat. This was a 'double ender'; There was no bow or stern on this boat as it loaded and unloaded people, cargo, wagons and the occasional motor car from both ends, depending on whether it was coming or going from the San Francisco or Oakland piers.

"Cinch 'er up tight, Mister Donohue!" came a voice from the other side of the boat. Mathew hopped over a coil of ropes and then helped to lower the steel apron, allowing the wagons and one motor car to pass with only slight jostling in the transition from water to land.

Matthew's nimble handling of the ropes at the pier revealed his skill. He was a quick study and with his previous experience on ferry boats, he had easily gotten comfortable with the workings of this side-paddle wheel steamer. This was just one of scores of ferries

Anthony Colburn

that crossed the bay from Oakland and Alameda in the east and Sausalito to the north headed for the landmark clock tower at the center of the Ferry Building.

The 'Golden City' was a handsome 210 ft. craft. She was built at the Risdon Iron Works in San Francisco in 1879 but was still in her prime. The steel reinforced oak hull held the boilers and coal bunker as well as the massive single piston engine. A 'walking beam,' mounted on top of the craft transferred the motion of the enormous piston protruding through the main, cabin and hurricane decks to the huge paddle wheels. Passengers could view the workings through windows at each level except the hurricane deck, which was off limits to all but the captain and crew. The accommodations were richly appointed with carved oak and leather seats, accented with brass rails and fittings. It was evident from its appearance and upkeep that the captain and crew were proud of her.

A fancy carriage moved out, carrying a fine-looking lady sporting a red hat with an Ostrich feather. At first the horse found the footing of the apron slippery from the condensation of the fog, but gained its footing again on the wooden wharf. As she passed, the lady glanced at Matthew, and their eyes met for an instant before the carriage dissolved in the fog.

"Someday," Matthew thought out loud, but then he noticed the other workers around him. Someday, he continued, this time to himself, I am going to be able to get Julia a hat like that.

Above on the cabin deck, the last of the passengers filed off, disappearing down the great cavernous iron-arched halls of the Union Ferry Terminal and down to the brick-lined beginnings of Market Street. After the trickle of passengers and a lone wagon boarded for the trip back to Oakland, Matthew had some time with his thoughts. He leaned on one of the ferry's lifeboat supports as it made its way back across the fog shrouded bay. Without having to strain to see his watch in the darkness, he checked the time, sliding a lever which chimed the hour and minutes; 9:23. They had just one more out and back run to make this cold, dank night before he would have a much-needed day off. The run to Oakland was uneventful but chilling, with the dense fog permeating even Matthew's heavy jacket.

"One more time…" he muttered, as they started the return trip toward the imposing clock tower, guardian of the entrance to the heart of San Francisco.

Matthew gazed ahead into the fog when suddenly, he thought he saw a flash and the concussion of gunfire, but there was no sound. He inexplicably dropped to his knees, a heavy sadness and confusion washing over him. Matthew looked at his hands and touching his thumbs to fingers, felt a warm thick liquid slowly covering them, but they were clean. He whispered, "What is happening?" in a strange way, more like he was asking himself a question than from fear or anxiety.

He stood up and tried to make out the faint forms around him; one, laying on the deck and others partially hidden under a wagon. He thought he heard shouting and more gunfire, then curiously, he imagined a golden glow, but just as abruptly as it appeared, it all vaporized and he was left alone in the middle of the deck. Matthew thought he heard something over the port side so he peered over the railing, squinting into the gloomy bay. Finally, he turned around and leaned on a crate, contemplating what had just transpired.

He pulled out his pocket watch once more, running just two minutes fast. He kept it that way since the huge clock at the ferry building in San Francisco read the same time and this is what all ferries used to stay on schedule. Matthew mused on the possibility of it being an intentional calculation by the bosses to keep the ferries ahead of schedule. After all, you have less complaints when the ferries are early than when they are late. He turned the watch over, revealing the scene of a ferryboat etched on the gleaming gold background; not the one he was working on, but a smaller, sleeker one plying smooth water with snowcapped mountains in the background. Matthew sat down on a sack of grain and recalled the day he got the watch, and the path his short life had taken.

"Whach'ya thinkin'?" Came a voice approaching from the stairs.

"I'm thinking, what are we doing here when we could be home in a warm bed," replied Matthew in a monotone. But his mind was even further away than that. He was thinking of his family, and Julia, and the gift…

Chapter 2

THE EAST SIDE

———◦◦◦———

Matthew Donohue was born February 20, 1885 in Carson City, Nevada to Robert and Dorothy Donohue. Robert was an Irish immigrant who worked his way west on the railroad. Hearing of the great riches to be had, he went to seek his fortune in the silver mines of Virginia City. He was trapped in two separate cave-ins and after the second one, which killed three of his friends, vowed never to step inside a mine again. He then found work with the Virginia and Truckee Railroad in Carson City for a time, but was killed when a car unexpectedly uncoupled and crushed him. Matthew was just eight when his father died and this drew him even closer to his mother.

Dorothy Donohue was a housekeeper who worked for James Fair, a United States Senator, representing Nevada. He was an Irish immigrant like Dorothy, and she felt she would have a stable job with a fellow expatriate, but he proved to be a prolific womanizer and she had to leave after one too many inappropriate advances.

Matthew had grown up on the east side of the Sierra Nevadas, a rugged mountain range which divides Nevada and California. The summers there are short and the winters, unforgiving, but he had a good childhood with lots of adventures. His mother's new boss, Mr. Bliss, had sons who were older than Matthew, and they took him under their wing after his father's death. Matthew was always willing to try anything, so the brothers took him along on their adventures as much as he could follow.

Anthony Colburn

One mid-summer day, the boys hiked up Clear Creek Canyon, following their father's flume used to help transport lumber from the Tahoe basin to Carson City. These timbers were destined to shore up the tunnels of the mines of the Comstock Lode around Virginia City.

"Bet you can't!" young Lee Bliss said. He was Duane Leroy Bliss, Jr., but everyone used his shortened middle name to keep confusion with his father to a minimum. "Bet you can't jump the next one!"

His older brother, Walter wasn't taking the bait. "You know that every third board is a big one, and the second one just went by!" The flume was a 'V' shaped ribbon of timbers supported like a rickety train trestle winding seventeen miles from Spooner Summit all the way down to the sorting stacks near Carson City. With a steady stream of water to lubricate them, huge rough-cut timbers would slide down to the valley. The last timber that passed by was going faster than any of them could run. It also had a strange wet, but burnt smell to it. Just then a huge board, as thick as young Matthew's body flew by. The odd sight of water sloshing over the side of the flume and smoke wafting into the cool morning air gave a hint of the incredible forces at work- gravity and friction, mitigated by the lubricating and cooling qualities of the water.

"Wow!" cried little Matthew. Suddenly, a feeling washed over him like a wave on the beach. In his mind he could see a large timber breaking over the flume, collapsing it as water gushed out and down the canyon.

"OK," said Walter, "the next one's mine."

Matthew shook his head, regaining his senses just as the vibrations reached a crescendo. Around the bend, sloshing and smoking, came a board that wasn't too big. Walt got a running start and leapt over the flume just in time to clear the tail end of the timber. He lunged, head first in midair and rolled to a stop against a bush.

"You cheated!"

"You didn't say what part!" Walt replied, dusting himself off.

After a short argument, Lee said, "OK, your turn!" Both brothers turned, looking at Matthew, but suddenly a loud crack came from somewhere down the ravine. The boys ran to a vantage point just in time to see wooden supports splintering and water gushing out of the flume.

That evening after Matthew's mother's duties were done for the day, they sat down to dinner.

"Did you hear?" she said, "a part of the flume collapsed today and sent a small flood down the canyon for a time. I overheard Mr. Bliss saying it might take a week to fix."

"Have you ever seen things in your head?" little Matthew suddenly inquired, looking straight into her eyes.

"What do you mean?"

"I mean have you ever seen things from far, far away or things that didn't happen but would come true later?"

"Sometimes…" she leaned over and gently took his hand. "Have you seen something?"

"Well, today I saw something up along the flume."

"Don't tell me you had something to do with it!"

"No, I was with Lee and Walt!" She was visibly relieved. "But I saw the flume break. I saw it happen in my head first and then it really did!"

Mrs. Donohue gazed into Matthew's eyes and smiled slightly, resting her hand lightly on his cheek.

Matthew's eyes started to well up as he confided, "I saw something else before, that was like that too."

She nodded slowly, wiping away his tears. "Was it about your father? You knew it was going to happen, didn't you?"

Matthew shivered and pulled back, startled by her reply. "I never told anyone before! How did you know?"

"By the look on your face. I suspected it then, now I think I need to tell you about a special gift you have."

Matthew was filled with confusion and curiosity. She took him over by the stove and sat with him on a rug.

"Mathew," she began, in a soothing voice, "you're a special person. I gave you a gift at your baptism. Remember going to the Handley's baby baptism last month?"

"Sure…" He could not fathom why a baptism would have anything to do with what he saw.

"Well, when the priest pours the holy water over the child's head, it blesses him in God's eyes. The same thing happened to you when you were baptized, but I had the priest do something more."

His brow was furrowed with confusion and suspicion now.

"At your baptism," she went on, "you had some special water to drink, too."

"Why would a baby need to drink anything 'cept milk?"

"Well, you're right, but this water had special powers."

Matthew was trying hard to think what this might mean, but before he could ask another question she continued.

"Far up in the hills above the village of Mullinavat, where your father and I were born, you know, in County Kilkenny, there's an ancient Holy Well called the Three Friars. It lies along a stone row with an arched opening protecting a pure spring. Just below the well is a Hazelnut tree with many clooties tied to its branches."

Matthew thought about the strip of cloth wrapped around the crucifix over his bed.

"People around the village said it had been there as long as anyone could remember. Old Mrs. Shea said her grandmother heard that it's been there for centuries. There are many ancient Holy Wells in Ireland, you know. Well, there is said to be a trout swimming in those waters that holds special powers from the Otherworld." Matthew made a skeptical frown.

"The story goes that over two hundred years ago, three friars stopped and splashed the waters on their faces and drank from that well and when they did, they saw their own deaths days before Cromwell's men caught up to them. They were given the vision but wouldn't believe it and that is why they died. It is said that from that time on, those who were worthy and drank from this spring and poured the holy water over their eyes, would be given the never-ending gift of seeing."

"I can see just fine!"

A slight smile spread across his mother's face. "Not that way. Seeing things from far away or seeing things that haven't happened yet, like when you saw the flume fall down, or when you saw your father..." Both of them contemplated when less than a year ago, Matthew's father and Mrs. Donohue's husband met his untimely end. Matthew saw it in a vision, but refused to believe it and felt guilty because he thought he should have been able to prevent it.

After a few moments, Mrs. Donohue regained her composure. "At your baptism, Father Carroll held a vial of holy water from that very spring. I brought it with me all the way across the ocean and this country, waiting for the right time..."

Matthew's eyes opened wider in wonderment, hanging now on his mother's every word. "...and at your baptism, he poured the water from that holy well into your mouth and eyes! Now you have the gift and it will be with you always"

Matthew was speechless. All sorts of questions were stirring in his young head but he could not articulate them. He thought back into the dark recesses of his memory, trying to differentiate between fantasy and reality and if he had foreseen any other events. It became too confusing so he had to be content for the time being to just let it be and get himself to bed. But still, after his mother had kissed him on the forehead and tucked him in, he lay there juggling his memories, trying to recall...

Matthew grew stronger and more confident with each passing year and the knowledge of his newly realized gift gave his life a sense of inevitability.

Ferryboat 'Tahoe' with Train on Pier

Chapter 3

TAHOE

꧁꧂

D uane L. Bliss Sr. had come West in search of success in the gold fields, but instead turned to the riches of its vast stands of timber. His wealth extended into the Comstock Lode of Nevada by virtue of the lumber needed to shore up the ever deeper and more dangerous mines. He also kept a home in San Francisco, designed by his then architect son, Walter.

As the Bliss boys matured, they started to help out more with their Father's business interests. They took Matthew along most of the time and gave him small jobs to do. One of Matthew's greatest adventures was when the brothers took him to Lake Tahoe to watch the reassembly of the grand steamboat 'Tahoe'. It had been constructed in San Francisco, then dismantled and transported by train through Reno to Carson City where it was then carried to the lake by teams of mules.

They rode horses, following the same trail the 18-mule team wagon used to pull the boat's massive boiler up to Spooner Summit then down the other side next to the switch-backing narrow-gauge railroad built to haul the logs up from the lake. Matthew spent the next three weeks at Glenbrook, watching the reconstruction of the vessel and helping put a gleaming white coat of paint on the hull of the sparkling new ship. On his time off, Matthew would wander along the shore of the lake, skipping stones, fishing and daydreaming about what it would be like to pilot such a fine vessel.

Near the end of June, 1896, the senior Mr. Bliss and all his extended family personally oversaw the launching of the vessel. It was Mr. Bliss' grandson, Will who got to do the honors of christening the ship (with a little help) with champagne broken over the bow. It was a grand sight, seeing the 'Tahoe' slip smoothly into her new home with people cheering and flags waving from bow to stern. With the gleaming new vessel safely tied up at the dock, a celebratory luncheon was held on board. There was plenty of room in the dining area and Matthew felt like part of the family.

That night after dinner at Glenbrook, Mr. Bliss offered Matthew his first real paying job. "Mister Donohue, how would you like to keep the 'Tahoe' ship-shape? You have been such a help to my sons that I think you are ready for more responsibility."

"Yes, yes sir!" Matthew blurted out, but after a moment of thought he said, "But what can I do?"

"Well," Mr. Bliss replied, glancing at a gold watch that hung from a chain in his vest pocket, "this is a beautiful vessel, but it will require constant care. Can you pay attention to details?"

"Yes sir!" He saluted like the sailors he saw in pictures of the battle ship 'Oregon' as it took its maiden voyage in San Francisco Bay. The next morning, before leaving for Carson City, Mr. Bliss took Matthew down to the dock where the 'Tahoe' sat, barely moving and perfectly reflected in its namesake lake.

"Here is what you need to do…" Mr. Bliss took the next half hour going over how to clean and care for all the brass fittings and fine woodwork, as well as cleaning the marble lavatories. "You will be an apprentice purser. Do whatever is asked of you and do it well! Work hard and you will someday be a deck hand or even engineer!"

"Gosh! You can count on me!" Mr. Bliss' approving grin showed under his long mustache.

Before long, the 'Tahoe' was underway with Matthew Donohue, 'apprentice purser', taking a daily route to different communities dotting the shore of the impossibly clear turquoise lake. At first, his work was seasonal, ending in September or early October so he could make it back to Carson City before the big snows came. His mother was proud of him but she missed having him close.

Matthew would spend many a winter evening around the fireplace telling her all the wonderful things he had experienced. He also proudly showed off the photographs of the lake and snow-capped peaks he took with his Kodak box camera she had given Matthew on his birthday.

By the time the 'Tahoe' was launched in 1896, the timber business had already begun to falter. There was not much timber left to be cut around the lake but Mr. Bliss had already shifted his interests in a new direction; the emerging tourist industry. He thought about Yosemite National Park to the south, which was proving to be increasingly popular. It was spectacular, but so was Lake Tahoe. Yosemite visitors had only the most basic of accommodations after a long, rough stagecoach ride.

Tahoe was only 15 miles from the Central Pacific Railroad lines at Truckee and Bliss already had most of the necessary locomotives, rolling stock and track from his logging operations on the other side of the lake. After a meeting with his sons, Bliss put his plan into action to make Lake Tahoe a true tourist destination of the first order.

In the summer of 1898, Matthew was taken off the 'Tahoe' for a season and made a deck hand on the barges that ferried virtually the entire narrow gauge logging railroad across the lake to Tahoe City, at the outlet to the lake. The plan was to build the narrow-gauge railroad along the Truckee River to the Central Pacific's line. This would open up the lake to tourists with a minimum of inconvenience.

At Tahoe City, Bliss was building a luxurious, yet rustic inn he would call the 'Tahoe Tavern'. Passengers would board the train to the lake then disembark, only having to take a few steps across a long pier to the waiting ferryboat 'Tahoe' to commence their tour of the lake. They would then ultimately, return to stay at the inn.

Matthew's duties on the barge included securing the ropes on the cargo and tying up the barge at the dock and running errands for the captain. On one such run from Glenbrook, Matthew overheard the other hands, talking about San Francisco and all the excitement there.

"That Barbary Coast is the best and the worst you could ever hope for!" one old-timer said with a touch of nostalgia. "I had me a woman what was no more up to my belly but what a bosom! Couldn't get closer than a foot from her sweet lips before I ran into 'em! What a night! My buddy, he had a fine lady too. She was one of them high kickin' dancers from gay Paree." But suddenly, his brow wrinkled in seriousness. "Never saw hide nor hair of him again. Some said he was Shanghaied! I woke up next mornin' in the alley with a damn cat licking my face! Guess I should count myself lucky though. All I lost was my money but oh, what a night!" The other men chuckled, only half-heartedly believing him. Matthew frowned. It didn't seem like that would be much fun to him. Besides, he had seen photograph post cards showing all the impressive buildings and rich people strolling in the parks. He was sure San Francisco was more like that. Besides, Matthew had had one of his visions about the city. He had seen beautiful colored buildings adorned with jewels, but could that really be true?

One day, as the barge eased up to the dock, Matthew noticed a boy about his age standing by a long stick with numbers on it gazing down the new railroad bed. "You get paid for standing there?" said Matthew with a tinge of sarcasm. The boy didn't respond but stayed very still, balancing the pole on the head of a spike. "I wish I had a job like that!" A man with a tripod whistled in the distance and at once the boy began to walk away.

"What I do," the boy responded, "takes skill and patience." Matthew smiled. He liked someone who was sure of himself.

One day, after Matthew had come back to Carson City for the winter season, his mother announced that she had been asked to be the head housekeeper at the Tahoe Tavern, which was almost completed. "You could stay with me," she said, "if you would like." Matthew was very excited to hear this because that would mean he could stay longer at the lake, possibly through the winters too. This was also a big promotion for his mother and he was very proud. "Mr. Bliss has been good to us," she told Matthew, "so we need to do our very best by him."

The next season came early for Matthew and his mother. That winter had been a mild one and the narrow-gauge railroad from Truckee to the lake finally opened up in late May. There was much work to do to prepare the Inn for its first guests, though. Along with the workers, the first train carried all the necessary bedding and kitchen utensils. Matthew helped his mother and the other housekeepers make up the beds and bring the last bits of furniture to the rooms. Amazingly, everything was ready for the first guests on June 1st, 1902, and it would continue to greet its well-heeled clientele for sixty-one more summers. All the employees stood proudly at attention that morning as Mr. Bliss inspected the new inn.

After touring the kitchens and looking in every single room of the inn, he turned to the staff and a large smile broke through his thick moustache. "Fantastic, just fantastic! We are ready to serve our customers!"

Matthew spent many an evening after work at the cavernous common room of the Tahoe Tavern bringing in wood for the large fireplace and listening to locals entertain the guests with music and stories from the area. Matthew's father had taught him fiddle tunes from Ireland and he was an accomplished player, sometimes joining in the merriment.

One evening, Ernest Pomin, captain of the 'Tahoe', came by to greet some of his passengers.

One tall man smoking a pipe inquired, "tell us of that island in Emerald Bay. One of your hands said it's inhabited by a ghost!"

The captain put one foot up on the rock hearth as his face took on a serious demeanor. "Oh yes. You must mean Captain Dick Barter."

"Captain?" one of the ladies said incredulously.

"That's right. Old Captain Dick was in her majesty's service they say- Came to these parts just before the end of that war over on the West Coast of the African Continent. He was a solitary sort, most of the time- Took to being an undertaker…" One older lady grimaced. "He liked his fun, though, and would row his boat out from the bay to test the liquor across the lake at some of the local watering holes. On one such trip, after taking his libations at the Tahoe House, he headed for home, but half way across the lake, his boat capsized." Matthew was fully engrossed in the telling as Captain Pomin's face was lit from the side by the slowly dying fire. "The captain managed to right the boat and continue home, but he was half frozen. Old Dick crawled into his bed and lay there for several days, unconscious." There was an air of uneasiness mixed with anticipation in the great hall as a few embers escaped the fire and rose to a height above the captain's head before they died. "When the captain finally awoke, he found that several of his toes were frozen and had become gangrenous. There was no one to help for miles around, so the only thing he could do was to… CHOP THEM OFF!" Everyone let out a collective gasp at the words that seemed to echo off the massive log beams of the inn.

"Did he die?" Matthew blurted out without thinking.

"No, but from that time on whenever he had visitors, he would tell his story and bring out a box to display his handiwork, saying, 'Them's my toes!'"

"That's disgusting!" a man complained and he and his wife took their leave.

"Well, I enjoyed the tale!" another man exclaimed.

"But it's all true! And that's not all!" continued the captain. "After his brush with death, old Captain Barter fashioned himself a burial chamber between two solid granite boulders on the island in Emerald Bay. Above it, he built a wooden chapel with a single cross. Whoever he came across from that time on, he would stop and tell them to make sure that when he died, he was to be buried in that tomb and to say a prayer for him in the chapel."

"Can anyone visit the tomb?" Matthew inquired, sensing the possibility of an adventure.

"Well, you can, but you won't find anyone buried there! See, the irony of it all is that one foul winter night in '73, Captain Dick was out on the lake again. There must have been a terrible storm because his boat was found smashed to pieces on the rocks at Rubicon Point...but his body was never recovered!" This time, the now larger crowd of guests and tavern workers alike let out a collective sigh. "And sometimes," he continued, almost in a whisper, "on cold winter nights, if you are about the waters of Emerald Bay, and there comes a mist born of the frigid air rising above it, you might see old Captain Dick's ghost, searching the island for his final resting place!" Captain Pomin looked blankly ahead as spontaneous applause erupted from the group. He took a short bow and began to mingle with the guests.

"There's nothing like a good ghost story!" Matthew told his mother as they walked around the front of the tavern, but her only response was a frown. It was a chilly night and as he looked out toward the lake, a slight mist was beginning to rise from the surface.

Chapter 4

ANDY

<hr>

One day after work on the 'Tahoe', Matthew went down to the outlet of the lake. The Truckee River begins its journey from this largest American alpine lake down to the desert beyond Reno, ending in Pyramid Lake. He was fishing for trout known by their red throat, which grow to a large size in the lake, then move into the river to spawn. In a large pool, Matthew could see three good-sized fish slowly moving in the crystal-clear water. He let line out of his reel and was about to cast when he saw a small splash. At first, he thought it was a fish rising to a fly on the surface, but then there came another, this time a succession of splashes that ran across the pool...a skipping stone. The fish scattered. Matthew was not amused, thinking it was a boy who liked to hang around him at the Inn. But as he squinted against the late afternoon sun almost lost amongst the granite peaks, he could see it was a larger boy about his age with a shock of golden hair.

"Hey there!" came the voice.

"Hey! You scared the fish!"

"Sorry," came the reply. "I was thinking about catching some for dinner."

"Yea, me too... Hey, haven't I seen you around?"

"Probably, if you paid any attention to the new railroad we built from Truckee."

"Well, I helped bring half the track and the locomotive over here from Glenbrook. I guess you could say I was paying attention to it!"

With that, Matthew met Andy, the surveyor's helper, for the second time. Andy was staying nearby in a boarding house for railroad workers. They became quick friends and nearly every day after work the two would walk along the lake or fish or swim, comparing their past and plotting a future of excitement and adventure.

One evening after work, as they sat on some boulders under the branches of a huge Ponderosa Pine overlooking the lake, Matthew proposed a hike to survey the area.

"What a 'ya say we hike over there to Ward Peak?" He motioned to the west where granite peaks stood in silhouette against the setting sun, still holding pockets of snow. Matthew had always wanted to head down to the Sacramento Valley and maybe to San Francisco and he heard you could even see the great Pacific Ocean from there.

"That's a long hike!" exclaimed Andy, but he was game. "We had better get an early start, though. We'd best go through Page Meadows and up the ridge. The creek bottom's full of brush."

With that, they turned back to the Tahoe Tavern and the cottage Matthew and his mother shared. Matthew and Andy searched through the pantry for canned meat and crackers that his mother kept for just such outings. Matthew produced a map, worn from being folded and unfolded, showing creeks and ridges and major peaks. They poured over the topographic features, recounting their earlier experiences.

Finally, Andy exclaimed, "Got to go now! Don't want to miss dinner! I'll save a couple of apples." Jogging along the beach, he headed towards town and the boarding house.

Early the next morning, a thin layer of frost blanketed the landscape. Matthew was not surprised- it was getting on toward the end of summer and at this elevation, fall would be just around the corner. Matthew met Andy on the bridge over the Truckee as the water slipped smoothly away from the lake. The sun was just hitting the ridges to the west and the two friends stepped lively out toward Page Meadows. Along the way, the two talked about what lay past the mountains.

"What'a ya want to go to 'Frisco for anyway?" asked Andy. "I hear there's robbers and all sorts of low life characters ready to take your money...or worse!"

"You've been reading too many of those dime novels again, haven't you?"

"Well, they wouldn't print it if it weren't the truth, would they?"

"I figure the only truth is what I know and see with my own eyes," Matthew replied confidently. They climbed on, slowed now by having to circumnavigate granite outcroppings, weathered by countless winters.

By noon, they were on the ridge headed north toward Ward Peak. Looking back, they could see the huge ancient bowl that held the azure waters of Lake Tahoe. Years of logging had stripped the landscape, revealing the bare skeleton of the geology that formed the basin. At the north end of the lake though, tall stands of ponderosa pine and fir were still left, hinting at the breathtaking grandeur the entire area must have had decades earlier.

Andy let out a long whistle. "Wha'cha think this was like before ol' man Bliss got to it?"

"I don't think anyone else would have done better by it!" Matthew replied. "At least he left a good stand down by Tahoe City." The pair spied the beginnings of the Truckee River and the small community hugging the shores of the lake. "An' anyway, he gave a lot 'a people work an' a fair shake, too."

Matthew suddenly felt a tinge of nostalgia, as if he were looking at this chapter of his life for the last time.

Finally, they reached the peak, really only a high point along the ridge stretching north and south. From this point, Matthew gazed to the north where he could just make out Lassen's Peak and beyond in the haze, the perpetually snowcapped Mt. Shasta.

Matthew felt a little light headed, so he sat down and took a drink of water from his canteen. As he tilted his head back, he noticed the billowing clouds transforming into thick grey plumes of ash blotting out the sun. Both Shasta and Lassen had volcanic origins and Matthew couldn't help but think that they might be the source of his vision.

When he turned as Andy sat down beside him, Matthew shuttered to see blood oozing from his chest. "Andy! Andy! Stay with me!" Matthew's hands were wet with blood.

"Hey! Look! I'm fine! What's going on? Here. Take another drink. Being this far up must be getting to you."

In a few seconds, everything seemed normal.

"Andy, promise me you won't get in any gun fights."

"O.K. I doubt I could hit a tree at five paces anyway! What's this all about?"

"I don't know. I just don't like to see anyone settling scores with guns."

"Don't worry 'bout me! I'm a lover, not a fighter!"

Matthew calmed down a little more now, remembering that he had absolutely no control over his so called 'gift' from that holy well back in Ireland. There seemed to be no rhyme or reason to these visions. He could never tell how far into the future they might reach, or if they would even come true or not. One thing he was coming to understand though, his visions almost always ended tragically.

After a few minutes rest, Matthew looked to the east, past the ridges bounding the lake. On that side, the great basin lay baking in an empty expanse for countless miles. It was sliced by the ribbon of rails laid down by Matthew's father and thousands of others like him years before. To the south, more nameless peaks poking out like the backbone of some prehistoric giant beast as far as the eye could see. Finally, Matthew fixed his eyes to the west. Granite outcroppings and small alpine tarns gave way to the blue-green forested foothills that were eventually lost in a brownish haze.

"Damned fires!" Matthew whispered under his breath.

The view of the Sacramento Valley and on towards San Francisco was hopelessly obscured by a sea of smoke. A forest fire emanating from somewhere to the north in the range of mountains between the expansive valley and the ocean was the culprit. The

Golden Gate of the Pacific Ocean would remain concealed from Matthew's sight for a little longer.

Washoe Indian and Baskets, Lake Tahoe

Chapter 5

FRIENDS

⟨∘⟩

Many well to do visitors of the Tahoe Tavern fancied themselves as enlightened, yet their actions sometimes proved otherwise. It seemed most tourists consumed too much food and drink, depositing their trash where ever they pleased. Matthew noticed more and more paper wrappers and especially bottles of every description, floating in the lake and littering the shores. Squirrels and sea gulls were starting to become a nuisance around the docks and inn. Also, guests were taking pieces of bark and cones off trees for souvenirs. Some of the pines around the inn had to be wrapped with burlap to discourage the practice. These were some of the tradeoffs for opening up the area to the fledgling tourist industry. Indian artifacts were also becoming ever more sought after by tourists as ancient ruins in Arizona territory had been discovered. More Easterners out to see the 'real' West realized how the Indian's life would soon vanish under the increasing weight of westward expansion, so interest in handiwork like baskets rose.

It was because of this, that Matthew came to know an Indian of the Washoe tribe called 'Dat So La Lee' by white men. Matthew knew her by her Indian name; 'Debuda', young willow, which suited her demeanor very well. Debuda would sit at the door of her small cottage across from the Truckee River as it left the lake and started its journey to the desert. She liked to sit in the morning sun and hum while her deft, strong fingers coaxed and cajoled willow twigs into beautiful shapes with intricate designs. Matthew met Debuda one late summer afternoon after his work on the 'Tahoe'. She was watching the people walk by, some staring disapprovingly and making rude comments about her personal hygiene. Matthew witnessed the exchange and approached her.

"I wouldn't pay them no mind." he said seeing that she was visibly uneasy.

"I not dirty! This is new dress!" Her Black hair was neatly cut straight across her wide forehead, the rest covered by a blue flower print scarf. Dat So La Lee's long-sleeved dress flowed down around three exquisitely crafted baskets at her feet. An Indian pattern belt defined her waist, revealing her ample size. He sat with her into the early evening talking to her about the old days before the white men and her secret to making the beautiful baskets.

"No secret," she said quietly. "Just take time to make it right way," and patience too. Some of Dat So La Lee's baskets took over a year to complete. Mathew was fascinated by her single-mindedness of purpose and would spend what time he could helping her.

One day, she announced, "I need to make one big basket this season. Need more fern to color with." Matthew was more than eager to help out so she described the fern to him. He set out to find some he recalled seeing, when he and Andy had climbed the ridge to the west. After searching for about an hour, Matthew came upon a patch of ferns shaded by tall mature pines.

He pulled up enough plants to fill a bag and when he returned, Dat So La Lee mustered a diminutive smile and said, "This will do for basket this year. Now I make you one."

Matthew was thankful but didn't really expect her to go through with it because she had many orders for her work that her benefactor, Mr. Cohn had requested. Summer flew by and autumn arrived early so Dat So La Lee moved back to Carson City for the winter. Matthew would sometimes pass by the display of baskets for sale at the tavern, marveling at the craftsmanship and wondering how she was doing.

The next season when Matthew went down to welcome Dat So La Lee back to the lake, she said, "Here, you take this." She held out a basket about eight inches tall, starting with a slender base that gracefully filled out and came back again to an opening about the same size as the base.

The designs on the basket reminded Matthew of grizzly bear claw marks but she countered, "Too many claws. What I see is trees on hills." Whatever the interpretation, the work was exquisite. Matthew was speechless so Dat So La Lee said, "From one friend to other." She never asked for anything and gave so much that Matthew was at a loss as to what he could do for her. After an awkward moment she said again, "One friend to other. You come by and we talk." So, Matthew continued to spend many hours that summer, listening to the old stories and playing bone dice into the night and they became true friends.

Chapter 6

RECOMMENDATIONS

Matthew's duties on the 'Tahoe' were varied and evolved as he gained experience. At first, he kept all the brass polished and there was a lot of it. Later, he helped stoke the two boilers with wood. It was hot, sweaty work, but Matthew could almost imagine that he was in the belly of a living beast. At one point, he even helped deliver the mail sacks and boxes for the people who lived around the lake as this was the only reliable transportation. Finally, Matthew was even temporary engineer on a few runs between the tavern and Glenbrook. He would take orders from the captain and regulate the amount of steam needed to maintain the correct pressure. Matthew would sometimes daydream as the graceful craft cut through the water, mirroring the fluffy clouds. Nothing could be better than to become captain of the 'Tahoe'.

Mr. Bliss was a fair and generous man and one fine August day, as the 'Tahoe' was under way to Tallac Resort, he strolled up the starboard deck, coming along side Matthew, then just seventeen. They both peered over the railing into the glassy waters of the lake. Matthew's hands started to stick to the brass railing from anticipation until finally, Mr. Bliss spoke.

"You know Mister Donohue, I have noted your good work on this vessel." Matthew was a little startled that he remembered his name. "You got this job because I think highly of your mother..."

What, Matthew thought, was coming next? What had he done wrong?

Mr. Bliss continued, "but you have shown yourself to be an exemplary hand. Did you realize I offer health insurance to my trusted employees?" He stopped to clear his throat and take in the sweet warm summer air. "For just fifty cents a month, you will be taken care of in any eventuality of sickness or accident, while in my employ."

Matthew was taken aback. He replied somewhat timidly, "Thank you sir, for thinking of me, but I don't expect I would need that kind of help for many years to come."

Bliss chuckled. "Just like me when I was your age. But you know, I was laid up for nearly six months with a fever when I was about your age, and if not for a friend nursing me back to health, I might well have died."

Matthew looked him in the eyes. "Just the same, sir, I might do better with the money."

Mr. Bliss' countenance turned serious. "Alright. If you won't take my help, you will have to accept a token at the end of your employment as thanks for a job well done. I know you are thinking of bigger and better things. Your mother told me as much last spring when I was inspecting the inn." They both returned their gaze to the azure lake for a few moments and presently, Mr. Bliss turned and shook Matthew's hand. "Good luck, then." and strolled toward the bow. He would never see Mr. Bliss again.

Matthew was determined to seek his destiny in San Francisco, a city where he heard, and believed, anything was possible.

A few months later, after Matthew's last day of work, he found a five-dollar gold coin and a pocket watch on his bed engraved with the image of a grand ferryboat in a placid lake and the word 'Tahoe' arching over the mountains like a cloud. With it was a note:

Mr. Donohue,

Keep your wits about you and look for the possibilities in every situation. Take these gifts- this coin to invest wisely and this watch to stay on time. When you get to San Francisco, look for a Mr. James Mulloy, at the ferry building. Give him this other note. He should be able to help you get started.

Sincerely, D.L. Bliss, October 23, 1905.

Matthew picked up another piece of paper that was written on Mr. Bliss' company stationary. It read:

Mr. Mulloy,

You should be getting this letter from Mr. Matthew Donohue. I have known him since he was a child and he has for the last few years, been deck hand and assistant engineer on my personal ferry vessel, 'Tahoe'. He is a dependable, hard worker and I am pleased to be able to call him my friend.

I would very much like you to find a place for him working for the Southern Pacific Ferries. He is more than capable and will prove an asset to the line.

Yours very truly,
Dwane L. Bliss, Sr.
President, Lake Tahoe Railway and
Transportation Company

Leaving Lake Tahoe was more difficult than Matthew had imagined. Besides leaving his mother, there was the 'Tahoe' and Dat So La Lee and the lake itself. His friend, Andy had already left to try his luck in the gold fields south of Carson City.

Matthew strolled toward the lake through the dry Ponderosa pine needles on the front lawn of the 'Tavern', recalling their aroma on hot summer days. But there was a nip in the air, signaling winter would soon have its grip on the mountains. He walked along the bank, hopping from one granite boulder to another, recounting his time with Andy, fishing and swimming in the frigid waters. How good it had felt to have his breath taken away as he dove deep into the crystal waters, then to lie on a boulder letting the sun bake him. Sometimes the lake lay placid, mirroring the clouds but sometimes its wrath crashed upon the shores like a wild animal. Matthew recalled once while onboard the 'Tahoe' how he was almost swept overboard by a sudden squall line that plunged down from Blackwood Canyon.

But it was time. Matthew was packed and his mother had made a lunch for him to take on the train.

"Don't forget your basket," she said as she put the exquisitely woven art in his pack sack. After a long hug, he looked back one more time and they exchanged waves. "And don't forget to write! Remember, you have a gift!" She stood at the entrance to the cottage and pulled her shawl over her shoulders as a tear rolled down her cheek.

He was on the threshold of manhood, excited to experience whatever life had to offer and at the same time apprehensive about the strange new world he was about to plunge into. He checked the time with his gold watch and boarded the narrow-gauge train for the short ride to Truckee with a five-dollar gold piece and ticket in hand, compliments of Mr. Bliss himself.

After he made the connection in Truckee, Matthew leaned back to take in all the scenery. It was slow going as the train started its tortuous switching back and forth up Coldstream Canyon to gain elevation. As the train cleared a tunnel, it came around a long ridge, high above on the south side of Donner Lake. All the stories of suffering and unspeakable horror that befell the Donner party so many years ago seemed like fiction to Matthew when he looked down on the dark blue jewel of a lake. He was reminded though, of many more small tragedies he had heard of throughout his days in the high Sierras. A man who was not prepared in these mountains was not long for this world, especially in winter.

The blackness of the railroad tunnels set Matthew's mind to wander to his childhood adventures and what would be in store for him in this next chapter. He tried to push his 'gift of seeing' the future to the back of his mind, knowing he had no control over what he saw or what the outcomes would be.

As the train finally burst out of the summit tunnel and began to descend the west side of the Sierras, he noticed a warmth in the air and the changing vegetation. Firs gave way to stands of pine and finally oaks and brush. The streams were crystal clear and very low, dribbling from one pool to another, but they would soon enough be covered by drifts of snow.

There were numerous stops at nearly every mining town with strange names like Cisco, Shady Run, Cape Horn and Clipper Gap. Finally, at Sacramento, as the train made a refueling stop, Matthew was able to stretch his legs.

Mr. Bliss had arranged for Matthew to stay the night at the Western Hotel on Second Street. This must be a fancy place, he thought, because there was a coach waiting to take customers to the hotel, only five blocks away.

As he rode, Matthew saw people of all description. Ladies with parasols shared the same board walk with grubby miners. Chinamen scurried along with bags of laundry, their long, braided queues swinging back and forth. He heard the familiar whistle of a ferryboat as it approached the levee, protecting the capital from its namesake river. Matthew was impressed with the hustle and bustle of the city. It was quite a bit larger than Nevada's capital, Carson City, with streets stretching east towards the foothills as far as he could see.

After Matthew got settled at the hotel, there was still much of the day left so he decided to visit the state capitol building. As he turned onto 'M" street, he could see the impressive edifice some eight blocks away. In front of the capitol, Matthew noticed tall, strange trees with no branches but many long, tough looking spear-like leaves, all erupting from the top. Matthew felt like he was entering the home of the gods as he passed under imposing white columns. The larger-than-life sculptures of robed figures peering down at him from the parapet were bathed in the late afternoon sunlight. Inside, the black and white checkerboard marble floor that made up the rotunda reminded him of the Bliss' kitchen floor in Carson City. In the middle, sat a most impressive statue that Matthew could only make out as a boy and a man on one knee offering a ball to a queen. He wondered what importance this statue had and why California would memorialize a queen. Matthew directed his gaze up to the curved ceiling, elaborately decorated with gold molding. Near the top, the sunlight pierced the round windows, giving a glow to the entire rotunda as well-dressed men and women walked purposefully between offices on either side.

Stretching out behind the building was a garden of trees and flowers. Most of the trees, Matthew suspected, were not native as he had never seen anything like them. His suspicions were confirmed when he saw at the base of each tree, a marker with the name and country of origin for each specimen. He could only imagine what a country like Siam would look like based on the flora, but its 'Golden Shower Tree' seemed appropriate for California.

That night, Matthew took a stroll along the board walkway back toward the train depot. There were hotels, bars and restaurants and much more activity at this late hour than he had ever seen back home. Gas lights illuminated ladies and gentlemen, reluctantly sharing the walkway with gamblers and their cohorts roaming from bar to bar.

Early the next morning after a good breakfast, Matthew slung his bags over his back and walked along the levy toward the depot. There was a river boat docked with workers rolling large barrels up a ramp and onto the deck. One of the workers was so dark Matthew could at first only make out his eyes and mouth. He had only heard of the Negro race and was amazed at his working pace, always hearing how lazy and unmotivated they were. Matthew was fascinated by his ebony skin, glistening in the cool morning air. He thought how it was best to experience things for himself and take criticisms with a grain of salt before he passed judgment on others.

A locomotive's whistle prompted Matthew to pick up his pace as it took on water and oil before departing. People were moving in all directions meeting relatives or standing in line to buy tickets. Porters were carrying luggage and other workers were loading and unloading crates and boxes of all sizes. A minute later, the train's whistle gave two short blasts and the conductor bellowed, "All aboard!" Matthew hopped on just before the train lurched forward. For a split second the locomotive's wheels spun, loosing traction but then held and the train was on its way once more. Now on the flats, the train moved much quicker than Matthew had ever experienced. In fact, this was the fastest Matthew had ever gone in his life, except maybe in a horse race he once had with one of the Bliss boys. At Benicia, the train slowed to a crawl. It had already crossed the Sacramento River once but they were now at a much wider part, the beginnings of the bay.

The conductor walked through the car shouting, "Carquinez Strait crossing! We will be transferring to the ferry in a few minutes."

The train inched its way down to water level along one of four tracks. Waiting for Matthew's train was a huge ferry boat fitted with tracks that reached from one end of the vessel to the other.

"Wow! That's a big boat!" He exclaimed without thinking.

"You said it!" replied a man in the seat across from him. "That's the largest train ferry in the world!"

The 'Solano' was almost two times the length of the 'Tahoe' and as he peered out the window, Matthew could see the vessel was nothing more than two huge engines and four smokestacks with four sets of tracks set on a massive hull.

A short jerk signaled that the train had been divided in half with Matthew's end slowly reversing its direction. The locomotive and the front half of the train slowly progressed onto the ferry while Matthew's half was shuttled to the adjacent set of tracks by a smaller steam engine.

"This is amazing!" thought Matthew out loud.

The man across the aisle smiled, knowingly. "This ferry can hold the whole train! Wait 'till you see this," as he pointed over his shoulder.

Another locomotive with a line of box cars inched up beside his train. Through the couplers, Matthew could also see more cars being pushed onto the fourth set of tracks. Matthew started to count to himself- That's ten passenger cars plus two, four, six, eight…twelve box cars on those tracks and let's see, looks like the same on the last tracks…That's thirty-four cars, two locomotives and two helper engines!

Matthew was still recovering from the contemplation of such a load when the Solano's whistle blew and the huge paddle wheels started to churn up the muddy waters. The crossing was smooth and surprisingly quick though Matthew soon realized there was a considerable current going out toward San Francisco Bay. Matthew was impressed with the maneuvering and docking of the behemoth and in short order, the train was on solid ground once more and moving away from the slip.

Ferryboats Leaving Oakland 'Mole'

Chapter 7

THE BAY AND THE FERRIES

It was mid-morning when Matthew departed the passenger train at the Oakland 'Mole' and saw the end of the Southern Pacific ferryboat, 'Bay City'.

"So, this is a double-ender." He half whispered.

He had made the short crossing of the Carquinez Strait up at Benicia in the huge ferry 'Solano', but the train was moved right onto the boat and no one was allowed to get out of their railroad car. But here, he stepped right out onto the dock and immediately felt the swell of another ferry's wake. The 'Bay City' was a fine vessel with an upper deck for passengers and the lower for freight wagons and more passengers. As he made his way amid-ship, he saw first-hand the huge single cylinder steam engine. The workings were all enclosed in windows that revealed the long piston rod transferring power up to a rocker arm out of sight on the top of the boat and finally back to another rod, turning the great side paddle wheels. All the moving parts were gleaming with a thin film of oil.

Matthew found a seat on the upper deck so he could get a better view of his final destination. There were gentlemen with bowlers and ladies carrying parasols but most were more plainly clothed working-class people chatting or reading the morning paper. Ahead and on his right as the ferryboat got underway was an island. Matthew sensed that the boat was headed much too close to its south side and asked one of the passengers about it.

"That's where the water's deepest," was the reply. Matthew would learn a lot about the depth of the bay soon. Right now, though, he was still working with the knowledge of Lake Tahoe and its thousand-foot depths. He would come to understand that fifteen feet was passable soon enough.

Once past this island, Matthew spotted another small rocky island, much further out in the bay to the north and west.

"That's Alcatraz. The Pelicans like it. Not much more than a rock in the middle of the channel," said the passenger once more.

In the distance, Matthew could make out a long roof line with a large clock tower in the center, gleaming in the morning light. There were perhaps ten or more slots for the ferries to dock, poking out into the bay like fingers of a glove.

"This is it." he said under his breath, a shiver of anticipation went rippling through his body. A low layer of fog began to creep over the hills in the distance. There was a whistle blast and the ferry's huge engine reversed, its paddles turning the water to froth. The vessel slowed to a crawl as Matthew closely observed the deck hands hurrying to make the boat secure with huge lines. He wondered what job he would be asked to do once he started. Matthew needed to find the Southern Pacific office but as he disembarked the ferry, he was pushed along by the crowd commuting to work in the city. They all spilled out onto the second floor, making their way towards the stairs leading to Market St. below, but Matthew paused at a flower vendor for directions.

"Could you direct me to the Southern Pacific office?" he inquired of a short, stout old lady carrying a basket of roses.

"You not know what you want!" she exclaimed, correctly appraising Matthew as a newcomer to the city. "Here. Have a rose." She stuffed a small red rose bud in his jacket button hole and immediately grinned her toothless approval. "Now you ready! You want I should tell you the office for the trains, or ferries?" Her accent was so thick it would have been impossible for Matthew to comprehend had it not been for his experiences working with the laborers building the Tahoe Tavern. She was definitely first-generation Italian. "Twenty-five cents, favore."

"Two bits?!" Matthew protested.

"Alright, for you, a dime."

Satisfied that he had been so savvy, he again pressed, "The ferry office?"

"Take hall. Five doors. A sinistra," the lady motioned to the left. As Matthew confidently strode down the hall, he heard the old lady crying out, "Beautiful rose, beautiful rose! Only five cents!"

The window to the office read: 'Southern Pacific Co. Ferries, Passenger and Freight.' Matthew slowly opened the door and as he approached the front desk, he couldn't help but notice a picture of a grand ferry spewing black smoke and sparks out its stacks with red, white and blue banners and flags draped over the entire length of the craft. Details of men and women waving hats and handkerchiefs populated every deck. Above it was a clock loudly ticking with the hour hand pointing to the Roman numeral, X.

"I am here to see Mr. Mulloy," he said as confidently as he could to a slightly built middle-aged man. He looked at the clock on the wall, then skeptically at Matthew while pulling out his watch as if to confirm the time and then replied tersely,

"Do you have an appointment?"

"Well, yes, sort of. I am Matthew Donohue." That didn't seem to impress the man in the least. "Mr. Duane Bliss told me to see Mr. Mulloy when I got to San Francisco—"

"Well! That's a different story! We'll see what we can do!" he replied with mock importance.

The man knocked on a door with frosted glass marked 'J.L. Mulloy' and didn't wait for a reply. Poking his head in, the man said, "Someone here says he knows Mr. Bliss."

"Well, send him in! Let's see what we have!" He opened the door wider to reveal a short fat man, older but not yet ready to retire, sitting on the corner of a rather plain desk but with many fine paintings of ferries hanging on the walls similar to the one in the outer room. The air had a thin layer of smoke emanating from the man's cigar. He took one long draw and slowly exhaled as Matthew's form cut through the haze.

"Sit down, boy! What can I do for you? Any friend of Bliss' is a friend of mine!" The clerk realized he had been too hasty in his assessment of Matthew and quietly drew the door shut.

"My name is Matthew Donohue—"

Before Matthew could take another breath, the man cut him off. "You mean of the Union Iron Works?"

"Well, I don't know..."

"Go ahead, go ahead." This time, the man was more patient as he rounded his desk and sat down.

"I worked for Mr. Bliss on his ferry boat the 'Tahoe'—"

"Oh, fine vessel, fine vessel! Made right down the bay at the Risdon yards. Did you know it was taken apart and shipped up there and then re...oh, you must know all that!"

"Yes, sir. As I said, Mr. Bliss told me to look you up when I got here."

Matthew handed him the letter. Mr. Mulloy slid his finger across it line by line, developing a slight smile.

"So, you want to work on our ferries?"

"Yes, sir."

"What can you do?"

"Well, on the 'Tahoe' I did almost everything from polishing the brass to engineer for a time."

"Well," he replied with a chuckle, "you might not start at engineer right away, but we always have room for a good deck hand! Are you a member of the union?"

Matthew looked puzzled.

"The ferryman's union. You can't work here without being in the union! Let me get you signed up and then you can see them down the hall."

It turned out that Mr. Mulloy had worked for Mr. Bliss when he first came to America from Ireland. He worked in the saw mill, then in Virginia City before coming to San Francisco. Mr. Mulloy talked for some time about his experiences in Nevada, and it seemed he had taken a similar path to the city as Matthew, only a number of years earlier. When Matthew finally said his goodbye's, he had gotten a short history of San Francisco and a primer on where to go and what to do.

"Good to have you with us!" Mr. Mulloy called out as Matthew left his office.

"Likewise." replied the now more polite clerk as Matthew entered the hallway.

Matthew had to smile, thinking, sometimes it *is* who you know not what you know that gets you noticed.

Down the hall, the Ferryman's Union door was covered on the inside with butcher paper making it impossible to see inside. Matthew debated whether to knock and finally he just went right in. It wasn't like the ferry office, with an outer reception area. It was just one small room with three desks taking up most of the floor space. A burly man sat at one desk near a window with mounds of papers in a basket.

"Did you ever hear of knocking first?"

"Yes, sir! I'm sorry sir." There was an awkward pause.

"And are you going to tell me why you are here?"

"I have just gone to work for the Southern Pacific Ferries and—"

"Say no more! Did they make you pay a sign-up fee?" Before Matthew could answer he shook his head saying, "No, no that's not it. You want an advance!"

"No," said Matthew, finally getting a word in, "I was told I need to sign up with the union before I can start work."

"That's right! Don't want the man to take advantage of you!"

Matthew was wondering which man he was talking about.

"What you need to do is fill out this paperwork an' you'll be set! Meetings are on the last Monday of the month."

As Matthew looked over the papers, he noticed he would have to pay something called 'dues'. "What does this mean?"

"It means that whenever the company tries to take advantage of you, we'll be there to protect you!"

"Says here that I need to pay every month," said Matthew cautiously.

The man was a little miffed. "Well, if you don't want the work, you don't need to join." Matthew acquiesced.

"Don't worry. You'll be glad you signed up. Us workers got to stick together." As Matthew turned to go, the man got up and followed him to the door. "Remember, last Monday of the month!"

With that, Matthew was now an official card-carrying member of the Ferryman's Union of San Francisco. He was to start work in two days which would give him time to find a place to stay and get his bearings.

View of Market Street from Ferry Building

Chapter 8

MARKET STREET

M atthew was first attracted to the wide thoroughfare stretching away from the ferry building to the southwest: Market Street. Ribbons of streetcar tracks shimmering in the late-morning sun, shot straight as an arrow as they vanished in the distance. Flanked on both sides were towering buildings …and people. People were everywhere; people riding in buggies and cable cars and the occasional automobile; people dodging all these just to cross the street or to enter and exit the buildings or just standing on the corners. Where were they all going…and why? Mathew felt like he had been in a backwater all his life and was just about to be swept into the main current.

From his vantage point, before he descended to street level, Matthew took stock of the layout of the streets. Market was the great divider of the city. To the south, streets ran parallel and at right angles to the broad thoroughfare, as one would expect. To the north of Market though, the streets all entered at a diagonal. Actually, it was Market Street that was skewed- heading off to the southwest. As a result, all the streets from the north created odd shaped buildings where they met Market. There were little slivers of real estate where fountains and sculptures separated the streets and triangular shaped buildings filled every inch of larger parcels. Matthew wondered to himself about who might be squeezed into one of those corner rooms.

Everywhere there was activity; cable cars, hacks, carriages and motorcars all jockeying for position as people entered and exited the great terminal. Pedestrians expertly dodged and weaved through the traffic like football players. Similar scenes were being played out all along Market St. as far as Mathew could see.

He watched patrons effortlessly hop on streetcars as they made the turn in front of the terminal. Suddenly, he became aware of the clock tower casting an ominous shadow on the cobble stoned pavement, almost as if it were directing Matthew to his fate. He took the long flight of stairs, emptying out into this new chapter of his life.

Looking out for the next car to come by after it had been turned, he had to run only a few steps to catch up before jumping on. Matthew sat on the hard wooden bench seats facing out, proud of finally entering the mainstream of life.

"Five cents." The operator of the cable car held out his hand. "Five cents!" he repeated, somewhat annoyed. Matthew dug in his pocket and produced a quarter. The man grudgingly gave him two dimes and a piece of paper. With only a few riders on his side, Matthew stretched out his arms along the railings on the back of the seat and looked up as the buildings passed, becoming larger and more ornate as the blocks melted away. On the right, was the Luning building and then on the left, the San Joaquin Valley Railroad building. Then a large fountain on the corner where Battery and Bush meet Market caught his eye. Huge heroic figures strained, working on some sort of mechanical device.

Without giving it another thought, he jumped from the moving car and narrowly missed being hit by a motorcar which was threading its way between two oppositely moving cable cars. At once, Matthew was aware that he had better keep sharp as he wound and dodged his way across the 100-foot-wide street.

The fountain's sculpture was heroic in scale- five muscled workers were actually endeavoring to punch a rivet through a thick piece of steel. The piece was dedicated to Peter Donahue, apparently a very important figure in San Francisco history. Matthew wondered if he was related to these other rich Donahues, but realized their name had the 'a' where his name had an 'o'. It was still possible, though; Many relations in the old country had names that were sometimes spelled slightly differently. Matthew jumped on the next cable car and took a seat.

"Five cents."

Not again! thought Matthew. "I already paid!"

"Where's your ticket?"

Matthew sighed and looked up to the roof of the car. Now he knew what that was for.

"Five cents or get off!" the man rudely announced. The other passengers stared at Matthew. He handed the man a dime and got a nickel back, along with a ticket and a scowl.

An older woman across from Matthew could see he was new to the big city so she leaned over and said, "Keep a hold of that ticket and you can go all over town without paying another cent!"

"Thank you, ma'am."

On the corner where Second and Post meet Market, stood his employer's headquarters, the Southern Pacific building. Opposite it on Post, the Crocker building stood, its upper floors dissolving into the encroaching mist. Then in rapid succession, the monuments to all the important newspaper giants; the Chronicle, Examiner and Call buildings loomed over the wide thoroughfare. Across from that, was the Grand hotel and next to it, one of the jewels of the city's crown, the Palace Hotel.

Matthew again instinctively jumped from the still moving cable car and scurried toward the entrance on New Montgomery Street. He stood before the Palace Hotel as if he were a conquering hero surveying his new realm. San Francisco's newest inhabitant strolled in as if he was born to be there, with all of his worldly possessions slung over his shoulder. He gazed, transfixed at the great open cathedral as he entered the Grand Court lined with its exotic palm trees and fine furniture. It was a mesmerizing experience with pillars and a glass domed ceiling seven stories in the sky, creating a huge indoor courtyard. Walkways gave every floor a view down to the court, with tropical plants and graceful statuary lining the conservatory level. What a place! What a Palace!

He sat down next to a potted plant with huge leaves to better take it all in while across from him, a man in a suit glanced disapprovingly over his paper, puffing on his pipe. Presently, Matthew heard a peculiar sound of objects sharply striking each other. It was the billiards room where well-dressed men stood, some talking and some leisurely eyeing their target, then with a crack, letting balls fly into leather pockets. Beyond it was the bar.

As he made his way toward the entryway, a young man dressed in a type of uniform, not military but somehow more official looking, intercepted him. "Are you a guest here, sir?" came the terse comment.

"No, but I was just admiring—"

"I'm sorry, sir but you must remove yourself immediately or I will be forced to call the authorities."

The erstwhile conquering hero was indignantly shown the way out. Thinking about it, what did he expect? Even the bellboys were decked out in the finest of uniforms worthy of one of Napoleon's lieutenants. He would find out later, that this was the residence of kings and presidents, opera legends and railroad tycoons while visiting the city. This was the place to see and be seen by the finest San Francisco had to offer.

Anthony Colburn

Palace Hotel and Lotta's Fountain

Chapter 9

JULIA

⌾⌾⌾

I t was on a warm autumn day like this that it happened. The old timers called it earthquake weather because the great quakes of '65 and '68 occurred on the same type of day in the same month. Matthew, having just been escorted out of the Palace Hotel, turned back onto Market and gazed across the busy street. A most confusing scent of flowers mixed with horse manure permeated the still air as he walked. Flower vendors were on the sunny north side of the great thoroughfare calling out to the passersby. Women, with parasols in one hand and the other holding handkerchiefs to their noses, scurried by. Paper boys held the Call or the Chronicle high above their heads, crying out the latest scandalous front-page news. Men in their bowlers dodged cable cars, horse drawn carriages and those new motorcars spewing so much smoke as to make one think they were about to catch fire.

A young woman was at an ornate fountain across the street, pausing to take a sip of cool water on this unusually warm day. Matthew spotted her long black hair cascading over her white dress and as she rose, she inexplicably looked directly across the broad busy street into Matthew's eyes. He was startled that she would notice him from such a distance and she was just as surprised too. They looked for what must have been only a few seconds, but it seemed much longer. Finally, her father and mother distracted her gaze as they pulled her away from the fountain and continued back up the street. Matthew quickened his pace on the opposite side of the street, keeping just behind the three, not believing his own actions.

I must not lose sight of her! he thought, as the trio rounded the corner and turned up O'Farrell Street. Matthew could not cross right away because of a fancy carriage that had just pulled away from the curb. As he strained to focus on the other side, all he could make out were flashes of gold paint and black leather and the sleek back of the chestnut gelding. He dodged a motorcar, or rather it dodged him because Matthew kept his gaze straight ahead as he negotiated the wide avenue. A bell brought him back to his senses- it was a cable car that had to slow down to keep from hitting him. The operator swore something he thankfully could not make out in passing, as he ran the rest of the way to the other side.

Just like that, he lost sight of her. Matthew decided they could not have gone far- maybe they had entered one of the many shops along the street. He methodically started looking in every shop on the side of the street he had last seen them. As he peered into the first window, Matthew came face to face with a corset and the startled shopkeeper inside shooed him away. As he continued up the street, out of the corner of his eye Matthew saw it again, the long, black, flowing hair cascading down the white dress, disappearing into a store. Matthew quickly crossed the street to better see the sign above the door- 'Thomas and Co., Musical Instruments for the Orchestra.'

Not wanting to seem suspicious, Matthew waited a few minutes, window-shopping at a haberdashery, eying the different bowlers on display. Finally, he could bear it no longer so he crossed the street and went right in. The first floor of the store was dedicated to mostly pianos and sheet music. He glanced down a row with racks of song titles but he might as well have been looking at the hieroglyphics of Egypt. Music was in Matthew's blood- he remembered his parents dancing to jigs and reels from their native Ireland and learning to play the fiddle, but as he leafed through the pages of scribbles and lines, it only reminded him of his limited education. The second floor was the mezzanine with a broad railing. Band instruments of all description hung and leaned on the walls. A shopper tried his hand at one of the cellos, plucking the heavy wound strings creating beautiful, low vibrations.

Softly, almost on cue, came tentative notes from one of the pianos, complementing the cello and then taking its own turn, like a carriage slowly making its way down a long lonely path in the dark woods, then entering a meadow bathed in moonlight. Matthew moved back up the aisle to see around the lifted top of the piano only to find that glistening black hair again. It was tied up in the back with a ribbon of deep crimson, the rest flowing over the girl's shoulders and breast, framing her pale face and steel-blue eyes; A girl of only fourteen or fifteen but with the countenance of a woman.

He stood like a cigar store Indian statue, moved but unable to move.

After a few moments, without taking her eyes off the keys the girl said, "It's Chopin. A nocturne."

Matthew finally found the faculty to speak and said, "It sounds sad."

The girl looked up and abruptly stopped, holding her hands just above the keys, trembling slightly as she gazed into his green eyes.

"My name is Matthew, Matthew Donohue," he said timidly.

"Welcome to Thomas and Company," she replied, somewhat more confidently. "My name is Julia. Julia Thomas."

Matthew didn't know what else to say. Here he was, struck as if by lightning- burning inside from some invisible flame- burning, yet comforting, as a hearth on a cold winter's evening.

Finally, Matthew exclaimed, "I'm new to the city and I wonder if you know of a good hotel."

"Just up the street is the American Hotel."

Making his way out the doorway, he managed a feeble wave and said, "Thank you again."

That was smart! he scolded himself, you talked yourself right out the door!

As he approached the hotel, he soon realized it would be far beyond his means. At the entrance, an attendant opened the door of a carriage and carried the bags in for a man of obvious means. One block over on Geary, Matthew spotted the Essex Hotel, which seemed to cater to a more frugal clientele. He made his way to the front desk only to find the proprietor demanded payment for the first three months in advance.

After a little more window-shopping, Matthew turned back past the music store. He tried as nonchalantly as he could, to glance in, hoping to spy Julia. She was helping a lady pick out some sheet music when she once again looked up to see Matthew. He bolted, but not before Matthew caught her slight smile.

Chapter 10

SOUTH OF THE SLOT

⸺◦◦◦⸺

As Matthew once again approached Market Street, he surveyed the signs crowding the sides and fronts of almost all the buildings: 'MJB coffee', 'Owl Cigars', 'Stanford Studio' and 'Hale's Department Store'. He made his way back down to the fountain where he had first spied Julia. Matthew hadn't noticed before, but the fountain actually looked more like an ornate cast iron lamp post, decorated with fierce lions guarding different views of the young West- one depicting men prospecting for gold and in another, a majestic ship in full sail. Constant streams of water spewing out of mouths of smaller beasts were caught in semi-circular bowls. In place of one of the views was the inscription: 'Presented to the citizens of San Francisco by Lotta 1875.'

"I know her!" He recalled workers talking about a girl entertaining in the gold mining camps. "Lotta Crabtree. She must have done pretty well for herself."

A well-dressed man walked by, and Matthew inquired about a suitable hotel. The man glanced at him but didn't even break stride.

A boy selling flowers saw the exchange and called out. "Hey! You wan'a find yourself a place?"

"Maybe." Matthew had by now become a little wary of unsolicited advice.

"What you need is to be lookin' south of the slot."

"Where?" He was more annoyed than curious now.

"The slot. The cable car slot, here in the street." The boy pointed to the metal sided gap in the street that produced a low-pitched hum.

"See, to get a place *you* can afford, is gonna' have to be south of the slot." The boy had Matthew rightly sized up as one of a multitude of immigrants that had come to San Francisco with more dreams than money.

"What you need is one a' them room an' board houses what gives you a clean bed *and* a good meal for cheap. Not gonna' get that on this side 'a Market."

Matthew decided to pursue his advice a little further. "So where would you recommend?"

"One a' them I-talian places is best for your money. Them ladies cooks more pasta than you can eat every time!" the boy said with obvious pride in his knowledge, "but most 'a them are way up north over to Saint Pete's. They're mostly all Catholics 'ya know."

"Yeh, I heard." Matthew replied, glancing back up Market.

"Here's what 'ya do; Take a right an' go down Sixth Street 'till you hit Natoma. If 'ya cross Howard you went too far. Head right down Natoma an' look for the sign says, 'The Venetian'. Hey, you need a nice flower to make a good impression! Only ten cents!"

"Five." Matthew coolly replied. As he picked a nice white daisy with a yellow center, he congratulated himself for not making *that* mistake again!

"OK," the boy relented. "An' remember, right on Natoma."

As Matthew crossed the 'slot' in the street, he heard the boy cry out, "Flowers. Get your fresh flowers! Two for a nickel!"

Making his way down Sixth, Matthew quickly realized a fact of life in San Francisco. 'South of the slot' was where you live if you had little means and sometimes little hope. The buildings were far less substantial, many just two-story clapboard houses. There were warehouses and factories and the smell of a stockyard drifting up from somewhere back toward the bay.

When Matthew rounded the corner on Natoma Street, he saw a small blue sign with a curious image of a man in a striped shirt standing at one end of a narrow boat holding a long pole or paddle of some sort. Over it were the words 'Venetian, Rooms to Let.'

Anthony Colburn

Matthew climbed the stairs to the main level of the hotel which was really just a large house with a half basement and two floors above. Once inside, the rich smell of tomato sauce drowned out the stockyard. He rang a small bell, left on a table, when all of a sudden, a cacophony of pots and pans falling led him to the next room. A short, rather rotund older woman still stood on a small stool turned to greet Matthew.

"Hello," he said, as he picked up a pot.

"Si, Signore? You want a room?"

"Si, I mean yes. How much?"

"What's your work?"

"I'm not working now but I will be Monday, at the ferries."

"Ah, the traghetti. OK. How 'bout three dollar a week?"

Matthew eyed the woman for a second and said, "Two dollar...I mean dollars."

"No, no can't take but two dollar-fifty. You pay three when you get work money."

"With dinner?"

"Si. Cena too."

"OK, then. Can I see a room?" The woman, still on the stool motioned for Matthew to take her hand as she eased herself down.

As she waddled down the hall she said, "I am Signora Marinelli, but you call me 'Nonna'"

"I'm Matthew, Matthew Donohue."

"Oh, how do I guess with all that red hair! From Irishland?"

"No," Matthew said patiently, learning from many encounters that red hair always seems to make people think he was from Ireland, "but my parents were."

"Oh, si. Well, here you are."

Signora Marinelli opened the door to his room. It was small and plain, with a bed and a picture of Jesus above it, a chest of drawers, and a chair. The south-facing window was open and through the flimsy curtains, Matthew could see across a fence, the back of another clapboard structure.

"Good sun!" the lady exclaimed. "Warm in winter!"

Matthew could tell though the place was old, it was well cared for. "This will be fine. Let me give you two weeks in advance."

"Grazi. Dinner is at seven. Lucky to be on same floor as kitchen. Bagno down hall, a destra." as she motioned to the right.

Matthew laid his bags at the foot of the bed, suddenly realizing he had spent the last of his money-except for the five-dollar coin Mr. Bliss had given him. He took out his pocket watch, observing the 'Tahoe' plying the waters of its namesake lake, then opened the case to reveal the time- 4:33. Seeing the sights of the city would have to wait 'till tomorrow.

Chapter 11

SAINT MATTHEW

⸺⊶◦◈◦⊷⸺

atthew looked up and down the street. There was a strange low rumble in the distance, coming ever nearer. It became deafening, like thunder, shaking the very foundations of the buildings. Cornices and facades tumbled into the street in front of him. Fire erupted from the middle of the street. There was no way to escape! Matthew bolted upright in his bed, sweat rolling down his brow. He felt his bed shaking and looked out his window through the thin curtains for evidence of the destruction. At that very moment he heard screaming, not those of victims of some disaster but that of children chasing each other down the hallway toward the bathroom, closely followed by Signora Marinelli's scolding Italian voice. Matthew let out the breath he had been saving in a long slow sigh of relief. The view out the window did not divulge the time of day. Colors and buildings faded into a light gray mist.

It must be late, Matthew thought. He quickly dressed scolding himself for wasting his last free day sleeping. He pulled out the 'Tahoe' and opened the cover. 6:17. He gently shook the timepiece and held it to his ear as it continued its steady rhythm.

"Have I slept the entire day away?" Matthew sighed. He stepped out into the hallway just in time to be almost run over by two children about eight or ten years old. Once again, Signora Marinelli shouted, half Italian, half in English. All Matthew could make out was something about being late for breakfast and another fragment about church.

It was Sunday- 6:17 Sunday *morning!* Matthew had the whole day ahead of him! Realizing he wasn't properly dressed to greet his landlady, Matthew quickly shut the door.

Almost immediately, Nonna knocked. "You come to eat, OK?"

"OK." Matthew searched for his socks under the bed. He peeked out the door making sure the coast was clear, then went down to the bathroom to shave. It had been a few days and Matthew's facial hair had grown to the point that you could almost tell it was there. He had to crouch a little or stand on his tiptoes to get an undistorted view of his face owing to the crack that ran diagonally across the old mirror. He started with one side and then the neck area and around to the other side of his face. As he held his razor up under his nose, something stopped him. "That doesn't look too bad," He whispered out loud. The hair was darker than the red mop on his head and it actually made him look somewhat older. He splashed the shaving cream off and looked into the mirror as a slow, satisfied smile spread across his face.

Breakfast was laid out in the middle of a small, long table with the robust smell of coffee permeating the room. The two children were chasing each other around the dining room table but stopped abruptly when Matthew entered.

Signora Marinelli was carrying some type of bread out from the kitchen and said, "Oh, buon giorno! We have pane, bread con marmellata! You meet my little bambinos. Come here Enrico."

The boy came forward with great confidence. "I am Enrico, named for the Great Enrico Caruso!" With that he sang a few words in Italian that sounded good to Matthew so he clapped approvingly.

"And this is Donata, a gift from God." The Signora's voice suddenly became softer. "A gift, when her poor mother..." she quickly made the sign of the cross with her right hand, "...was already gone. Kicked in the head by a horse, but she was ready and they cut Sweet Donata out...a gift." Signora Marinelli was visibly saddened by the retelling. Matthew didn't ask who the mother was, but he thought she might have been the Signora's daughter.

On the table was a pot of coffee and another pot of something hot Matthew could not make out. He poured out the rich brew and before he could ask, Signora pointed to the other pot and said, "Latte. You like with Caffe?"

"OK." Matthew didn't want to appear impolite. She poured a little into his cup and instantly the deep dark coffee blended into chocolate brown swirls.

"Caffe latte!" She grinned, showing one gold tooth and a space where another had been.

"Oh. Right. Coffee with milk." The meal was not what Matthew expected. A type of jam was spread on the hard bread, washed down with the milk-coffee. At the mill worker's dining hall at Lake Tahoe, breakfast was an all-you-can-eat affair with bacon, eggs and pancakes piled high.

"All the others, gone to work. You don't go?" Signora Marinelli asked as she sat down.

"No," Matthew replied, sounding grateful, "today I have free. Monday is my first day."

"Oh, buono! You come to church!"

Matthew was a little stunned. "I don't know—"

"You from Irishland, you Catholic, si?"

He hesitated, "Yes, yes I was baptized—"

"Buono, buono come to church! We go at eight."

Matthew felt like he had just gotten caught up in a dust devil, the kind he remembered would appear in the dirt streets of Carson City on a summer day. He and the Bliss boys would chase them and sometimes find themselves in the middle of one, leaving them all turned around and laughing. That seemed almost a dream now, as much of a dream as the girl he met just yesterday, Julia.

Matthew didn't exactly have church clothes, but he did have a clean white shirt with button-down collars, a new pair of work pants and a dark blue suit-jacket. Signora Marinelli wore a light blue dress with a white shawl and a lacy white hat with small blue flower designs and the children wore their school clothes. The four set out down the street, paralleling Market. Both Enrico and Donata skipped along the street through the grayness of the damp fog with Matthew and Signora following.

"You know," she began, "is not so easy to go to this church, but my church is so far. I need to be closer…"

"Aren't you Catholic?" Matthew was astonished. He quizzed himself, wasn't everyone from Italy a Catholic?

"Oh, si. But this is the Irishland Santo Patrizio Catholic church. My people, Santo Pietro y Paolo, but is so far…" She motioned to the north.

St. Patrick's church was just a short walk down Mission St. to fourth.

On the way, they passed the U.S. Mint. It was an imposing building, with two tall chimneys in the rear and large Greek style columns guarding the front. The early morning sun was finally burning through the fog, illuminating the East-facing front of the edifice in all its grandeur. This was indeed a place that seemed impenetrable.

"Do they really make money here?" Enrico asked as he and Donata made a detour up the steep front stairs.

"I believe so." Matthew said, "and they bring much gold and silver from the mountains to melt into coins."

"Really?!" cried Donata. Matthew dug into his pants pocket and produced a gold coin.

"Who is that lady?" Enrico asked.

"That's Lady Liberty."

"Is she really that young?" Donata inquired.

"No, that is when she… I mean, it… was made right here at the mint, 1901. That means this coin was made five years ago." He flipped the coin over to reveal the denomination.

"Wow! Enrico's eyes widened. Five dollars?!"

"Yep. But that's all I got, till I get my first pay from work." Matthew was glad to have some spending money, but he felt a twinge, remembering Mr. Bliss' letter, but today after church, he was committed to going sightseeing.

Saint Patrick's Church was beautiful, with a slender steeple which, if taken by itself, would be as tall as the church proper. Just below it was a large clock showing just three minutes before eight. Matthew glanced at his watch and noted that it showed 7:54.

"Maidin mhaith. Go raibh Dia le at." A voice from out of Matthew's past seemed to greet him. He nodded, still confused at the familiar yet foreign greeting. Matthew was thrown back to his childhood when his father would gently nudge him awake, greeting him in the same manner before he went off to work. Matthew looked up to see the face of a late middle-aged man with a ruddy complexion. He entered the church hand in hand with his wife who was smiling broadly, followed closely behind by their two teenage girls who giggled shyly as they passed him.

Never before had Matthew stepped into such a building. The first thing he noticed was the quality of the light. He was surrounded by rows of windows high up the walls. Each window glowed with the natural light of the early morning sun and each told a story of the history of Ireland. To the right were images of 'Lir', the god of the seas, and his children who were turned into swans until the time of Saint Patrick. Matthew remembered being told this story by his mother in Carson City and later thought of it when he noticed a flock of swans on Lake Tahoe one late summer day. Then there was 'Connla of the fiery hair'. He glowed in all his stained-glass glory, longing for the fairy maiden, bidding him to go away with her to the land of the ever-living. Matthew mused on the thought of Julia being like the fairy maiden and he, the fiery haired warrior, but he was soon distracted by the giggles and whispers of the girls in the pew to his left.

As he walked down the center aisle with Signora and the two children, she pointed and whispered to Matthew, "Look, there. That is your name saint," In the center stained-glass window of the sanctuary, was the unmistakable image of Saint Patrick, holding the staff he used to help vanquish the snakes of Ireland. Flanking him were the authors of the gospels, Matthew, Mark, Luke and John. He was a little embarrassed to see his name in church.

Only seconds after they found their seats, the mass began. The altar boys, dressed in their long black Cassocks and starched white Surplices led the priest to the front of the altar. He knelt and kissed the altar and began the service, with his back to the congregation.

"In Nominee Patris, et Filii, et Spiritus Sancti." Almost reflexively, Matthew answered, "Amen," with the rest of the congregation.

Throughout the mass, Matthew gazed at the stained glass and soaked in the ambience of the church, bits and pieces of the proceedings coming back to him through the haze of long ago. When time came for communion, Matthew followed along, up to the beautiful golden marble altar railing, forgetting that he had not been to confession in years.

When the mass was finally over, they made their way out into the brilliant sunshine. Ahead, men and women were greeting the priest. Signora Marinelli took the priest's hand and announced,

"Father Walsh, this is Matthew..." She paused, glancing to Matthew with inquiring eyes.

"Donohue."

"Oh, si. Matthew Donohue, from Irish land!" Before he could protest, father Walsh firmly took his hand and said, "Dia duit!" Matthew nodded, afraid to respond. "Monsignor John Walsh. County Wexford. Have you been there?"

"No, I'm afraid not. Much the same weather as here, I suspect," Matthew responded in his best Irish brogue. He didn't know how to defuse the lie, so he just decided to let it be.

"Ay, though a few more people here!" the father returned, as they both chuckled. "Will we see you next Sunday, then?"

"Ay," said Matthew as he turned to accompany Signora and the children down the street.

Chapter 12

THE SIGHTSEER

⸻

This was Matthew's day! He was young and healthy with a five-dollar gold piece in his pocket and the whole city to explore! Signora Marinelli gave him a piece of the morning bread and some cookies and told him to steer clear of the area down by the docks.

"You keep away from that part!" she said in her thick Italian accent. "That Barbary Coast place! No good!"

"What's so bad about it, Nona?" inquired Matthew, wanting to compare the stories he heard on the barge at Lake Tahoe to hers.

"No law! No rules! They do what they want! No one to stop! Girls, drink, gambling. No good!"

That piqued Matthew's interest, but he assured Signora he would not go there and set off toward Market Street. After a sip of water at Lotta's Fountain, Matthew decided that since he was so close, he would go back up O'Farrell St. to just nonchalantly look in the direction of the music store. Maybe by chance he might see Julia again. As he approached on the opposite side of the street, he strained to see through the reflection in the glass of the front windows.

"Are looking for something?" A clear feminine voice came drifting down onto the street from somewhere above.

Matthew looked up toward an open window and squinted from the now late morning sun in his eyes.

"I said, are you looking for someone...I mean something?"

"Why yes, as a matter of fact I was," Matthew was in full control of his wits now and he knew who he was talking to. "I was looking for some sheet music by Show-pan."

"Oh, yes. We do have some on hand. I will be down in a minute to help you."

Matthew slowly crossed the street feeling rather tentative. What have I gotten myself into?! he thought. I don't know the first thing about this girl! He tried the door but it was locked. "How stupid can I be?!" he whispered. It was Sunday and the store was closed. Julia had just happened to be reading by her open bedroom window when she saw Matthew below.

He cupped his hands against the store's window peering under the 'closed' sign. Finally, Julia came down the stairs from the upper story above the music store. It seemed to Matthew that she almost floated as she descended.

As she opened the door, he prepared his excuse. "I am sorry for the inconvenience…but my friend wanted to know where he could find that night music to practice."

"Does he have his own piano?" Julia was suspect but beginning to enjoy this little masquerade.

"Uh, no. He has a fiddle, though."

Julia giggled. *Fiddle?* Well," she continued, "maybe he can transcribe it from the piano."

"I'm not sure he can tell the music notes written down, but he has a really good ear."

"Well, it would be very difficult to learn a piece by ear alone, but if your friend knew the tune, he might be able to pick it out."

"Maybe so!" Matthew was digging himself a pretty deep hole by now but he continued, "if you would play a little bit, maybe I could hum it to him."

"Alright. Which one do you think he would like?"

"That slow, sad one. Kind of lonely but pretty."

"Oh, you mean the one I was playing when you were here last?" Julia slid onto the bench in front of one of the pianos. "Chopin never gave titles to his music. It's just known as 'Nocturne, in B flat minor, Opus nine, number one'."

"Right…That one."

"Chopin wrote this for Marie Pleyel, the wife of a well-known piano maker. In fact, she was a very fine pianist herself… and very beautiful. They became close friends. Chopin was given a Pleyel piano to perform on for free to help promote them. Only a few years after her marriage though, her husband divorced Marie because he said she had been unfaithful." Julia glanced up at Matthew as he ruminated about what she had just said.

"Do you think—"

"No one knows. But it does make you wonder…This is a Pleyel." Julia rested her slender fingers lightly on the keys and Matthew closed his eyes as the music started. He could see a carriage drifting through the fog, and then the impression of a small waterfall and a meadow began to take over his thoughts, but there was a tragic feeling to the notes, like something was about to come to fruition, yet falling just short. The music grew in intensity only to recede once again back to the original melody.

"Julia! What are you doing?" Matthew's beautiful picture was shattered by the words of a man still wearing his Sunday suit, as he made his way down the stairs from the upper level.

"I'm sorry, father…I was just—"

"We're closed on Sundays, sir. Perhaps you can come back another day."

"Yes. Sorry sir. I was just asking about directions to the Orpheum Theatre." Matthew had heard that operas were staged there and it sounded like people of distinction would go there.

"Yes. Well, you won't find anyone there until two p.m."

"No sir. Sorry to disturb your Sunday, sir." As Matthew made his way to the door, he turned to Julia. "That's a pretty long name for a tune. Does it have a *regular* name?"

"I don't think so, just dedicated to Marie."

"Well, I'll tell my friend to come around to listen to it again…I mean I'll tell him *again* to come around to listen to it. Thank you. Goodbye."

As Julia closed the door, she continued to watch Matthew until her father summoned her back up the stairs.

The visit had been a total fiasco, but it didn't seem to bother Matthew. He had spent more time with Julia today than he had ever before and the scent of her still lingered in his nostrils. This day could not be any better!

A street car passing by going up O'Farrell, caught Matthew's attention and he wondered if it would take him to the park so he decided to inquire at a candy shop a few doors up the street. Everything looked so inviting and as he looked over the high-priced confections, a lady waited on him.

"May I help you?" she asked mater-of-factly, suspecting he was not really looking to buy.

"Well, actually I was wondering how I might go out to the park on the cable cars. Will this line take me there?"

The shop keeper's expression remained unchanged. "Best go back to Market and take the McAllister car. You do know where Market is."

"Yes. Thank you. Didn't mean to bother." With that, Matthew turned back down O'Farrell and back past the music store. He glanced in at the piano bench where Julia had been sitting just a few minutes before and looking up, he noticed the curtains of Julia's room, fluttering slightly in the fresh breeze.

As Matthew walked slowly toward Market, his thoughts drifted back to Julia and the music and Chopin, and Marie…The raspy horn of an automobile bouncing across the cable car 'slot' prodded him back to the present. Matthew looked down Market Street past the fountain, toward the Ferry building.

All at once, a strange feeling swept over him like that which you get when you are sure you have done something before but you know you hadn't. He could just make out the clock tower and it already looked very familiar, but all the buildings along Market leading up to it seemed somehow different, taller, newer and sleeker. Lotta's fountain was still the same but everything around it made it look very old and out of place. Trees lined both sides of the street with broad, red brick walkways for the people. There was the noise of hundreds of strange sleek automobiles. Matthew closed his eyes a second and let out his breath. When he looked again, everything was back to normal. Is this in my future? He asked himself. Matthew had come to terms with his 'gift', accepting it for what it was and not trying to alter or preempt it.

He had followed the candy shop keeper's suggestion and walked the five blocks down Market toward McAllister Street. Along the way on the south side of Market, was an imposing building with a sign over an arched entry that read: 'California Academy of Sciences.' What sort of school can that be? thought Matthew, as he watched a small group of very somber older men enter.

At McAllister, Matthew caught a cable car that had just made the turn off Market. As he settled in on one of the seats facing out, he heard a rough voice call over the merry clang of the car's bell, "That'll be five cents!"

Matthew reached deep in his pocket and suddenly realized his only money was the five-dollar gold coin. He slowly pulled it out of his pocket, eyeing the profile of the heroic woman's head then the eagle, with outstretched wings.

"I only have this," Matthew sheepishly replied as he handed over the investment to his future.

The operator of the cable car frowned as he searched through his pouch for change. "You just off the boat?" the gruff man inquired.

Matthew took off his cap and scratched his head reflexively trying to think of just what he meant.

When the man got sight of Matthew's hair he softened. "You from Ireland, then?" The man's voice revealed the unmistakable accent that gives away all people who grew up in their mother country and did not immigrate until after they had matured.

Matthew twisted his hat with both hands and looking into his eyes replied, "Yes, sir."

Suddenly the man's demeanor softened. He looked on the lad more as a father would look upon his son. "You keep that coin and make a name for yourself now!"

"Yes sir!" Matthew replied with a smile, putting on his Irish brogue.

The man returned the smile and the coin as Matthew turned back just in time to see a monumental building with a huge dome and tall columns with spires.

"What's that?" he asked his new friend.

"Why that's city hall. I'd be thinkin' they'd never finish, but it gave us good work!"

"You built that?"

"I helped. Did stone cutting for the foundations, 'till my back let out."

Matthew was impressed. He hoped one day he would be part of some really big project that would stand so majestically.

"It's sure to be here long after we are all dead and gone!" the cable car operator pronounced proudly.

The trip out to Golden Gate Park was full of new sights and sounds. The government buildings along McAllister Street gave way to businesses and finally homes with delicately painted finials and railings. They proceeded at a brisk pace always slightly up hill. Presently, Matthew saw coming into view, white columns and what looked like tiny white stone huts perched on a small hill.

"What are those?" Matthew inquired.

"Why, that's where everyone would like to end up, I'd wager... If you have the luck! That there is the Calvary Cemetery. You got to be Catholic now, aren't you?"

Matthew quickly thought about the morning just past.

"I was at mass just this morning at St. Patrick's!"

"Good then! Use that gold piece wisely and we'll see you there!"

As the car moved by the cemetery, Matthew could see there were monuments of all sizes and shapes, looking like the owners were all competing for the living's attention. As the tracks made a jog down to Fulton Street, the operator of the car spoke again. "The Masons have that space." Matthew knew of the mistrust Catholics had for the Masons and wondered if they really were trying to destroy the Church. He remained silent in thought.

Soon, they were moving along the tree lined north edge of Golden Gate Park. Ladies and gentlemen in their Sunday best were strolling into the park at Second Avenue.

"Are we close to the Conservatory?" he asked the man.

"Ay. Just there." as he pointed to the glass dome of the Conservatory of Flowers peeking out from among the trees lining the park.

Matthew had seen a post card of it at the Tahoe Tavern, left by a tourist on the table around the great fireplace. This is one of the places he promised his mother he would visit. He knew it would gladden her heart to know that he was getting to see some of the finer things San Francisco had to offer. He had planned to find a post card to send back to her as soon as he could and one of the Conservatory would be perfect.

Matthew hopped off the cable car while it was still moving and waved.

"Remember, use that coin wisely!"

"I will!" he shouted back as the cable car rocked back and forth down the street. "I didn't catch your name!" but the car was already too far away.

So, here he was at the famous Golden Gate Park, wrestled from the sand dunes just three decades earlier. The flora of the park was new to Matthew, having lived all of his life up until this time in the alpine environs of the Lake Tahoe basin and the high desert fringes of Nevada. As he walked, Matthew recognized some trees as pine but of a different species than he was used to. There were other trees, tall and straight with bluish-gray bark that seemed to be in a perpetual state of shedding. Its leathery leaves were long and slender and as he walked on, he noticed a very pungent and pleasing aroma. Matthew crushed a leaf in his fingers and found it to be the source of the smell. Also, there were strange small cone shaped pods, emitting the same scent.

This would make my room smell nice, he thought as he stuffed a sample of the pods and leaves in his coat pocket.

Approaching the Conservatory, Matthew realized he had been coming at it from an angle and as he turned a corner, protected by an exotic looking palm tree, he realized the building was much larger than he had imagined. The Conservatory of Flowers was a long Victorian style structure with a central domed area that served as the entrance. Reaching out on both sides were wings over one hundred feet in length. It sat overlooking a sloping lower level, with all manner of impeccably kept flower beds and exotic trees.

This time, Matthew would have to part with his gold coin; it was 10 cents to gain entrance. He balked, remembering Mr. Bliss and what the operator of the cable car had said. The coin was beginning to take on a sort of significance Matthew didn't really understand, but he was determined to keep hold of it, for now anyway.

He strolled down the broad stairs toward a causeway with a pedestrian tunnel under it. Walking under the road, he could hear echoes of what seemed like music coming from somewhere in the distance. As he turned toward the sound, he encountered more strange plants creating a canopy over the path. There were short stubby palm trees and vines with delicate purple clusters of blossoms. At the end of the path, was a grand sunken concourse lined with trees laid out in a grid pattern. By this time, the music had stopped and the crowd was dispersing. A fountain in the center of the concourse sprayed the occasional passerby each time the wind caught it. At the far end, a large band shell with statues in relief of some sort of goddesses, hovered over the stage.

While the band members were putting away their instruments, Matthew again heard music, this time much fainter, yet closer. It was a violin, sounding sweet and slow, reminding him of the music Matthew had heard at the music store.

He walked once again toward the music and found a thin man sitting on a bench playing his instrument with its case open at his feet. Every once in a while, a gentleman or lady would drop a coin in the case.

Matthew stood for some time, listening and eventually the man stopped playing and said, "Well, what do you think?"

"Think?"

"Yes! Do you think I'm good enough?"

"Of course! That was great!" Matthew started clapping.

"No! I mean good enough to warrant a dime or two?"

"Oh! Yes, you're very good, but I'm afraid all I have is this." Matthew produced the five-dollar gold piece.

The man's thin lips formed a grin. "That would do!"

"Right. Sorry to be a bother, but I play the fiddle too, and I—"

"You play the *fiddle*!?"

"Well, yes. You see my father left me this fiddle—"

Once again, the man interrupted. "Could you show me some fiddle tunes? I am a classically trained musician and I play *violin*." The man straightened his shirt collar. "These days I've been a little down on my luck...Whenever I play out here like this though, people want to hear *fiddle* tunes. Do you know any? Could you show me some?"

"Sure!" This one is called 'Red Haired Boy'"

"I wonder where you got that from," said the man with a wry smile.

Matthew put the bow to the strings and realized there wasn't much friction. He reached for the case and the man immediately grabbed his hand.

"That's my dinner money!"

"Sorry! I just need some rosin..."

"So, you do know a thing or two!"

Matthew started in with a lilting tune similar to a sea shanty that had two distinctive parts. As he played, a couple strolled by and paused. The man reached into his pocket and tossed a dime into the case with an approving smile.

"See! They love that music!"

Matthew continued, and before long there were two more couples gathered around the bench. He played another tune with a melodic up and down run.

The couples both contributed coins to the case and Matthew tipped his cap to them at the end of the song.

"That was wonderful! I love how you used those double stops!"

"What?" Matthew knew nothing of music talk but he knew the technique passed down to him by generations of Irish fiddlers.

"No matter. Now show me that first tune again!"

Matthew spent the next hour tutoring the man who was really quite skilled with a violin, but needed to get the feel for fiddle playing. In between, Matthew would play another song and passersby would invariably drop a few coins into the case. He shared his bread and the cookies Signora Marinelli gave him from breakfast and they talked about the city and Matthew's new job and Chopin.

Finally, Matthew said, "I really have to get going...I didn't catch your name. I'm Matt."

"It's Sam. Samuel Epstein. And thank you so much! Where could I find you again?"

"I'm staying all the way across town; south of the slot. Maybe I'll see you here again, then."

"I plan on being around here or the Conservatory most Sundays. That's where the well-heeled gather. Alright then, here!" The man reached into the case and brought up a small handful of coins.

"I really couldn't..."

"Come now! You disserve it! Besides, I'm only giving you a third of what was thrown in!"

"Alright. I guess I could use it."

Matthew took the coins without counting them and said his goodbyes, turning back toward the Conservatory, not expecting to see the man again.

As he walked, the jingling of the coins prompted Matthew to take stock of his new found wealth. Two quarter dollars, two dimes and three five cent pieces! What luck, finding a way not to have to use the gold coin with money to spare!

Anthony Colburn

This time he followed the road back to the Conservatory. The thoroughfare was full of buggies and bicycles and on either side, pedestrians of all description.

What a wonderful day! The colors and smells and sights of the city seemed to inspire possibilities in Matthew's every step.

He strolled once again up the steps of the Conservatory of Flowers, flanked by palm trees and flower beds. He stepped confidently up to the front door and reached in his pocket, purposefully revealing his wealth to the attendant. Matthew picked out one of the dimes and gave it to him, tipping his cap as he passed.

Entering the Conservatory of Flowers was like traveling half way around the world with each step. As Matthew entered, he immediately felt, for the first time in his life, the almost oppressive sensation of the humidity in the air. He looked up and in the center of the thirty-foot-high dome was a huge plant looming over him with three-foot-long leaves. He felt a drop of water on his head and turned around only to be bombarded by three more to his face. Each enormous leaf had water on the very tips of their pointed ends, waiting to assail any person under its sphere of influence. At regular intervals, a large electric fan swiveled around to disturb the leaves and another round of this indoor rain fell on the unsuspecting visitor.

There was another somewhat smaller plant with leaves just as long but narrower. It had a long central stem bending over from the weight of what looked like bunches of long greenish-yellow fruit, all turned upward. He wondered if they were edible but didn't ask for fear of seeming backward.

Moving down one of the wings he passed flowers of all description. One had a blossom almost erotic in nature. No doubt, he surmised, to entice bees to their nectar. Another had orange petals that seemed to stack one on top of another until finally reaching a blue zenith.

As he admired them, he overheard one lady exclaim, "What a perfect Bird of Paradise!" Matthew looked up, scanning the glass paneled dome, but didn't see any.

At the end of the wing, he came upon a small pond with huge water plants crowding the surface of the water. Their circular leaves sat flat on the surface concealing the gold fish under them. Most also had a showy purplish or pink flower rising above the surface of the water. What a fantastic world there must be out there to explore! Matthew thought to himself.

A Conservatory attendant walked along the ornate, metal grate pathway. "Four forty-five! The Conservatory will be closing in fifteen minutes!"

Where had the time gone? Matthew had only seen a portion of the Conservatory and it was almost closing time! No matter, he thought. I'll ask Julia out here another Sunday. We can have a picnic and listen to the band and look at the flowers. A vendor outside the doors had just the post card he was looking for; a hand-colored photograph of the Conservatory with ladies and gentlemen strolling along the paths in the foreground. He headed over toward Folsom Street to catch the cable car back to Market, happy to be out of the tropical humidity of the Conservatory and back into the fresh sea breeze. Matthew realized now that to see all San Francisco had to offer would take many days and he knew just the person he wanted to share it with.

At the City Hall, Matthew jumped off his car and walked slowly by the gigantic building, especially admiring the stone work. The pillars reached fifty feet or more with the central dome towering a hundred feet above that. On the very top of the dome was a sphere with a statue maybe ten feet tall. It was hard to tell much about the statue from the angle and the closeness, though. This was really meant to be seen from a distance to get the full effect. He headed down Eighth Street, thinking to himself how relatively easy San Francisco was to get around and with water on three sides, the city would never get much larger. As he headed down Natoma Street, he turned around and spied, between a warehouse and over the roof of a boarding house, the majestic dome of the city hall. Like a mountain... Matthew thought, best seen from a distance. Ahead, he could just make out the blue and white sign, two blocks away.

Chapter 13

THE FERRY

--------◦◦◦◦--------

Matthew wandered through paths lined with exotic plants forming an arch. Hearing his name, he turned to look back. It was Julia! He walked slowly at first, noticing the strange aroma of the leaves, then at a faster pace, closing his eyes in anticipation of meeting her sweet, full lips. As he ran, the sounds of a fiddle drifted in the distance.

Then, his eyes popped opened. Had this been another one of his 'visions' or just a dream? The sky was a strange, light green but as Matthew focused, he could make out that it was really the cracked ceiling and walls of his room with its one window and thin curtains. The sky outside looked gray. Matthew lifted his head revealing his pants hanging on the bed post. He dug in the pocket for his watch. 5:11 exactly. Matthew had just nineteen minutes before he would be late for his first day of work on the ferry! He flew out of bed and threw on his clothes. He didn't bother to shave; He could still go a couple of days before it really showed anyway. Matthew hopped out of the boarding house still pulling on one boot, prompting Signora Marinelli to poke her head out the kitchen door. Soon he was running down Natoma Street and as he turned the corner on Sixth, he could hear the clang of a cable car but which way was it headed? As he neared Market Street, Matthew saw the car had come down from the direction of city hall toward the ferry building. He pressed on as fast as he could but the car was almost as fast as him. He turned down market about one hundred feet behind the cable car, waving and shouting. The operator slowed slightly to allow Matthew to catch up and jump on, planting himself next to another young man.

"Pretty lucky."

"Yeah, and my first day of work," Matthew puffed, almost out of breath. He handed the car operator his fare and bent over to tie his boots. "Don't want to be late."

That was about the extent of their conversation and for the next twelve minutes the cable car swayed back and forth as it came ever nearer to the clock tower of the ferry terminal. The young man stepped off at Beale Street and by the look of his clothes it appeared he was headed for the iron works. As the cable car slowed, making ready to turn for the return trip back down Market, Matthew jumped and started to run once again. He headed straight to the number four slip to meet his new assignment-the 'Golden City'. The hinged metal apron that made for an easy transition to the boat's main deck was being lowered by a man of around forty years, with the look of about fifty years' experience.

"Matthew Donohue reporting for duty, sir!" Matthew snapped his right hand to his forehead.

The man glanced at him with a bemused grin and said, "It's not me you want to be saluting!" pointing up to a small room on the top deck. "See the captain."

Matthew found the stairs to the next level and then a small ladder to the top deck. The captain was just stepping out of the pilot's cabin when they met.

"Matthew Donohue reporting for duty, sir!" The captain was a short, stout man with steely eyes.

"And not a minute too soon!" He looked Matthew over. "So, you will be the new hand, then. I am Captain Turner. You may call me Captain Turner. See Mr. Roberts at the fiddley."

Matthew looked puzzled. "The fiddley, sir?"

The captain was a little irked. "Just go down to the main deck where you see the big machinery!"

"Yes sir!" replied Matthew with a snappy salute, "And thank you, sir!"

The captain started back toward the pilot house waving and mumbling something. Matthew wasted no time making his way back to the main deck and the man he mistakenly saluted.

The fiddley was the perfect place to view a working example of the industrial revolution. Enclosed in glass, was a huge piston connected above to a sort of gigantic iron teeter-totter which was in turn connected to another rod, just as he had seen on the ferry he took from Oakland a few days earlier. Matthew was impressed at how well cared for all the inner workings looked.

"What a machine!" exclaimed Matthew. He marveled at the precise fit of the moving parts and the enormity of the piston.

"That'll do the work of about fifteen hundred horses! I'm George, by the way, George Roberts."

"Matthew, Matthew Donohue." George extended his hand and Matthew met his with a firm grip.

People had been gathering behind a gate that separated the vessel from the dock, and when an attendant opened it, the passengers streamed onto the second level deck. The lower deck of the vessel was for baggage and wagons with the occasional auto car. You could drive eight teams of horses with good sized wagons on with just a few feet to spare. In fact, as Matthew was standing by for orders, three freight wagons and a milk wagon came aboard. A low-pitched whistle announced the vessel's imminent departure, which made the horses a little skittish. George placed blocks in front and behind the wheels to keep the loads from shifting as the horses stomped the wood deck, then he walked Matthew to what would be, after the ferry got underway, the stern.

"So, what do you know about ferry boats."

"Well, I was a hand on a ferryboat on Lake Tahoe for almost eight years."

"Really! Well, I guess you know a little bit about it then. I always wanted to see Tahoe. Is it as blue as they say?"

"More!" Matthew proudly replied, "and you can see a hundred feet down into it!"

"Well, you won't have that luxury 'round here!"

Matthew took a glance over the starboard rail only to see the turbid blue-gray water and his own choppy reflection.

George untied the rope, crossing in front of the lower deck and rolled it up. "Get ready to cast off!"

Matthew sprang over to the heavy rope that was looped over a cleat and unwrapped it.

"Cast off!"

He threw the heavy rope onto the ferryboat and walked along the dock for a short while before hopping on.

Matthew was finally underway! He knew he would do well-he had the confidence of both youth *and* experience on his side. Once on their way to Oakland, Matthew reported back to George.

"Let's go below. I want you to meet the men that work in the belly of this boat."

At the fiddley, he followed the man down a steep ladder, the temperature getting noticeably warmer with each rung. A hissing sound with a slow cadence drowned out most of the man's words but he did catch the introductions.

"This here's Bob. He's the muscle of this boat." Matthew caught a glimpse of the man's face, while he shoveled coal into the boiler furnace.

"Nice to meet you." The fireman paused and just stared and nodded to Matthew. As he shut the door, Matthew saw that his arms and face were smeared with sweat and coal dust, glistening in the light of the single bulb illuminating his station.

"An' your engineer there, is Angelo. He takes the pilot's orders and runs the ship's engine." Matthew gazed at the controls that looked much like those of the 'Tahoe'.

"You just-a do what you are told," Angelo said, "and you work out-a fine."

Matthew grinned at the obvious Italian inflections in his voice. As he followed his tour guide back up the ladder, Matthew could hear Angelo shout out something and immediately Bob started shoveling again.

"Here, take this manifest to the captain and meet me back at the fiddley."

"Yes…" Matthew stopped himself in mid salute as he met George's peeved expression.

Back on the second deck, people of all description were seated or standing, leaning on the railing or milling around. Business men and ladies with children, China men with their large bundles of clothing, even a few military personnel from the Presidio at the railing, looking toward Goat Island. A vendor roamed the wide walkways, selling coffee and biscuits.

As Matthew passed through to the top deck, he could finally see the true expanse of the San Francisco Bay. It had two main fingers; one running north and south separating San Francisco from Oakland and Berkeley and the other which wrapped around an island to the north, then turned east and out of view. Matthew surmised that somewhere around that bend was where the railroad ferry 'Solano' did its work. The two arms met around this large island and swept toward the golden gate past Alcatraz.

Matthew spied two tall sailing ships under way toward the narrow 'Golden Gate' headed out to sea, and wondered what adventures lay ahead for the crew. Were they headed up the coast to take on redwood lumber in Eureka or were they off to the Orient by way of exotic Hawaii, or maybe they were whalers headed for danger and excitement on the high seas!

His thoughts were interrupted by one short blast of the vessel's horn followed by its gradual turn to starboard. The 'Golden City' passed two ferries approaching San Francisco on its port side. As he looked back, Matthew could see two more ferries on the same route as theirs and one other approaching San Francisco from the north. From the vantage point of the pilot's house, he could see the reason for the turn. The 'Golden City' would be skirting the south side of Goat Island and by looking at the wash of a ferry in front of them, Matthew could tell they were taking the same course.

"It's like a road in the water," Matthew said as all the activity finally dawned on him.

"What's that?" Captain Turner yelled.

"Nothing, sir, just looking…" as he handed the papers to the captain.

"And take a good one! This is the kind of day that makes it all worthwhile!"

Matthew and Captain Turner both stood for a short time admiring the view, one with the knowledge and respect of years on the bay and the other with the wide-eyes of a greenhorn. Matthew turned three hundred-sixty degrees, taking in the hills beyond Oakland to the east and the morning light striking the hills to the north. He then turned his gaze to the city with its tall buildings, huddling along a strand he recognized as Market Street. Looking south, Matthew could make out seemingly endless rows of orchards.

"What a sight!" Matthew finally remarked.

"That it is! Best be getting back to your duties, now."

"Yes sir!"

Matthew descended to the second level again and decided to walk to the front of the boat. He still had a hard time deciding which end should be called the bow and which should be the stern. As he passed the people, he could tell that he was almost invisible to them. He tipped his cap to a pretty lady who seemed to look right through him. A gentleman walking toward him, would have hit him had Matthew not side stepped at the last moment. He was starting to get the feeling that these were different people and they didn't mix with his type. When he reached what would be for the next few minutes anyway, the bow, he spied George on the lower deck, motioning him to come down.

"There's more to do than admire the pretty girls on this boat!" George said only half seriously.

"Sorry."

"Oh, that's alright. Won't get anywhere with the likes a' them anyway. Now see here. When we're underway, especially on a foggy run, you need to know where the sounder is." George went to a closet door that revealed a weight with a long chain.

"See here, see this mark?" Matthew looked at a white mark on the rusty chain. "That there is five feet down. And this double mark; That's ten feet. Every five and ten feet you have these marks."

"So, are we going to check how deep the bay is?" asked an astonished Matthew.

"That's right! If you go off course in this part of the bay, you might be running aground before you could spit, 'specially at low tide!"

Matthew was still trying to get his head around the idea of a bay of this size being so shallow. At Lake Tahoe, when you get a hundred feet off shore, you were in five hundred feet of water!

"We're drawing about ten feet on a normal run, so you can't stray too far off line."

Matthew stood for a second, peering over the railing still thinking of the crystal-clear waters of Lake Tahoe.

"This here's the coal hatch. Won't need to deal with that too much." George opened the door, flush with the deck, with a special hook and Matthew peered down into the darkness.

"That chute goes right into the coal bunker. We can take on five tons, no problem." Matthew thought about Bob below and how many scoops it would take to shovel five tons of coal.

"We get our coal from Dunsmuir's over at those docks." George pointed to a tall building with a large sailing ship tied up to it. "But the damned stuff burns too cold! Look at the stack." Matthew looked at the bellowing, thick black smoke that trailed behind the boat for a considerable distance. "If we had oil like the trains, we'd be burning cleaner an' gettin' two hundred more horse power to boot!"

"Is it too expensive?" Matthew replied, thinking about the oil.

"It's refitting the boiler that's expensive! Back in '88 the 'Julia' blew her boiler 'cause they didn't refit her to take the heat." Matthew's thoughts switched straight to his Julia. What a wonderful idea to name a ferry boat after his new love! "Let's go over to the fiddley."

Amidship, the glass enclosed inner workings of the engine was open to view. A few children with their fathers were gawking at the enormous steam piston. It drove the walking beam above which powered the crankshaft in a mesmerizing up and down motion, finally propelling the great paddle wheels.

George had to raise his voice to be heard. "At the end of this run, I'll show you the greasing points and what needs cleaning." George pointed to a locked door used to gain access. "Over there's the head." Matthew knew what that was. "You clean up after yourself. After that you'll clean the passenger's too." Matthew peaked in and saw a small sink with a toilet seat in the up position.

"Can I?" Matthew motioned to the small room and George consented.

"But don't be too long. We'll be coming up on the mole pretty soon."

Matthew entered and latched the door shut. He inspected the seat as he lowered it and sat down. As he relieved himself, his thoughts were drowned out by the thumping of the huge paddle wheel just on the other side of the wall. When he finished, Matthew pulled the chain and peered straight down to the frothy water of the bay. That was a lot different than the lavatories on the 'Tahoe'. It had a holding tank that was emptied at the end of each day. When Matthew emerged, George was talking to one of the passengers about the fiddley.

"Do you want me to go up to the main deck and clean the lavatories?"

George looked puzzled, then realized Matthew's mistake. "This *is* the main deck. That there's the cabin deck and the top one with the pilot house is the hurricane deck. No passengers are allowed up there."

"Sorry, sir. I mean, sorry." Matthew was a little flustered. He knew enough about how a ferry boat worked, but he didn't like not knowing the terms. As he made his way to the cabin deck, he made a vow to himself to learn quickly.

When Matthew reached the lavatories, the men's side had a sign that read 'in use' so he started with the ladies' side with the sign that read 'available'. The lavatories for the passengers were much nicer with brass fittings and smooth varnished seats. When he finished cleaning, Matthew opened the door, almost hitting an elderly lady in a full ruffled dress.

"Would you watch yourself?"

"Yes ma'am, sorry, ma'am."

"I should say! The kind of help one gets these days!"

Matthew didn't let the experience faze him. He had a job, a place to stay in an exciting city and he was in love.

The 'Golden City' was approaching the Oakland mole and Matthew was called down to the main deck.

"Here's where it can get a little tricky," George said as the boat approached the slips. "It'll get tighter as we come closer until we're in like a glove. Don't let yourself get caught in between. Last year, a poor bloke over on the Key Route made that mistake and he was lucky to survive without his legs." Relishing his propensity for gore, he continued, "Heard of one man, went down head first and lost it. Had to fish it out of the bay with a net!" Matthew wasn't going to have that problem. He was nimble and could jump like a frog when needed but when he looked over the side, he saw some sort of flotsam that made him think twice.

As the ferry got closer, the paddle wheels were thrown into reverse. There was an audible 'clunk' as the piston changed direction. The ferry continued forward at what seemed to be much too fast a speed, but presently the paddles did their job, slowing the 1,000-ton boat.

As the 'Golden City' started to skid against the port side of the slip, George yelled, "Take that rope and jump, but stay clear of those cleats!"

Matthew threw the rope over one shoulder and took a few

running strides. As he leapt, he remembered what he had learned from his work on the lake. "Look to a point on the other side," the engineer of the 'Tahoe' would say, "and you'll never land short." His jump was so long that he landed halfway across the dock.

"Well! We won't be having a problem with this hand!" exclaimed George.

Matthew quickly wrapped the rope around the far cleat just as the craft touched the front bumper.

"Good job! I think we have a real ferryman! Now quickly make fast the starboard line!" George threw the rope and Matthew caught it face high and deftly guided it to its place. The two men then proceeded down either side of the craft, securing two more lines. At first, the dock groaned from the weight of the 'Golden City' rubbing against it but it quickly subsided as the vessel's wake disappeared.

George had been holding back the crowd amassing on the main deck stairs. "Just hold on now, folks. Gotta get these wagons off first!"

The horses moved forward hesitantly, pulling their loads in short jerks. One lost its footing as it came upon the metal apron causing the other horse to rear. In a short time, the teamster regained control and eased the wagon to the dock. The other wagons proceeded without incident followed by the passengers. Matthew marveled at how a boat of this size could be affected by the shifting of its passengers to the bow. It was easily two feet lower now with all the pedestrian traffic than when the boat was first tied up. Finally, the boat was emptied of its load, but as quickly as Matthew could say 'San Francisco', another round of wagons and people approached. The passengers were allowed to board first, moving to the cabin deck by way of the two wide stairways on either side of the craft.

George seemed a little uneasy as he scanned the docks. Finally, he said,

"Keep an eye out for stowaways, now. I have some business to attend to." Matthew stood to the port side as he took stock of their new cargo streaming in. Matthew was continually amazed at the diversity of the people. He looked suspiciously at one young man with a bundle over his back and reflected on if he had looked like that to the crew just a short time ago.

Next, the wagons were directed down the middle of the craft to the new bow of the boat. Matthew and another hand put blocks on the wagon's wheels, as three short blasts from the horn prompted the paddles to slowly start their churning back toward San Francisco. Matthew was getting concerned, knowing he should cast off the lines soon when George finally came running along the deck. Matthew caught in the corner of his eye, a feminine figure in the shadows, waving.

"Cast off!" George yelled as he jumped on and started to raise the apron.

Matthew quickly complied and before the great paddle wheels could begin to propel the vessel, all lines were loosened from their moorings and thrown back on deck. Matthew effortlessly bounded across the three foot and ever widening gap and proceeded to coil the lines, making them ready for their next task. George took another look toward the mole and met Matthew's eyes as he turned back, in an awkward moment of silence.

"Well then! Everything's ship shape! How 'bout I show you around a little more." George took Matthew back down below deck to the engine room. Angelo had his ear up to the brass speaking tube and immediately moved a lever from slow to half and yelled into the tube, "All ahead half!" Gauges to his left recorded the boiler pressure and he pushed a lever forward.

"One more round!" he yelled to Bob across the hull. He turned and opened an iron door, revealing an orange/yellow glow that lit the cramped room and illuminated the fuel. The coal bunker narrowed into a small depression from which Bob shoveled a heaping load of the black rock. No sooner had he thrown this into the glowing fire than more coal tumbled down into the depression.

Bob repeated this fourteen more times, then kicked the door shut and leaned on his shovel. "That'll get 'er going!" He took out a grimy rag and wiped his brow.

Matthew spied in the dim light, the coal chute toward what was now the stern and he pondered the possibility of a man maybe accidentally falling down the chute if the hatch on deck were left open. Angelo turned a brass valve, letting more water into the boiler and pulled on another handle.

"See, there's more to running this boat than just shovelin' coal. You got 'a keep enough water heated, but not too much or you could blow up the whole boat!" Matthew decided there was more to piloting this boat than just steering it. He thought too, that a railroad locomotive's engine must work much the same way.

Once again George and Matthew climbed the ladder back to the main deck, and he again appreciatively breathed in the cool, crisp sea air.

"Take a look here." George opened a door on the port side revealing a generator humming away. "That's the power for all the lights. As long as we have steam, we have lights. Check that it's spinning freely every run." He moved over to another door, this one locked with a sign that read 'keep out'.

As he rummaged around in his pocket for the key, George said, "any trouble an' you be sure to get me. This here's for 'mergencies." George opened the door revealing a rack holding three pistols and a rifle. Below them were some flares and a good-sized barrel half filled with oil.

"Emergency?" Matthew was trying to decide what would constitute a bona fide emergency that would require the use of firearms.

"That's right! The 'Encinal' had gunplay just last year. Two men fighting over a woman, most say she weren't worth it. They were such poor shots, both missed but one went overboard. They didn't have a problem getting the gun away, but the other sap almost drowned. Now that's a problem we could handle, but then there's the real 'mergencies."

Matthew looked hard into George's eyes trying to ascertain his next words. "Take ramming, for example. When the fog gets thick as soup, you hope an' pray 'ya don't get rammed or ram some boat yourself! Anyways, if something like that, what puts the whole boat in danger happens, we would light these here flares. Or you can roll out this barrel to the bow an' light her up."

Matthew thought for a second. "But only the captain decides..."

"That's right. If you are the one that sees the danger, tell the captain right away. George pointed to another brass tube on the starboard side. He'll decide one way or the other."

Matthew was thinking of one time on Lake Tahoe when captain Pomin had to make the decision to abandon ship or not because the 'Tahoe' was taking on water. An early winter gale swept in from Fallen Leaf Lake almost swamping the boat until he could turn it into the storm and make it to shore. Matthew thought about how much responsibility falls on a captain's shoulders.

"Me an' the captain are the only ones with keys for this door, but it's still his decision to open it. An' just so you know, the captain's the only one with a side arm on his person, an' that's how it should be, too."

"What about crimes like stealing and fights?"

"Well, if it's bad enough, we got the OK to tie them up 'till we reach shore and then we let the police take care of it. But it would be pretty stupid to try something. Not much room to run, if you know what I mean."

Matthew thought about some criminal trying to swim to shore with all his clothes and boots weighing him down. Pretty stupid, Matthew chuckled to himself, nodding.

"As for the life boats, we got two on either end. Take a look." George untied a rope and let out some line. The lifeboat descended about a foot. "Let out the line and turn this. It'll push the bow over the railing. Let out the rest of the line and she'll be sitting in the water. They only take about fifteen or so each but I wouldn't worry. If we sank right now, and the 'Golden City' was resting on the bottom of the bay, God forbid...bet we'd still be high an' dry on the hurricane deck!

As the 'Golden City' neared the ferry building, Matthew could make out the clock tower reading 10:37. Passengers on the main deck began gravitating to the stairs, knowing that they would be disembarking on the cabin level. Three short blasts of the horn signaled the 'Golden City's' paddle wheels to be reversed, and they slowly eased into the slip. Once again, Matthew effortlessly hopped onto the deck and secured the lines. The passengers streamed out to the second level of the terminal while the wagons departed below. This was the routine to be played out each and every day- rain, shine, or fog. Matthew knew he would be good at his assignment.

Anthony Colburn

Chapter 14

HIGH SOCIETY

⸻⸻

One evening, just before his birthday, Matthew had gotten off work and was heading down Market Street for home. He noticed much more activity than normal as well-dressed people were streaming out onto Market Street just past the Palace Hotel. There were fancy carriages and even a couple of motor cars coming from Third Street. Restaurants and night clubs up Kearney and Geary Street were lively. Matthew was intently watching the people crossing in front of his cable car when all of a sudden, he saw a splash of black hair flowing down a beautiful white gown. He flew off the cable car and into the throng, crossing Market. Finally, when he had pushed his way to the other side of the street, he caught a glimpse of the woman again going up O'Farrell St…with a man! As he ran to catch up, Matthew was trying to think of what kind of excuse he could use that would seem remotely feasible that he just happened along at this time. Without thinking, he called out, "Julia!" The man and woman turned to the call and seeing no one they recognized, continued up the street and past the music store. It was not his love, but a middle-aged woman of some means and her escort, old enough to be Julia's father. A flush of embarrassment overtook Matthew and he was angry that his jealously could so easily influence him. But he hadn't seen Julia since before Christmas. Her father caught them behind the store talking one evening and sent Julia up to her room. He told Matthew in no uncertain terms that she had been betrothed to another and that he should not come around anymore.

Matthew sat down across from the music store and gazed up at Julia's window. Soon, more people approached from the direction of Market. It was the Thomas family coming toward the music store! Not wanting to look like he had been lying in wait for them like some common criminal, Matthew slid between two buildings out of sight.

"What a splendid performance that was!" said Julia's mother, Grace. "Isn't it wonderful when the hero finally gets his love?"

"Some hero!" replied Mr. Thomas. "The problem with Hoffman was he never knew who he was in love with! Just dumb luck that the drunk got his girl!"

"Well, he was deceived so. I'm glad Lindorf got his comeuppance!"

"I liked Olympia!" chimed in Katy, Julia's little sister.

"You would like anything with dolls in it!" replied Julia dismissing her.

"Now girls! It was a fine performance! That's what counts! How would you like to see a truly world-famous opera?"

Mr. Thomas frowned, "What do you mean, Grace?"

"Well, you know the great Caruso is coming to town with the whole Metropolitan Opera Company! They are going to do 'The Queen of Sheba' and 'Carmen' in April! We should go! How about 'Carmen'?"—

"Let's go on opening night!" interrupted Julia. "You know I love Caruso and that's always the most exciting performance!"

"*If* we can get tickets! I'll see what I can do..." Mr. Thomas fiddled with his keys and finally opened the door while he said under his breath, "Just what the girls need, a philandering gypsy as their heroine."

Matthew drew back in the shadows, hoping he wouldn't be noticed. As he watched Julia and her family retire into the store, Matthew thought about the Grand Opera House. He had passed it many times before as he sometimes would travel down Mission Street on his way home, so he decided to go by again this night and see what all the fuss was about. The Grand Opera House on Mission Street was between Third and Fourth, right next to the imposing Call Building and just a block west of the Palace Hotel. The façade was made up of impressive columns fifteen feet high which patrons would pass through. As Matthew passed by, a couple of men were exiting by a side door.

On a whim, Matthew approached them and inquired, "what could I do to get tickets for 'Carmen' on opening night?"

The men chuckled but one of them saw the seriousness in his face and walked over to Matthew to introduce himself.

"Can you come around this time tomorrow night?"

"Yes, sir. I live just a few more blocks down on Natoma."

"The name's Doran, John Doran. I'm the head usher and I'm responsible for cleanup after the shows. One of my boys quit last night and I need someone right away. Can you be here tomorrow night at 10:30?"

"Yes sir! I don't need to be paid, just a ticket to 'Carmen' opening night, this April."

"Need to see her bad, do you?"

"Yes sir."

"Well, you're not the first. Tell you what. You show up here and work for the next five nights an' I'll give you a ticket. Won't be the best seat in the house, but you'll be in!"

"That would be fine, sir."

"You're gonna have to start saving up for some good clothes, too. You won't find many working types at these shindigs!"

"I can get some!"

"Good! See you here tomorrow night, then! I didn't catch your name..."

"Matthew, Matthew Donohue, sir"

"Alright, Matthew Donohue. Just come to the side door here, knock and ask for me."

"Thanks again sir!" Matthew shook his hand with a little too much vigor. "I'll be here!"

"10:30."

"Yes, 10:30. Thanks again!" Matthew still had a hold of the man's hand.

"OK, OK. Just don't be late!" As the men walked away, Mr. Doran said to the other. "He can do my work and I can get home at a decent hour!"

"But what about the ticket?" the other man said.

"I got a free ticket from Mr. Dillon and I'm going to see it from the back of the hall anyway. I'll be ahead both ways!"

Matthew headed on down Mission with a spring in his step. He could hardly believe it! He was assured a ticket to the very Opera Julia was going to see! Matthew took a detour up the steps of the U.S. mint building, bounding three at a time.

"Won't her father be surprised when he sees me coming down the aisle! Then maybe he'll see I'm as good as anyone else!"

But somewhere around Sixth Street, Matthew's euphoria suddenly evaporated. "What will I wear?" he said out loud to the empty street. "What have I gotten myself into?" The rest of the night and into the early hours of the next morning, Matthew wrestled with this predicament in his dreams. The moment he awoke, he was consumed with another dilemma, how to get Julia to forget her fiancé!

The next evening at the end of their last run, Matthew, his matt of red hair spilling from under his hat, met George at the center of the ferry. The trip had gone along uneventfully, although the 'Golden City' was nine minutes late. As he climbed down the ladder from the pilothouse, the captain was cursing to himself.

"That blasted Goat Island!" he said, now out loud, "It creeps up on me every time in this God forsaken fog, especially on the outgoing tide!"

"Aw, we-a miss-ed it by a mile!" The thick Italian voice preceded the form of Angelo, as he ascended from the bowels of the boat, his face smudged by coal dust, glistening on his sweaty brow.

"How would you know?" George teased. "You were ten feet below the water line!"

"I feel these-a things," he responded matter-of-factly, wiping the sweat from his face with a clean rag. "I know-a my boat. I can count her heart-a beats!"

"Ha!" scoffed the captain. "That, and a nickel will get you down to Lotta's fountain! You'll be counting your *own* heart beats when we run aground! You can tell old Hearst the story yourself! He'll print anything that'll sell a paper!" Matthew chuckled at the truth in his ranting.

"You know, he practically started that Spanish-American War mess single handedly! That bastard! My nephew...lost to that damn yellow fever in the Philippines! Never even got a shot off! What the hell did we ever gain..." His voice trailed off until finally, his mind wandered back to the present. "I can't keep to my schedule in this blasted fog! And I won't cut that corner again just to make up five minutes!"

"OK, OK, Capt'n..." George said, trying to calm him a little. "We wanna' keep our feet dry just as much as you. You don't have to talk us into it."

After the last of the passengers disembarked, Matthew made the rounds, making sure no one was left in the lavatories. George said it *had* happened. An elderly man once nodded off and made two trips before he was found.

"Get your bag, Matt," yelled George. Matthew had been day dreaming again as the fog and the hour tended to dull his wits. "...Unless you are planning to bunk here for the night!" Matthew picked up the bag and obediently followed his friend. The two entered a small room, smelling of sweat and tobacco, labeled 'Southern Pacific Ferry Employees Only'. They signed their time sheets and headed for the front door.

"Hey Matt!" came the familiar voice of the company timekeeper, "Don't forget that pack sack!" He had left it once again, this time on the bench by the time sheets.

"Man, I really need some sleep!" Matthew thought to himself as he said goodbye to his fellow workers and walked through the ferry building's tall arching entranceway facing Market Street.

Matthew usually found the back of some wagon hauling produce or meat to and from the wholesale warehouses for a ride partway up Market, but this time of night they were few and far between. And this wasn't the best place to be walking alone, even if you were a man in your prime. There were rumors of gangs of Italians and Chinese who would roam the streets after hours but Matthew didn't believe it. After all, men like Angelo, the engineer on the ferry and his clothes washer Sophia and Signora Marinelli were good hardworking people and he never heard of any Chinese gangs outside of their own part of town. After walking a few blocks and looking down Front Street, he saw a small group of men walking his way. Matthew finally decided discretion was the best choice this night so he hopped one of the few cable cars headed up Market at that hour and plopped down on the hard wooden seat. Glancing back at the imposing two-hundred-thirty-five-foot tower of the ferry building, it commenced its chiming on the hour; 10:00 exactly- or more exactly, two minutes early.

The ride home was uneventful as the chilling fog had already turned most people indoors hours earlier. Matthew's thoughts turned to Julia and how he could manage to change her mind about that other man. It was strange, he thought, that she had never mentioned she was interested in another. Julia's father didn't have much patience for Matthew either, mostly he thought, because of his status, or lack of it.

As he approached the Palace Hotel, he could see a glow from its grand entrance piercing the fog. Matthew decided to walk the rest of the way just so he could soak in its ambience. At the entrance stood a man in the hotel's uniform waiting to assist any patrons. The man cast a suspicious eye on Matthew as he walked slower and slower. Matthew could see the great common room with its exotic plants and plush rugs. Oh, to be married here, in the midst of all this grandeur! he thought to himself. That would give Julia's father cause for celebration!

"May I assist you?" The uniformed man coolly inquired.

"No thanks. Just making my way home."

The man invited Matthew to move along. "Good evening then, sir."

As Matthew strolled by on the opposite side of the street from Lotta's fountain, he replayed almost like a moving picture in his mind, the first time he saw Julia.

But then, he suddenly remembered the Opera House! I have to keep my head screwed on straight! he reminded himself as he rushed back down 3rd Street. The work at the opera house wasn't all that hard. First, Matthew had to empty all the ash trays in the lobby, polish the brass handrails along the stairs and then, after picking up the dropped programs and wrappers, he would take a carpet sweeper to the entire house. The balconies and the stairs were the most tedious, but Matthew kept his mind on the prize. But then there still was the matter of the clothes.

Drum Bridge, Japanese Tea Garden

Chapter 15

A FREE AFTERNOON

M atthew instinctively woke up at 4:30 a.m. It was hard to break a six day a week habit. As he lay there looking at the cracks in the ceiling resembling South America, Matthew plotted out his day. He would join Signora Marinelli and her grandchildren for church, mostly for the connection he felt to his father when he heard Gaelic spoken at St. Patrick's. Then, he would meet Julia behind her father's music store in the alley and confront her about this fiancé of hers. Julia's family would be going to church too- the Thomas family was Presbyterian so they would be home later than Matthew. He wanted very much to take Julia to the park and listen

to the band there and stroll among the flowers in the conservatory…
and make her forget about that other man!

At 1:00 p.m., Matthew headed toward O'Farrell Street and the
music store. He had kept his church clothes on and was intent on
asking Julia's father for his permission to take her to the park, just
as a friend.

When he knocked on the music store's door, Julia's sister Katy
popped her head out an upstairs window.

"Julia! It's your frieeend, Mattheeew!"

Oh great, he thought. What a wonderful way to be announced!

Julia's mother came to the door and looked pleased to see him.
"Good afternoon, Matthew. Won't you come in!"

Why would Julia's mother be so pleased to see me, Matthew
pondered, if Julia was engaged to another?

As he followed her up the stairs to their third-floor home, Mr.
Thomas met him two steps from the top.

"Good afternoon," He said, looking down at Matthew, somewhat
less enthusiastically than his wife.

"Good afternoon, sir."

"What brings you around this fine day? More sheet music?"

"Oh, father!" Julia had just come down the hall from her room.
"How are you, Matt?"

Mrs. Thomas said, "Why don't you come in and sit down. Here,
have a cookie."

The parlor was nicely appointed with paintings of the mountains and a rugged beach scene along with a photograph Matthew
recognized. The early afternoon sun warmed Matthew's back as it
just started to make its way through the west facing window.

"That's a nice picture of Lake Tahoe," Matthew finally said,
trying to end an awkward silence.

"You know where that is?" Mr. Thomas said rather skeptically.

"Yes sir. I was a hand on the 'Tahoe'…finest steamer on the lake
and I lived at the Tahoe Tavern for almost eight years."

"*Really…?*"

"We would like to see it someday," Mrs. Thomas chimed in, obviously more impressed than Mr. Thomas. "What's it like? Is the water really as blue as they say?"

"More," replied Matthew enthusiastically. "Some days, it's a pale aquamarine and other days, as deep blue as your eyes."

Mrs. Thomas blushed. "Oh my!"

Matthew had never delivered a better line in his life. "And clear. You can see one hundred feet down. The best way to see it is on the 'Tahoe'. Here, take a look at my watch." Matthew proudly showed off his pocket watch to the whole family. "Mr. Bliss gave me this watch as a going away present."

Mr. Thomas inspected the timepiece. "This is a 'Patek Philippe'. Is it a minute repeater?"

"Yes." replied Matthew, surprised that Mr. Thomas would notice.

"Bliss. I've heard of him. He has a home over in Pacific Heights. He's in lumber."

"Not so much anymore. At one time, he supplied almost all the timbers for the Comstock mines, but now he is favoring tourism as a business for the future." Matthew could not believe how authoritative he sounded.

"Very interesting." Mr. Thomas was warming up to Matthew a little more after seeing that watch and dropping a name like Bliss.

"Did you see any Indians?!" Julia's sister Katy had been reading too many dime novels with blood thirsty natives ravaging the settlers.

"Well, I knew one Indian very well. She is a basket weaver from the Washoe Tribe. Her name is Dat So La Lee and she made me a basket. Would you like to see it some time?"

"Oh, yes, yes!" Katy leaned wide eyed, toward Matthew. "How about bows and arrows?"

"Sorry, no."

"Can Matthew come over and show us the basket, daddy? Please?"

Mr. Thomas had been painted into a corner. "Oh, I wouldn't want to bother Mr. Donohue..."

"That would be no problem at all, sir."

"It's settled then. Do come back and show us your basket," Mrs. Thomas replied eagerly. "Now what are you planning for this afternoon?"

"Well," as Matthew, turned to Mr. Thomas, "I was wondering if Julia could accompany me to the park to listen to the band and go to the Conservatory of Flowers...just as friends, of course."

"But, there's the fare for the cable cars and the fee for entering the conservatory..."

"That's no problem, sir."

Mrs. Thomas interrupted, "That would be wonderful, wouldn't it dear!"

"Please father," Julia interjected. "It's such a nice afternoon and you said just the other day I should get out more often."

Mr. Thomas was out numbered. He knew he was beat but he had to get one concession. "Alright. But I don't think it's fair to leave poor Katy here cooped up in the house."

"Oh boy!" blurted Katy.

"Alright then. You had better get going if you want to hear the band. Here's the fare for Katy."

"I couldn't sir..." protested Matthew.

"Don't be so chivalrous. You had no idea you were getting Julia's little sister in the bargain."

Matthew was searching his brain for the word *chivalrous* but the way Mr. Thomas had used it made him believe it must have been a compliment.

"Thank you, we'll take good care of her."

"You just remember to take good care of Julia, too!"

"Yes, sir!" Matthew had to fight the sudden impulse to salute.

Mrs. Thomas sprang into action. "You girls get changed into something more appropriate for the park! And remember to put on some comfortable shoes!"

"Be sure to be back before dark!" Mr. Thomas yelled at the trio as they scurried down the stairs.

"Don't worry!" Julia replied, hurrying out the door.

Matthew and Julia walked together while Katy skipped in front of them all the way to Market Street.

"Let's take this one!" Katy yelled as a cable car approached.

"No, silly," replied Julia. "That one's continuing out to the Mission district. We want the one that says McAllister. Now look at that one. See that sign, up at the top." As another car came down Market, Matthew waved it down and they hopped on.

"Fifteen cents!" It was the familiar voice of the operator Matthew had on his last excursion to the park. "Oh, it's you! And you have some pretty company this time! For you, no charge!" The two sisters looked at each other in amazement.

"No, don't be so chivalrous. I plan to pay my own way from now on!" Matthew paid the man with a quarter and said, "Keep the change." He tipped his hat, pulled on a lever and they were off.

"That was sweet of you." Julia said as she squeezed Matthew's arm.

He leaned back, and for the rest of the way out to the park, they engaged in small talk befitting the day. He was determined to get to the bottom of this engagement thing though, but any time with Julia…

When they reached the spot where he had departed before, Matthew said, "OK, now."

But Katy protested, "couldn't we go out to the 'Chutes'? It's just a little bit more!"

"What's the 'Chutes'?"

Julia responded, "It's an amusement park- rides and a penny arcade and the like. I think you'd like it. And besides, we could have a little time to ourselves with Katy on the rides."

"OK. But we can't take too much time."

"Oh, boy!" Katy squealed.

The 'Chutes' was located on Fulton Street between Tenth and Eleventh, near the end of the cable car line. The charge was ten cents per person and all of a sudden, Matthew began to think frugally.

"Let's go on the chute!" Katy said gleefully.

"You go ahead," Matthew countered. "Here is a dime."

"Oh, no! I got my own money! That way, you can't tell me I can't!"

With that, Katy hurried to the line that snaked up the long stairway to the top.

With Katy out of ear shot, Matthew saw his chance to confront Julia. "Have you set a date?" he coolly inquired.

"Hold on tight!" yelled Julia as Katy waved. "What date?"

One boat was slowly pulled up an incline as another at the top was getting loaded with smiling and waving young riders.

"I mean a church date. You will surely have the ceremony at your church, won't you…"

"Have what!?" Julia was getting a little aggravated with this cryptic line of questioning.

With a sudden swoop and breathless screams from the passengers, the boat started its precipitous journey down the watery ramp. Matthew and Julia watched with some trepidation as it hit the pool below and skipped, out of control, until the nose dug into the water. The riders were ringing wet but laughing.

Matthew continued, "Why didn't you tell me—"

"Tell you what!? I declare, you are making no sense at all!"

Now Matthew was the one who was upset. "It would seem to me that you could have had the common decency to let me know that you already had a beau and you were engaged to be married!"

"What!?" Julia shrieked, her eyes turning a frigid blue.

"Your father let me know before Christmas…"

"Oh! So that's it! That's why you haven't been around to see me!"

"Well, yes…"

"What did he say to you?! No, let me guess. He said that I already was engaged to be married and that you shouldn't come around anymore, right?"

"Well, something like that…"

"Oh, he is going to get a piece of my mind! Whenever anyone shows the slightest interest in me, he tries something like this!"

The next boat seemed loaded a little heavy to starboard and as it hit the pool, dug in too soon and one unfortunate soul flipped out into the water. Attendants quickly threw a lifesaving ring and, in a few seconds, the waterlogged boy was safely on soggy ground. The crowd walking up the stairs cheered and the boy waved. Katy's boat was next.

Julia was livid now, "Let me tell you. I am a young woman who can make up her own mind about who she wants to see or not... and I want to see you!"

"Good! That's good!"

Julia took his hand in hers and squeezed it tightly.

"I do hope everything will turn out alright..." she said, looking up to her sister's boat.

"Me too." Matthew wasn't talking about the ride. "Don't worry, I think it will be smooth sailing from now on."

Julia glanced at Matthew quizzically. "And father might get a little angry. But don't worry, he'll have other things to worry about!"

Suddenly, Matthew was much more concerned for Katy's welfare. "Hold on tight!" Katy's boat careened down the chute and skipped across the pool with no mishaps, much to Matthew's relief.

When they met her at the exit gate, she was jumping up and down. "That was SOO much fun! Let's go together!"

"Not today!" said Matthew. "We need to get to the band concourse before they are done playing."

"How about the Mystic Mirror Maze! Please? Just one more thing!"

"OK, OK. Point us in the right direction."

The three entered a maze of mirrored corridors, slowly at first, because every turn looked like a dead end. Matthew moved carefully, feeling along the way while Katy blithely hurried ahead, giggling, sometimes hitting a mirror instead of a pathway. Matthew turned one corner and saw what he thought was Julia's reflection. He put his hands up and abruptly ran into her, his left-hand landing on her waist and the other, dangerously close to her breast. For a split second, just like on Market Street, Julia and Matthew's eyes met and this time, their bodies as well. Matthew timidly stepped back.

"Sorry…"

"Don't be." Julia said softly.

As they left the amusement park, Matthew and Julia were walking together, now in a different way.

Just as he thought, the band was almost finished when they finally approached. Matthew and Julia sat on a bench near the front on the right while Katy sat on the grass covered embankment. The band was playing their last tune, a Straus waltz and Julia swayed with the music.

"Let's dance!" she declared.

"I don't know…"

"Oh, come on. I'll show you!"

She climbed the stairs that led to the tall Greek columns on the sides of the band shell and motioned for him to follow.

"Feel the rhythm?" Matthew had a good ear and felt the strong first beat followed by two lighter ones, repeating over and over. "OK. This hand on my waist," she motioned for Matthew's right hand. It landed hesitantly, on her sloping hip. "A little higher. Now take my hand, and point me in that direction and slide to the beat! This is a waltz; one, two, three, slide, two, three…"

After a few tentative steps, Matthew was actually dancing—with Julia! He had only done this in his day dreams on the ferryboat. They shuffled and twirled down the colonnade as Julia held Matthew's hand and rested the other on his shoulder.

"This is the 'Waltz of the Flowers'," She explained, as Katy began dancing around the couple with her imaginary beau. When the music stopped, the crowd applauded as much for the young couple as the band. But Matthew stood there, still holding Julia, their eyes transfixed on each other.

After the crowd began to disperse, Matthew started for the conservatory.

"There's still time to see the flowers. I want to show you—"

"I've seen the flowers many times. I would like to show *you* something."

They turned up the steps and crossed a broad walkway toward an unusual entrance. A large wooden roof, flaring out like a pointed hat with fierce carved faces guarded the doors of the entrance to a mystical, foreign world. It was late March and as they entered, everywhere stood trees with the most exquisite, delicate white and pink flowers. These are not apple trees, Matthew thought, as he turned to take it all in.

Almost as if Julia had read his mind, she said, "These are Cherry trees, brought all the way from Japan."

As they strolled down the narrow paths, he was enchanted by the miniature landscape with its expertly pruned trees and bushes and the ponds with strange golden fish lazily moving their fins. Every rock was set just so and every leaf seemed to be in order.

"How did they do this!?"

"The Hagiwara family keeps it. They even live right here at the garden. It was created for the 1894 Midwinter Exposition, but it is much more impressive now." Julia took Matthew's hand. "Let's go this way. I want to show you something." The path led to a bridge that crossed a narrow part of the pond.

But this was not just any bridge. It took off almost straight up and made a gracefully arching half circle across the water. The bridge was so steep that it had cleats so you could maintain your footing while crossing. Katy went first and reached the apex, peering down at her reflection. She created a small ball of spit on the end of her tongue and let it drop to the water.

"Katy!" scolded Julia, "Remember your manners! This is also someone's home!" She carefully descended to the other side and followed a gold fish that was slowly swimming along the bank. When Julia and Matthew reached the top, they paused and turned, looking over the low railing into the water just as Katy did. Hundreds of cherry blossom petals floated on the surface, pushed along by the lightest of zephyrs like tiny sail boats.

"This is called the 'Drum Bridge'," Julia said in a soft voice.

They simultaneously turned toward each other and found their lips just inches away. Julia looked away, then returned slowly back up into his eyes and gradually closed hers as Matthew leaned to meet her open mouth. They continued to hold on to the railing, her head tilting slightly as Matthew's lips caressed hers.

He could feel her warmth and softness, wishing this moment would never end. As they parted, their lips seemed to cling for an instant. Matthew smiled as Julia's eyes opened, her glistening hair falling off her shoulder. Once more, they gazed at their reflections in the still water below.

A small building with a thatched roof, open on all sides, lay just beyond the bridge. "That's the tea house. Would you like to try some?"

"That would be nice." Matthew thought of the tea his mother sometimes served on cold winter afternoons back in Carson City.

An attendant approached the three at the entrance to the tea house wearing a strange, flower patterned silk dress that restricted her stride and motioned for them to sit down. "Please take off your shoes." Matthew looked around and saw other people, sitting on pillows on the floor had done the same, so he did too, thanking himself for putting on socks without holes this morning.

Noting his wonderment of the attendant, Julia said, "She's wearing a Kimono, a traditional dress in Japan."

"Those shoes don't look any too comfortable." Matthew observed as she shuffled away in wooden sandals with elevated cleats.

Soon, she returned carrying a small tray with a steaming pot and three tiny, handle-less cups. Also, on a small plate, were three strangely folded cookies.

As they drank, Julia recounted her family's trips to the park and many more sights she wanted to show Matthew. Katy didn't want tea, but quickly broke open her cookie and pulled out a small piece of paper.

She squinted and read, "*You will be happy with your a-ccomplish-ments.* What's accomplishments mean?"

"It means you will be proud of what you will do with your life,"

"That's nice. I'm going back down to look at the gold fish."

"Alright, but don't stray too far and don't bother them."

After a few cups of tea and conversation about Matthew's work on the ferry, they reached for their fortune cookies.

Julia opened hers first and read aloud, "*Look to the future, but not too far.*"

"That's a little bit mysterious,"

"They're supposed to be," returned Julia. "Read yours."

"*You will feel both great joy and sorrow.* That's no great revelation. It's not what happens to you that's important, it's what you do about what happens that makes a difference."

"You should be writing fortunes!"

"I'll write my own," he replied, as he looked deep into Julia's eyes.

As they left the Japanese Tea Garden, Matthew's ear picked up a familiar sound. "That's 'Red-Haired Boy'."

"Well, *you* certainly would know!"

"No, I mean that tune on the fiddle. Do you hear it?"

Back on the concourse, between them and the Egyptian Museum, stood a musician playing the violin. Passersby would stop for a few seconds and some tossed coins into his open instrument case.

"Let me introduce you."

Julia was puzzled. As they walked up to the man, Matthew hailed him and he stopped his playing. "Samuel, how have you been?"

"Matthew! What a pleasant surprise! Well, what do you think?"

"Nice to see you again, Sam. You play that better than I do!"

"You are too kind! And who are these two lovely ladies accompanying you?"

"This is Julia and Katy Thomas." Samuel made a short bow. "Their father has a music store on O'Farrell."

"Oh yes, I know of it." Then he turned to Matthew once more. "Do you have any more Irish music for me?"

"How about 'Whisky Before Breakfast'? It's in D."

"That sounds like a good Irish tune!"

Matthew showed him the tune and like before, he picked it up very quickly. After he had mastered it, Matthew asked if Samuel could show him how to play a certain Chopin Nocturne.

"I'm helping a friend learn it." Matthew said as he looked back at Julia and winked. He could only play it from his memory and missed some important notes, so Julia would interrupt from time to time.

Finally, Samuel said, "this is a piano piece. A violin cannot do it justice." He was right. "Say, do you still have that five-dollar gold piece?"

"Right here!" Matthew produced the golden coin.

"You make sure you keep it, for good luck!"

"Don't worry!"

As they parted, Julia said to Matthew, "You certainly have a way of making friends! There's one more thing I want to show you."

They turned back past the Tea Garden and went up an incline until they were at the edge of a small lake with an island in the middle.

"This couldn't be natural," exclaimed Matthew, inspecting the topography around the lake.

"No, it was also made for the 1894 World's Fair. Let's take a boat ride and then we can go up 'Strawberry Hill'." They rented a row boat and Matthew got in first and took the oars. Julia and Katy sat at the back.

"Let's feed the ducks!" Katy cried.

"With what?"

Matthew replied, "Well, actually, I brought along some cookies for us to eat but they seem to have been smashed…"

"That's great!" Katy answered, but Julia looked at her crossly.

"OK. Once around the island!" He put his back into it and they smoothly got under way. Even though Matthew stayed to the right like all ships should, he still had to dodge some boats traveling in very haphazard directions. All along the way, Katy threw bits of cookies to the ducks and even a few gulls who tried to get in on the action. There was a gracefully arching stone bridge joining the island that had two curved openings so narrow that Matthew had to pull in the oars to navigate through to continue. After the boat ride, they walked over the same stone bridge and up 'Strawberry Hill' to the top.

"You'll love the view," Julia assured Matthew.

As Katy ran ahead, Matthew replied, "I do right now."

Matthew couldn't believe his eyes as they reached the top. A small octagon shaped castle with open arches greeted them. They climbed the stairs to the parapet and gazed across the park back toward the city and the bay.

"This is incredible!"

"I knew you'd like it."

As they took in the view, a finger of fog started to encroach on their afternoon. Matthew took Julia's hand and drew her close, brushing her hair from her face. He felt her warm sweet breath and her full, sensuous lips once again.

Still embracing, they turned to the west and seeing that the fog would hasten the sun's setting, they started down the hill.

The fog seemed to have changed Julia's demeanor. "We should be getting back. I need to have a talk with father."

That night, as Matthew cleaned the Opera House, he could think of nothing else but his day in the park with Julia, and the future he was planning with her.

The Cliff House from the Sutro Heights

Chapter 16

A PROPOSAL

⌇⌇⌇⌇⌇⌇⌇⌇⌇⌇⌇⌇

Matthew could hardly wait for the week to end. After work on Saturday, he cleaned the Opera House for the last time and Mr. Doran gave him his ticket. It had red borders with the words 'Carmen' and the date printed along with the seating number and row. Matthew carefully placed it in his shirt pocket and buttoned it down. He had been asking all the people working at the opera house about the best places to take Julia for an afternoon and where he should go to pop the big question. Although there was much dissention about restaurants and movie houses, as for a romantic day outside, there was wide agreement. After Golden Gate Park, the Sutro Heights and the Cliff House were it.

Sunday morning was almost gone. Matthew was so exhausted from his work on the ferries then going to the opera house until after midnight every night that his body had to catch up. Slowly, he opened one eye to the now familiar pale green that was his room. There was no need to look at his watch. The sun easily penetrated his room through the gossamer fabric covering the window. It cast shadows that were very short, revealing that the sun was almost directly overhead. He slowly rose and checked the pocket of his shirt. There it was; the ticket! So, it wasn't a dream! He turned it over, revealing the word 'Carmen' and 'Conreid Metropolitan Opera' and best of all, 'Enrico Caruso'! Julia loved the Italian tenor's voice. She had phonograph records of his great performances and had played a few for him. Matthew then thought about Signora Marinelli's little grandson and how he got his name.

April 17, 1906. Tuesday. That would be the big night! Matthew had it all planned. After the opera, he would invite the family for a late-night feast at the 'Darbee and Immel Oyster Grotto', the next block up from the music store. He would stand and offer a toast to the great Caruso and his fine performance, compliment Mrs. Thomas on her lovely dress and then coolly and eloquently ask Mr. Thomas for the hand of his daughter, Julia, in marriage!

But there was still the little detail of asking Julia! Matthew slowly shuffled down the hall to the bathroom. As he peered between the cracks in the mirror, he could tell that his face had been neglected for this last week. Matthew drew a bath, using all the hot water he could, scrubbing and soaking until the work week was washed away. He faced the mirror once more and went to work, carefully scraping off the stubble. Matthew had left a note and some money with Signora Marinelli earlier in the week to have his best clothes washed and pressed and there they were, neatly folded on the chair.

Matthew hoped Julia had gotten his note about today. He picked up the basket Dat So La Lee had given him, intending to give it to Julia as an engagement present.

Anthony Colburn

As he headed out the front door, Signora Marinelli called out. "You need'a get more to eat, you know!"

Matthew turned up O'Farrell with anticipation and some apprehension. Maybe she didn't even get the note. Maybe they would have to babysit Katy again. And maybe she would just say NO! He put those thoughts out of his head as he rang the bell to the store.

"Hello!" The familiar melodic voice came from a window three stories above. "I'll be down in a minute!"

Matthew waited anxiously on the sidewalk. He leaned on a lamp post and watched the traffic pass, trying to look nonchalant.

At last, the door handle moved. "I'm ready!"

"Where's your sister?"

"She went to Oakland with my parents to visit my aunt."

"Then it's just us?" Matthew tried to hide his elation.

"That's right. Are you disappointed?"

"You'll do!" Matthew returned sarcastically. "What about your father?"

"I told him you were related to the ship building Donahues. That changed his tune!"

"I'm going to have to look into that!" He produced the basket from behind his back. "This is for you. Remember that Indian basket maker I told you about, Dat So La Lee. She's my friend and she made it for me. I hope you'll like it too."

"Like it?! It's beautiful! How did she color it?"

"She uses natural dyes from plants. See this here," pointing out the dark designs, "It's from a fern."

"Thank you so much! I will cherish it always!" She threw her arms around Matthew's neck then went back upstairs and returned in a few seconds. "OK where are we going to go?"

"Let's take the line out around Point Lobos. It has some nice views," Matthew said rather matter-of-factly, though he had never been that way.

It was a fine day, just warm enough to not need a jacket, although they both took one along. As they traveled around Point

Lobos, Matthew gazed at the land north in Marin County beyond Fort Point. Julia could tell in Matthew's wide open green eyes that he had never seen these places before.

At the Sutro Heights depot, they departed and strolled toward Palm Avenue. At the entrance stood a wooden gate with fancy finials and statues on every spire with two imposing sculptures of lions resting on both sides. The avenue was true to its name with palm trees flanking both sides. Matthew smiled, thinking of the first time he saw a palm tree at the state capital. They walked up to the conservatory which was as impressive, if not as large as the one in the park.

"This is all a private park?" he asked suspiciously, "built for public use?"

"That's right. Mr. Sutro was a very magnanimous man." Matthew looked at Julia, trying to decipher the word. His goal was to add a new word to his vocabulary each day. "Generous," Julia said finally.

"Oh, yes. Quite." Matthew was a little uneasy because of his lack of formal education, but Julia appreciated his efforts and Matthew could sense it.

As they strolled hand in hand among the many statues lining the grounds, Matthew started to talk about Lake Tahoe and the beauty of the area.

"It is so refreshing and alive up there!"

"Don't you think this is refreshing?"

"Of course, but in a different way. The sea breeze and the salt air are, but it never gets too cold and it never gets too hot here. There are times in the fog when you don't even know whether it is day or night. And there are so many people!"

"And so many opportunities." Julia was wondering where this talk was headed.

"If you saw it, you would understand."

"I'm sure I would, but there are good things about all places," she said in a conciliatory tone.

Anthony Colburn

Their walk had taken them to a semicircular rock wall overlooking the impressive Cliff House and Seal Rocks with the grey-blue Pacific Ocean stretching out toward Japan.

"This is the Parapet," said Julia. "We used to come out here and watch the tall sailing ships come and go. I would wonder if they were on their way to China or coming back from their adventures in the Hawaiian Islands. I hear the native women there are quite beautiful."

"As are those of San Francisco," Matthew said, getting his courage up. Julia took Matthew's arm as they turned and watched a large steamer slowly paint its wake across the watery landscape.

The Parapet had many statues of classical figures lining the edge, looking down on the Cliff House and facing out to sea. Matthew got out his camera his mother had given him and took a couple of pictures.

"I think I'll send one to my mother. She'd like this view." As he took a photo, the scene through the view finder seemed to metamorphose. The waves and the rocks were still there, but the ornate structure below appeared to shrink into a plain flat-topped building. There were sleek motor cars parked in front but when Matthew looked up, all was just as it was before. All Matthew could do was wonder what lay in store for him and Julia.

Another couple saw Matthew and Julia and asked if they wanted a photograph together.

"That would be very nice!"

So, they stood arms around each other's waist with Julia reaching over to Matthew's chest with her other hand.

The woman commented, "such a lovely couple."

After enjoying the view a few seconds more, Matthew said, "Let's go down to the Cliff House. I hear there is a camera there that is so big, you can get inside!"

As they strolled along Serpentine Drive, they paused at a bench next to a statue of two wood nymphs. Julia sat with her parasol at her shoulder but Matthew immediately knelt on the pathway. At first, Julia thought he had dropped something, but then suddenly realized what was coming. She drew in a breath and sat motionless, her widening eyes staring into Matthew's.

"Julia, you are one of the most generous, kind and *magnanimous*, persons I have ever known," her face flushed with a demure smile, "and I have never known more joy and delight being around you." By this time, Matthew's knee was getting damp in the crushed sandstone drive. "I want you to know that I will always love you and I can't imagine living the rest of my life without you. Will you do me the honor of becoming my wife?"

Julia's mind was racing. All she could get out was a soft, "Yes."

"Good. That's good! Now your father can say you're engaged as much as he wants!"

Julia giggled as they both rose to an embrace, a melding of body and soul that they had never before experienced as her parasol dropped to the ground.

"But I have no ring…"

"That's alright," Julia softly whispered, "just have something by the time you ask him."

After a few moments, they continued down Point Lobos Road. Matthew felt as if a great weight had been lifted off his chest. Going on, they sometimes walked and sometimes skipped.

"We need to go there sometime," Julia said, as they walked downhill past the 'Sutro Baths'. "Thousands can swim at the same time!"

Matthew looked at the Greek style entrance and peeked down the stairway of the glass domed structure and made a face thinking of what that would be like compared to a solitary dip in Lake Tahoe on a hot summer day.

"Let's go in and take a look!"

"I don't know…" Mathew scratched his head. "Besides, we don't have swimming suits"

"We don't have to swim. There's lots to see inside. Let me show you. And just to let you know, you have to use the swimming suits they provide here."

"OK. But no swimming."

Through the entrance, Matthew and Julia immediately descended stairs to the ticket booth. On both sides of the broad staircase were tropical plants similar to the ones Matthew had seen at the conservatory and warm humid salt air wafted up as they walked.

"This is the museum," said Julia as they passed a huge stuffed sea lion.

"Where did Sutro get all this stuff?"

"They say he travels a lot and always brings back something from wherever he visits."

"He must've been a lot of places!" Matthew replied, thinking of how he could ever get the means to travel someday.

As they continued to walk down the wide corridor, they passed all manner of preserved wild animals. A Polar bear shared the space with objects collected from those same regions of the North. Beautiful wild spotted cats guarded glass cases full of native costumes and weapons from the equatorial regions.

"I'd like to spend our honey moon in Hawaii." Julia said out of the blue.

"Why Hawaii?"

"I don't know, it just seems like a place you can let time stand still and not worry about the rest of the world for a while."

"It would take some time to get there too," said Matthew, thinking more practically. But then he too got into the mood. "But it would be nice to lay with you on the beach with the warm waves splashing over us."

Julia smiled and wrapped her arm around Matthew's waist as they walked. "Let's go down to the promenade level."

As they descended, Matthew saw stretching out before him, the expansive arching glass and steel roof casting a cool, even, almost dreamlike light on this level. Everywhere were exotic potted plants and people leaning over the railing looking to the pools below.

Matthew whistled, "Wow! You weren't kidding when you said big!"

The pools stretched out over three hundred feet with one large 'L' shaped pool enclosing five other smaller pools. The Space looked like an aquatic circus with patrons going down slides, swinging on rings and trapezes then falling and diving, oblivious to the crowded water below. The sound was deafening with screams, yells and whistles reverberating off the glass dome.

After a minute or so of this, Matthew was ready to take his leave. He motioned to Julia and they started hand in hand, back up the stairs. Matthew was glad to finally be back out in the fresh air as they continued down toward the Cliff House.

The Cliff House was more like one of the mansions on Nob Hill multiplied tenfold. There were five levels with multiple turrets and spires in the most ornate 'French Chateau' style. It hung there at the high-water mark, its foundations clinging to the rocks over-looking the breaking waves and 'Seal Rocks' just off shore. Matthew and Julia walked onto the enclosed porch and strolled around its perimeter, taking in the view.

"We must be on the third level," said Matthew. "I want to see if we can find the 'Camera Obscura'. It's supposed to be in one of the turrets." They continued down an interior hallway passing various dining rooms marked 'private', finally reaching the large main dining room. It seemed a little crowded, so they decided to come back after their search. On the fourth floor, they entered an art gallery with more private dining rooms off to the side. Out some double doors was an outside porch, offering even better views, being one floor higher and totally open to the elements. The seals on the rocks just a hundred yards off shore offered their part to the din of gulls and people playing on the beach punctuated by the crashing waves below. But their quest was even higher so they went back through the gallery and up a narrow flight of stairs.

"This must be it!" remarked Matthew excitedly. He went up first, only to have to retreat to let a party of four descend. "Once more?" he said, this time letting Julia lead the way. The fifth floor held even more rooms with each turret being a room of its own with curved windows.

"I wonder where the camera could be?" Matthew puzzled. Finally, they passed a turret room that had an even narrower staircase, just for one person at a time with 'Camera Obscura' written above the door. This time, Matthew went first, following the spiraling stairs hugging the cylindrical walls.

"Wow." said Matthew almost in a whisper.

"Ohhh." returned Julia breathlessly as she arrived.

They were in almost total darkness with all the windows blacked out and just one single light source emanating from the top of the conical ceiling. They gazed at the almost magical sight in front of them. On a large polished metal concave drum, was the image of the outside world in panorama! The 'Camera Obscura' needed almost total darkness so the lens could record the image which seemed to float down, resting on the drum. They were mesmerized by the image as waves crashed and gulls flew across the surface of the drum.

"What a wonderful sight!"

"I agree." said Matthew as he leaned over and kissed her.

With his eyes closed in the darkness of the room, and holding Julia so close, He let his thoughts transport them to Lake Tahoe. There they were, Julia in her white dress and parasol and Captain Donohue in his uniform waving as he took the wheel of the 'Tahoe'. Suddenly, a blinding light cut his movie short. Another couple had found the door to the room and after they squeezed up to their level, Matthew and Julia descended.

"How lucky we were to find that room! I enjoyed every second up there."

"Me too."

They made their way back down the floors until finally reaching the main dining room where they had a light dinner and enjoyed each other's company immensely. As they were leaving, Matthew found a souvenir shop.

"Mother has never been to the Pacific Ocean," remarked Matthew as he picked up a shell. "I think she would like this."

"You really are so thoughtful." Julia suddenly proclaimed, "I want to put my feet in the sand!" So, they went down to the beach and walked along the broad expanse toward the base of the Cliff House.

The constant breaking of the waves made it impossible to talk softly, so Matthew yelled at the top of his lungs as he spun around, "I am the luckiest man in the world!"

He raced the surf up the beach taunting it to try to get him wet and then dared it by following the receding water back down the sand. Eventually, the relentless sea won and he was wet up to his knees. Julia was more cautious with her dress, but she let the waves cover her ankles as she wiggled her feet into the soft sand. They wanted to go around the rocks at the base of the Cliff House, but the tide was too high and the sea temporarily had its way. After getting back to the walkway, they took turns cleaning and tickling each other's feet.

Returning home as they rocked along in the cable car, Matthew said, "I suppose you would like the ceremony to be at your church."

"Yes, and I need to think of how many people and where we can have the reception. Would there be many of your friends or relatives?"

"I'm afraid there aren't too many of either that I can get a hold of. Maybe we can have a small wedding."

"I don't think you would say that if you knew my mother better!"

As the cable car proceeded to the center of the city, they smiled at each other, both thinking of how their lives would be changed forever, each having a very different vision of what that would look like.

Virginia and Truckee Railroad Locomotive #12 'Genoa'

Chapter 17

A VALUABLE CARGO

A crystal clear, frigid early April morning greeted all those waiting to board the northbound train on the east side of the great Sierra Nevada mountains. Towards the glow of the impending dawn, a mountain sheltered the remnants of one of the largest silver strikes in history and beyond that, desert for as far as the eye could see. In the opposite direction, the Sierras, shooting up like a geologic picket fence, already bathed in sunlight for a while, but it wasn't going to be enough to shake the icy grip winter still had on it.

Steam and smoke belched from the Virginia and Truckee engine number twelve, 'Genoa', as she momentarily slipped and then caught traction on the ice-cold ribbon of steel. This American-Standard type locomotive had been working the rails between Virginia City, Carson City and Reno for over thirty years, but even now, the twentieth century was promising to change this technology forever. She would soldier on though, for a few more years, her brightly polished brass fittings and white painted wheels revealing the pride the railroad still had in the hard-working veteran. The methodical chuff of the wood fired iron horse slowly picked up its cadence as it pulled out of Carson City, bound for Reno. Along with a mixed consist of passengers, freight and mail, there sat in the baggage car, a special shipment- gold bullion, just starting its long, perilous trip to the San Francisco mint from the Carson City assay office.

The silver boom of the 'Comstock Lode' had long since tarnished in the hills around Virginia City but to the south, gold fever was beckoning, this time in the desert boomtowns of Tonopah and Goldfield. For an instant in time in 1906, Goldfield was the largest city in the state with 30,000 eager prospectors, swindlers and shopkeepers. In that year alone, they coaxed over $7,000,000 of gold out of the desert landscape but just four years later, less than 5,000 souls would be hanging on. Tonopah would fare better, yielding nearly 1,000,000 ounces of gold worth over $20,000,000 in the first decade of the new century alone. In a small window of time, from 1902-06, all movement of precious metals from this Nevada mining region made its way north to the U.S. Assay Office in Carson City. The gold ore was brought up from the deep shafts of the mines, crushed in stamp mills to a powder, then dumped into a cyanide bath which drew out the precious metal. It was finally melted into bars and sent off to the assay office. The Carson City facility had closed its doors to the minting of coins some thirteen years earlier, so the bullion was now sent on to the mint in San Francisco by way of Reno to be made into legal tender.

Shipments followed a patchwork of railroads from the narrow-gauge 'Tonopah & Goldfield Railroad' to the 'Carson and Colorado Railway', the 'Virginia and Truckee Railroad' and finally to the mainline 'Central Pacific Railroad', part of the transcontinental link to San Francisco.

Labeled as machine parts in an oversized crate so as not to attract attention, the gold, collected from various mines, would safely navigate the mountains of the Sierra Nevada then continue down to San Francisco bay at Oakland. The only persons who knew of the crate's true contents were the Carson City assay office Superintendent, Roswell Colcord, the San Francisco Mint Superintendent, Frank Leach and the three guards. Once the train made its way to the bay, the train would creep out over the long wharf or 'mole' as it was known at Oakland, which was in effect, a long extension of the rail line jutting more than two miles into the bay. The crate would then be transferred to a waiting horse drawn wagon to make the bay crossing on the ferry and finally, driven to the mint on Fifth Street.

The guards wore plain work clothes to avoid attracting attention to their cargo- twenty-five, 400 oz. bars worth over $200,000. The ingots were stamped with their mining company's marks; the 'Mohawk', 'Florence' and 'Jumbo' mines around Goldfield and the 'North Star', 'Desert Queen' and 'Mizpah' in Tonopah. Because the crate weighed over 600 pounds, it was fitted with steel wheels to facilitate the transfers.

About a half hour into the trip, the sun finally broke over the Virginia Range to the east and soon Washoe Lake glittered, reminding one of the guards of the silver strike he was too young to know. He leaned against the sliding door of the baggage car gazing out one of the small windows.

"My old man could've been one of those rich bastards sitting up on that hill in 'Frisco right now..."

"Yea, and mine would'a been president if he could'a got a vote!" The owner of the second voice was a smallish wiry man with a handlebar moustache with the best of his years behind him. He slowly pushed himself up so his head cleared the crate. "What time 'ya got, anyway," he said in a semi-annoyed manner.

"It's only half past six," replied Andy, the daydreaming young man. "And what do you know of the Comstock anyway? I heard tell they brought you in from Denver just for this run."

The older guard grinned, "I know enough not to throw my life away just digging a hole in the ground!"

Andy made a move for him but stopped short when a rifle barrel came down on the crate between the two. A man just on the other side of his prime but still a formidable figure, stepped up.

"Is that the only thing you two can think of doin' to keep warm? Get some rest. Before you know it, we'll be in Reno and we won't have much shut-eye after that 'till we hit 'Frisco."

"Well, he could'a..." mumbled the young guard.

"Yea, yea," replied the voice sinking back behind the crate.

As the train pulled out of the small Mormon settlement of Franktown and up the grade, the old guard quipped, "Didn't know you were so well thought of, Frank!"

The big man was not amused. He just kept his eyes on the barren landscape, rubbing the baggage car window to clear away the frost and glancing at his pocket watch. Soon the train slowed for Steamboat, a stop that used to carry passengers from Reno to a grand hotel with hot springs to rejuvenate the tired and infirm in the healing waters. All that was left now was a post office and some outlying ranches.

"Do you remember when there was boiling water and steam everywhere?" asked Andy.

"Yeah, I even spent some time soaking my bones in that water. Said to cure whatever ailed you."

"What happened to it?"

"Earthquake! The very thing that made the springs bubble up right there in the first place," Frank pointed to a barren patch of ground with deep fissures.

Anthony Colburn

"...just took it away in the blink of an eye. Then the hotel burned next year. Some said squatters cookin' in the empty rooms started it."

The young guard looked blankly at the unremarkable landscape, absorbed in thought as the train got underway again. Andy wondered if the forces of the earth could someday drain Lake Tahoe. He also wondered where his friend Matthew was and what he had made of his life. For his part, Andy was satisfied with his decision to leave Lake Tahoe and he dreamed of having a ranch up near the mountains along the Carson River someday.

The train ambled on through the brush studded landscape toward its final destination, its thick black smoke creating a stark contrast to the almost cobalt blue of the high desert sky. In less than thirty minutes, they would reach Reno and wait for the westbound Central Pacific train.

Reno was a bustling town at the foot of the Sierra Nevada range where the Truckee River flows down from Lake Tahoe and on out into the desert, finally emptying into Pyramid Lake. The town started as 'Lake's Crossing', where an entrepreneurial man first constructed a toll bridge and later made a deal with the railroad to put a depot stop there. It serviced the ranchers and farmers of the area as well as travelers on the railroad. Soon, Reno came to be known up and down the line as a town where just about anything goes.

"Well, this is it," Frank said matter-of-factly as the train crossed the ice-fringed Truckee River and turned parallel to the east-west tracks of the Central Pacific.

Sam, the older guard from the Denver mint curled his moustache and thought for a second. "Where can we get a good meal? We only got a half hour before the 8:15 westbound gets here!"

Frank calmly replied, "Don't worry, I'll get something for all of us over at Kate's. First thing, we have to get these bars- I mean machine parts onto the loading platform."

After the passengers disembarked, the train eased up to the platform on the mainline side and the three men started pushing the heavy cargo off. The conductor strolled by and noticed the stenciled label 'Hendy Iron Works, San Francisco'. "I thought they *made* machine parts, not bought them."

"Yeah, that's right," said Frank, "but they sent the wrong ones, so these are being brought back for an exchange." The conductor thought for a second. "That's some awful heavy parts."

Sam retorted, "If you ever saw a stamp mill work, you'd know why." After the conductor's curiosity was satisfied, he walked on to the V&T office, glancing at his watch.

"We make a pretty good pair of liars!"

"Yea," Frank replied, "but we best be talking less than more if we want to make it to 'Frisco. Don't wan' a cause any suspicion. Be back in a few minutes with some vittles."

Frank quickly crossed the main line and then the narrow-gauge Nevada, California and Oregon tracks and proceeded past the plaza and up Center Street. On the corner of Fourth and Center stood a boarding house with a restaurant on the ground floor. 'Kate's Best Room and Board' adorned the window and the smell of fresh coffee and bacon permeated the brisk air. A slight blanket of frost covered the boardwalk, with footprints revealing that only a few souls had yet ventured out this morning for breakfast. Frank entered and sat close to the door. Presently, a woman of ample proportions sauntered up. She was pretty with curly straw-colored hair and looked younger than her forty-some years.

"Haven't seen you 'round these parts for some time, Frank. Wha'cha been up to?"

"Been down to Tonopah and Goldfield."

She looked to the south. "That's a long way to go to chase gold."

Frank had to think fast in order to keep her off the subject. "Not for me. Everyone that has any gold is wanting to build and there ain't too many that know how. You can make a pretty good living in carpentry these days."

Kate looked out the window, then smiling, back into his eyes. "You always were good with your hands." Frank wasn't expecting the reply, and self-consciously turned back to his menu.

"Workin' with the Virginia and Truckee now. Got two helpers back at the warehouse in need of some good cooking, quick."

"Well, you came to the right place for that, too. What'll it be?"

Frank searched through the menu for his favorite. "Mutton and biscuits with gravy," he announced. "Three orders."

"A little early for supper, don't ya think?" she said, as Frank glanced nervously over the top of the menu.

"We gotta make it last for a while. Still get your meat from them Basque folks up by Honey Lake?"

"Yeah. It'll be just a few minutes. What are your friends doin'?"

"They gotta move a crate, so I came ahead to get the food. I'll take it down to 'em so they'll get it good and hot." Frank felt a twinge of uneasiness, feeling that he may be revealing too much.

Kate glanced back as she went into the kitchen, catching Frank leaning around a chair to get a better view somewhere below her waist. As Frank looked around, he noticed a couple of men seated at the table closest to the kitchen who looked like they were on their way to the fields. He could tell they were greenhorns from the new boots and clean clothes.

The older of the two men approached and inquired, "Excuse me, sir. I couldn't help hearing that you spent some time in Goldfield. We're headed that direction and we were wondering what news you might have."

Frank looked up from under his black, sweat stained hat. "If it's gold you're lookin' for, best place to find it is in the hotels and saloons, or in a trade…You'll find better money from that than being lowered into some hole every day."

The man was taken aback. He took a step back and had turned away before a hesitant "Thanks" came out.

Frank stared through the window and thought back to his younger days when the West was still wild and he was 'green'. Frank was born in Virginia City in 1874, just one year before the great fire that leveled the town. His father was born in the lumber and mining camp of Roopville up north of Reno and rushed to the Comstock Lode to find his fortune when he was just eighteen. There he met a girl in the saloons who became Frank's mother. They never married, but stayed friends and Frank knew his father as a good-natured man who helped with his schooling. He last saw his father just before the 'Great White Winter' in 1889-90 when almost all the livestock in the state perished. His mother later moved to Marysville in California. Frank tried his hand at mining for more than two years but found it too dangerous and unsatisfying. In 1903 though, he found himself once again in the middle of a great strike, this time to the south in Goldfield. This is where he met Andy.

Andy had lost his parents to consumption in the 'White Winter' when he was just four years old. He had an aunt in Salt Lake City, but she showed no interest, probably because she had seven children of her own. A Mormon family near Franktown took him in and raised him as their own, even though they already had five children. It was a hard life and Andy never took to the religion so when he turned twelve, he left for work in the woods of Lake Tahoe. Andy had no idea what hard work was until he reached Glenbrook, but a timber faller took him under his wing as his helper. His timing was always a little off though, and in just a year, all the timber had been cut and the mills were closing down. Andy knocked around Lake Tahoe working as a surveyor's rod man creating the route for the railroad from Truckee and later helped in the construction of the Tahoe Tavern. That's where he met Matthew Donohue and spent many days together exploring the area. When word came of the strike in Butler in the Tonopah district south of Carson City, Andy decided to trade the ten-foot snow drifts of Tahoe for the heat of the desert.

Frank had vowed to himself not to go back to mining, so he turned to carpentry. One day, as he watched the miners emerge from the hole in the ground known as the Mizpah Mine, he noticed a young man with large hands striding toward him. Frank talked the young man into going into business with him and he and Andy developed a steady carpentry business. The team built homes and hotels and supplied the local undertaker with coffins. They even had the occasion to make Virgil Earp's coffin, brother of the famous Wyatt Earp, when Virgil succumbed to pneumonia in 1905. Finally, Frank moved back north and settled in Carson City to work as a carpenter and part-time crew on the Virginia and Truckee Railroad. He let Andy know about the guard position and personally vouched for him to the officials at the assay office. It was Andy's mother though, who got him the guard position, as she worked for Mr. Yerington, the manager of the Virginia and Truckee Railroad.

When Kate came out with the food, it was already 8:10 a.m. Focusing back to the present, Frank took the boxes and hurriedly slapped two ten-dollar gold coins on the table. He gave Kate a kiss on the cheek and as he headed for the door he said, "That should cover the plates and forks, and a down payment for my next visit, too." Kate just stood there shaking her head, as a slight smile stole across her face.

Luckily, the 8:15 express was a few minutes late. Frank crossed the tracks just as he heard a whistle in the distance. Sam and Andy were on the platform leaning against their valuable cargo looking a bit more relieved at the sight of him. Before Sam could get a smart remark in, Frank said, "Had to look up an old acquaintance while I waited for the food."

When the train pulled up to the station, Frank met the conductor who directed him to the baggage car that would hold the valuable cargo. The three strained to load their shipment of 'machine parts' and secured it with blocks of wood and chains. After they got underway, the crate substituted for a dinner table.

"Only fourteen hours to go…," said Sam as he grabbed a rag for a makeshift napkin. "Good thing this was a light winter. I remember back in '80. Dumped fifteen feet that April alone!"

Andy's eyes widened, "How did the trains get through?!"

"Didn't. Least not for a couple of weeks, till they got those Chinamen diggin' down to the tunnels."

Andy's eyes dropped to the crate, and not wanting to imagine those conditions any longer, changed the subject. "How much 'ya think this is all worth?"

"Well," replied Sam, "gold is about $20 an ounce these days and each bar is 400 ounces and there's twenty-five bars…"

Andy looked up as if he was searching his mind for what to do with the figures and finally resigned himself to the fact that the number would be too great to ponder.

Sam continued, looking more serious, "You know, you're not on this trip by accident. The government checked you two out pretty good before you got the job. Didn't want a bunch of stiff collared guards causing a big stir, neither. Sometimes the best security is goin' along like machinery parts."

The trip progressed uneventfully up the long steep grades along the Truckee River, then began winding in and out of deep granite filled ravines, still choked with snow and ice. It was midday, and the glare off the snow was too much to bear for more than a few seconds, but just before the snow sheds, Andy looked out to a flat, long, leaf-shaped expanse of snow.

"What's that, a frozen lake?"

"Not only that. It's just about the sorriest place this side of the great Salt Lake desert. You heard of the Donner Party, ain't you?" Andy looked at his boots and nodded. "Well, that's what they call Donner Lake, now. Beautiful spot in the summer time but no place to find yourself with winter coming on."

He was thinking of his step-father and the stories he told of that ill-fated group and how he had long ago vowed to himself never to travel these mountains in the winter. This was bad enough- even in the bright light, the snowdrifts looked menacing. Then there were the tunnels that bored straight into the granite mountainside, black holes in a dazzling white world. Each tunnel promised minutes of choking acrid smoke. Even with the lantern lit, it looked like a dark sinister fog descending on the guards. Then they would pop out, suddenly thrust into the blinding sunlight, but thankful to be breathing fresh air again.

"How many more hellish tunnels do we have to go!?" pleaded Andy. He had never been west of Tahoe and the trip was losing its charm by now.

"Well, if my count is right," Sam twisted his moustache to help him think, "I'd say that was tunnel number ten so we only have twenty more to go!" Andy had a blank look of astonishment.

Frank interrupted, "No, really, the tunnels are counted from west to east. We started with tunnel fourteen and we just went through number ten. Most of the tunnels are short 'cept for number six, Summit Tunnel. Over 1,600 ft., not counting the snow sheds. We should keep our eyes peeled for any suspicious goings on around that tunnel."

At the summit tunnel, everyone just hunkered down with his own thoughts and waited for the darkness to be over. Under the crate, a faint creaking sound was just barely discernable over the rumble reverberating off the tunnel walls.

"What's that?" Andy nervously inquired.

"Just us rats," came Sam's voice.

Once more, the train burst out into the open and all came back to normal. Frank checked the doors on both ends of the baggage car as they picked up speed.On the west side of the Sierras, there seemed to be more snow but it was also starting to melt. Along the tracks, Andy could see rivulets flowing over and sometimes falling beneath the ice and snow and here and there he could see bare rock.

As he looked to the west, Sam could see well out into the haze of the Sacramento Valley. "That's the worst of it," he declared, "but now we have about a hundred stops between here and Oakland!"

Again, Andy's inexperience allowed for this huge number so Frank interjected again. "Well, maybe not quite a hundred, but there are plenty and we got to keep a look out for any suspicious characters."

Finally, the snow-white world of the mountains began to give way to the greens of early spring. Torrents of water followed the train's progress next to the tracks in an unnamed gully. At Dutch

Flat, Andy kept a keen eye through the baggage car window on a China-man who just sat cross legged, with his head down, motionless.

Sam glanced over and said, "No need to bother with that one, Opium got him under control."

Then came stops at Gold Run, Colfax, Lander, and Auburn. Finally, as the train spilled out onto the flat Sacramento Valley, the sun sank below the defining hills surrounding San Francisco Bay. As the train came to a stop, just visible in the encroaching dusk, there stood all alone, the silhouette of a low, broad mountain and a little more to the right, a notch where the Sacramento River turned toward the bay.

"That's where we're headed," Frank proclaimed as if he were guiding the first explorers, "The mountain of the devil and Carquinez Strait!"

"They can all go straight to the devil for all I care if I could just get me a good meal!" an irritated Sam shot back.

"I swear, about all 'ya think of is your stomach!" Frank said under his breath.

"And the gold," came an even less audible response.

Right across from Sacramento's depot was a café.

"Sit tight," Frank announced. He slid the baggage door open and in a few minutes, he returned with an armload of food. "They keep it warmed up for folks like us," he said as Andy and Sam started in on ears of corn.

Before he even took two bites, Sam suddenly said, "Almost forgot. Got to send a telegram to the mint in 'Frisco!"

Andy could see him through the half-closed curtain as Sam hurried over to the Western Union office. Andy entertained himself as he ate, by watching the rush of people leaving and boarding the train. Where have they all come from and where can they all possibly be going? he thought. Then, Andy's attention returned to Sam as he left the office. Curiously, he gave a tip of his hat as if greeting a lady, but there was no one passing by.

The whole stop took less than ten minutes, just enough to top off the tender with water and oil. As Sam jumped back in the baggage car, it was evident he had done more drinking and smoking in his life than running as he coughed and wheezed to catch his breath.

"What you lookin' at?" he said, glaring at Andy as he lit up another cigar.

As the train got underway again, Andy noticed two men, both about Frank's age but bigger, with non-descript work clothes jump on the slowly moving train just behind the baggage car.

"What would two men like that be doing, hitching a ride this time of day?" asked Andy, turning to Frank.

Before Frank could respond, Sam interjected. "Just railroad workers headed back to the Oakland yard, I s'pect. I've seen it lots of times. Men are needed in Sacramento for a few days then they go back to their regular jobs."

That response didn't sit quite right with Andy and he asked, "I thought you were from Denver."

Sam bristled, "You callin' me a liar? I've made this run from Denver plenty 'a times. How 'bout you?"

Andy recoiled, "just askin'."

Andy had never quite warmed up to Sam. He just didn't seem like what a U.S. Mint man should be. With his incessant fiddling with his moustache, he looked to Andy to be always planning something. At length, he decided that Sam just had a lot of responsibility as they all did ensuring that the gold got to the mint in San Francisco safe and sound.

Frank gazed at the stars beginning to appear in the increasing darkness, and trying to break the uneasy silence said, "Were you old enough to remember that thing... happened at Candelaria, Andy?"

Andy thought for a second. "You mean that light in the sky? Heard 'bout it but didn't see it myself. I was pretty young. My folks did and said it was a sign...from God."

Frank, still fixed on a star, said, "It was late winter. '94. There was a light dusting of snow. I was walking down West Street in

Carson when I noticed the snow started to glow. I looked up and saw a blue-white light streaking across the heavens." Frank traced a graceful arc with his hand. "It only lasted 'bout five seconds but it was enough to make you wonder. Men over in Candelaria thought it was the end of the world. Said a big explosion lit up the whole sky, an' everything was shaking, earthquake like. Never found what it was, though. Probably one a' them meteors you hear about every now and then."

Sam looked skeptical. "Did 'ya ever see one once it was on the ground?" Frank shook his head. "Well, if I can't hold it in my hand it ain't real. Take these here 'machine parts'. Now that's the real thing"

Andy looked puzzled but then remembered.

"If you were to pick up one 'a these parts, you would be surprised just how soft the metal is. An' they're valuable. You could shave off a bit of it with a knife if you wanted to pay for some new boots, or a bit more would get you a good horse."

"What about one a' them new horseless auto-mobiles?" Andy asked with an enthusiastic smile.

"Aw, those things won't never take hold. Where 'ya gonna drive 'em outside the city? Anyway, they always break down."

"Well, I still want one. 'Sides, they're getting better all the time. So how much gold would that take?"

"Thirty or forty ounces I 'spect." Andy fixed his gaze on the crate. "All it would take is one or two of those bars and you'd be fixed for life!"

Frank chuckled, "Yeah, one or two 'a those bars would fix you for life in San Quentin, too! Let's just keep our minds on the job. Only a few hours to go anyhow."

The train made good progress now, stopping at Davis, Elmira and Cannon as the western sky grew progressively darker. Finally, the whistle indicated that they were slowing down for Benicia. The train would be taken across part of the bay to Port Costa on a huge ferryboat. It was already in place as the train rounded the bend to the water's edge. In the faint electric lights around the dock, Andy could just make out the ferry pilot's cabin and just below it, the word 'Solano'.

"This is just 'bout the biggest boat I s'pect you ever seen!" said Frank as the train came to an abrupt halt.

"That's a fact!" exclaimed Andy almost in a whisper, as his eyes widened. Sam chuckled as he waxed his moustache. The train had to be separated in two parts. The locomotive and the first five cars moved gingerly onto the huge vessel. Andy could see there were four tracks, including the ones they were on. One of the deck hands motioned for the engineer to inch forward until the locomotive came up against a large beam set across the tracks. Huge chains keeping the locomotive about thirty feet from the other end of the boat, secured it. At the same time, another smaller locomotive, Sam called it a 'boat goat', pulled the remaining cars back and then pushed them onto another track so they were across from the first set. It seemed a little strange to Andy to look across to people seated in cars that had been trailing them for so long. There were men in suits puffing on cigars and families with children peering back at him through the darkness.

"Let's take a look outside," Andy said, as he leaned for the door but Frank put his hand on his shoulder.

"Can't do any sight seein'. This is the hardest part of the trip."

"Sorry, It's just…"

"I know, you just ain't never seen such a big boat!" Sam mocked. Presently, the 'Solano' gave a long low whistle while the paddle wheels struggled against the cold dark waters of the Carquinez Straights. Slowly at first, but then with increasing speed, the 'Solano' got underway. Going down stream with the current of the Sacramento River and the ebbing tide, the boat quickly made the less-than-one-mile crossing. There was an almost full moon reflected in the ferry's choppy wake as the men stood, feeling the predictable sway of the cars on the tracks give way to a slow smooth pitch. Just as it got up to speed, the boat had to start slowing by reversing its engines and by the time they reached the opposite shore, the huge paddle wheels were beating the water into a froth. The railroad and ferry crew made short work of putting the train back on firm rails at Port Costa and they were soon on their way once again to Oakland.

Curiously to Andy, the western horizon was beginning to get lighter and he turned to Frank. "Why is it getting brighter out there?"

Before Frank could respond, Sam let out a big belly laugh. "You really are a greenhorn! Them's the lights of the big city, boy! Watch him, Frank! You don't want him wandering down to that Barbary Coast…taken in by some lady of ill repute!"

Andy glared but Frank just said, "That's enough, we'll be done with this job soon and that's all that matters."

"I'm not worried," Andy replied calmly. "I got a friend working on the ferries. He'll show me around the city!"

Andy didn't care to be in the company of Sam a moment more than he had to by this time. He kept wondering to himself, how a man like this got to be in the employ of the government.

Finally, the train pulled into Oakland and came to a 'wye', slowly backing up to the man-made spit of land jutting out into the bay. The terminus was a large arching metal structure able to accommodate four trains at a time. Sam went to meet the horse drawn wagon that would take the precious cargo to its final destination while Andy and Frank released the chains and blocks.

All the passengers left the train first. There were business men in their suit coat and vests, couples with their children and a small group of working-class men maybe returning from Sacramento. The porters hurried to unload the luggage as the last of the passengers walked by the gates to join other people from Oakland waiting for the soon to be arriving ferry boat.

"Got to sit tight," said Frank. "Nothing worse than getting this cargo on that wagon and having to wait fifteen minutes, exposed."

Chapter 18

A FATEFUL CROSSING

⸻

The 'Golden City' eased up to the Oakland mole with its paddle wheels in full reverse. Matthew Donohue hopped onto the dock like he had hundreds of times before, securing the lines.

"OK, now it's time to get going!" said Frank. He opened the baggage car door while the wagon backed up with one man at the reigns, and Sam and another man walking beside it.

The driver showed his U.S. Mint badge and said, "Any troubles?"

"Nah, pretty quiet all the way." Sam looked at the other man, who nodded.

The three assisted by the other mem shoved the crate over and onto the wagon, compressing the springs considerably while the two horses stamped their hooves uneasily. The wagon progressed without incident onto the deck and proceeded through the center of the craft to the San Francisco end. Matthew saw the wagon come aboard, with Sam directing it to one side, almost directly over the coal chute hatch while another wagon full of building materials was maneuvered to the other side. Then, walking up behind the wagon came Andy, Frank and the other U.S. Mint man.

Matthew glanced over at the men and could hardly believe his eyes! He hadn't seen Andy since he left for the gold fields years before.

"Well, what 'd ya know! Look what the cat drug in!" yelled Matthew as he jumped back on deck.

"Is that you, Matt!? What luck, getting your boat!" Andy turned to his fellow workers. "This here's Frank and Sam." Andy continued,

"We've been riding in stinkin' baggage cars since Carson City!" Frank frowned.

"Can I have a few minutes to catch up on old times, Frank?"

"OK. But remember..." He held his finger up to his lips.

Matthew and Andy gave each other a hearty hug near one of the life boats.

"Wait a few minutes while I help get us underway."

Andy watched with pride in his friend's skill as he did his duties. Just like on the 'Tahoe', he thought.

After they were safely under way toward San Francisco, they sat down on the main deck near the fiddley.

"So," Matthew began, "what 'a ya been doin' with yourself?"

"Well, I hooked up with Frank, down south 'a Hawthorn, by Tonopah. He's a real good guy. Got me out of the mines and working with him in carpentry. An' believe it or not, I got to meet Wyatt Erp an' his brother, Virgil, rest his soul."

"What!?"

"That's right. Wyatt ran the Northern Saloon in Tonopah an' Virgil was deputy sheriff in Goldfield, but he took sick an' died, an' we were his official coffin makers!"

"Well, that's interesting. But what are you doin' hauling this crate all the way from Carson City?"

Andy took Matthew by the coat and pulled him closer. "I know you 'bout as good as anyone an' I'd trust you with my life..."

"What's wrong?"

"Nothing's wrong!" Andy said almost in a whisper now, even though the sound of the huge engine would have drowned out any eavesdroppers. "It's our cargo!"

"I was wondering. How many men does it take anyway just for some machine parts? An' what's with the guns?"

"Here's the thing." Andy looked over his shoulder again. "We got us here a real treasure!"

"What!?"

"Shh! That's right!" He continued, leaning over to Matthew's ear.

"That crate is carrying twenty-five bars of pure gold!"

"Why!? What's going on?" Matthew's eyes widened. Andy had to put his hand over Matthew's mouth to keep him from saying anything else.

"Came from the mines 'round Tonopah and those parts! Picked them up at the assay office in Carson City and now, here they are!" Andy motioned discretely towards the crate on the wagon and the men leaning against it. "We're all U.S. Government agents! Sworn to see that the gold stays safe! All we got to do now is escort the load down to the mint on Fifth Street!"

"I don't think I should be hearing all this!"

"Don't worry, what can happen now? We're almost home! But, I sure do feel a lot better knowin' you're onboard. You got to show me around San Francisco tomorrow. We got a day or two before we have to go back."

"OK. We can go out to the park and I think you'd probably like to see the ocean…"

"Does it really taste like salt?"

"Yup. You know the mint's pretty close to my place. You could probably stay with me."

"You're the best!" Andy patted Matthew on the back as they got up.

"Let me show you the rest of the boat."

As the ferry boat passed Goat Island and turned toward the ferry terminal, Matthew could see the tower with its huge clock reading 10:05.

He looked at his watch and turning to Andy said, "They keep that thing a little fast, just to make sure we're not late."

At the same time, Sam, checking to see no one was watching, casually nodded to the man leaning against the wagon. He slid under and started to open a hatch in the bed of the wagon, but it was stuck. He had to pry it open with a knife and the noise alerted Frank.

"What was that?" he asked Sam.

"What. That? That's just the boat creaking and groaning. You're getting awfully touchy!"

The man under the wagon finally pulled the door open and then started to work on the crate. Sam had already loosened the boards while they passed through the tunnels in the mountains, but it still took some effort. All of a sudden, a piece of the crate came loose and fell with a thud on the deck.

Frank, who had gone over to the other side of the deck, leaned over and seeing the man, gave out a yell, "Hey, you!" and started to run toward the wagon. He drew his pistol but stopped short as he felt the cold steel of another barrel at his temple.

"Just take it easy, Frank! I told you not to be so touchy!" Sam eased the gun out of Frank's hand and escorted him behind the wagon next to the railing as the vessel's bow cut through the smooth water.

"Who put you up to this, Sam? You've been with the mint for twenty years!"

"It's my own idea! After all this time, they wanted to just throw me out with the trash! Well, I'm just saltin' a little something away for my retirement! I've been playin' this like a fixed game of poker 'cause I'm holdin' all the cards!" He tauntingly handed Frank a deck of cards he had in his pocket. "Straight flush! Ace high!"

"You'll never get away with this! How are 'ya gonna get off this boat with all that the gold?"

"That's the beauty of it! We won't!" Frank was confounded. "You see that hatch down there?" Sam pushed Frank's head under the wagon with the barrel of his gun. "That's the hatch to the coal chute. See my friend there? He opened it an' he's just about done prying open the bottom of the crate. In a minute, all the gold bars will drop down the chute and into the coal bunker! But with all that commotion, I'm afraid the horses will most likely get all spooked and dump the crate overboard. What a pity, losing all that mining machinery. It'll be in all the papers! We'll lay low, then when the 'Golden City' goes for its overhaul next month, we just fish them bars out of the coal! Pretty good huh?"

Then Sam got serious. "No one has to get hurt! Go along with us. You may even get a cut if you help us out! What did the railroad ever do for you anyway?"

Frank looked Sam straight in the eye. "They trusted me,"

"You really are the real thing, ain't you?"

Finally, the boards were freed. The man under the wagon reached into the crate and pulled out a bar. Even at night, it shone with an unnatural brilliance. He guided it to the chute and reached for another. Suddenly, a board snapped and the whole load gave way and cascaded down on the hapless man. He screamed as the gold bars crushed his chest and one leg.

In a flash, the driver of the wagon jumped off and helped remove the bars, continuing to guide them down the chute. The scream alerted Andy and Matthew and they came running while a crowd started to gather on the cabin deck.

Frank used the distraction to try to wrestle the gun from Sam. As they fought, the other man drew his gun and fired at Andy and Matthew. The first bullet whizzed past Mathew's ear, but the second shot found its mark. Andy stumbled and fell, almost into Matthew's arms.

"Help Frank...for me, Matthew!" Those were his last words.

A dazed Matthew held Andy's blood-stained body close. "Andy! Andy! Stay with me!" Matthew looked at his bloody hands in horror, instantly recalling the same words he had uttered on the mountain top when he had foreseen Andy's death. But he was already gone and Matthew slowly lowered him to the deck.

Andy's murderer quickly finished pushing the bars down the chute when a shot rang out from the hurricane deck, dropping him like a sack of grain. Matthew wheeled around to see Captain Turner, still pointing his gun.

The spooked horses reared and bolted, tipping the wagon onto the railing and the crate fell into the bay, bobbing off into the darkness.

By this time, the ferry's horn had sounded and the paddle wheels were spinning in full reverse.

Sam and Frank continued to struggle but in an instant, it was over. There was a crack from the pistol and Frank turned to brace himself against the overturned wagon, struggling to remain upright. He took two steps and fell on his side. Sam jumped overboard into the dark water followed by more shots from the captain from above.

Matthew ran to Frank's side and held him up. He just pointed to the coal chute and let out his last breath. Matthew thought he heard a cough from out in the bay but as he turned, all he could see was the water lapping against the pieces of the crate.

It was all over in the space of fifteen seconds. As a stunned Matthew sat on the deck, George finally made it from the opposite end of the boat. The crushed man lay moaning and coughing up blood.

"What happened to him!?" George was trying to make sense of the whole scene- Three men lay dead on the deck, one was crushed and near death, the wagon was tipped and hanging over the side and Matthew was just sitting in the middle of it all.

"I think the wagon must have run over him." Matthew said, regaining his composure.

George calmed the horses and unhitched them from the tangled mess.

Captain Turner made his way to the main deck and posted hands to keep the passengers from getting down the stairs.

"I think I might have winged the one that jumped. What caused all this carnage?"

Matthew thought quickly. He saw the cards strewn on the deck. "I think they were fighting over a card game."

"What men won't do to lose their life over! What a waste! How's that one?"

"It looks pretty bad. I don't think he'll make it," said George.

"Well, keep him comfortable as you can. We'll get back underway. Signal shore to have a hospital wagon waiting when we dock, Mister Donohue!" The captain ran over to a speaking tube and ordered the engine room, full speed ahead then headed for the hurricane deck.

Frank, Andy and the wagon driver's bodies were carried out of sight of the people above on the cabin deck and covered with a cloth. The crushed man was made as comfortable as they could, covering him with coats and a blanket.

Matthew and two other hands righted the wagon. After it was pulled away and tied down, Matthew went over to clean up around the broken railing. Under some of the clutter, he thought he saw a golden gleam. Moving some boards away revealed the source- a huge gold bar! He knelt down, concealing it from view.

All sorts of ideas started to race through Matthew's head. Were there really twenty-five bars of gold in that crate? Where were the others? Did the rest fall into the water? Did anyone else know about the real contents of that crate and if so, they must assume that it got dumped in the bay!

As Matthew's head was spinning with questions, he glanced over in the direction of the coal hatch. A fragment of wood kept it from being completely closed. This seemed odd to Matthew because it was flush with the deck when it was closed and it took a hook to open it. He knelt over the hatch and pulled out the wood. It was a piece of the crate!

How could it have possibly gotten stuck in the coal chute hatch… *unless* it was already open!? He thought he said it to himself, but he couldn't be sure.

Matthew took off his coat and wrapped up the bar, then casually walked over to his pack sack and dropped it in.

What are you doing!? This time he was sure he said it to himself.

Someone must know about the gold, but they also must think it was lost overboard! I'll just take it for safe keeping, until the authorities call for it. Matthew wasn't concerned about the flawed logic of that thought. He just comforted himself knowing he was doing the right thing.

By the time the ferry docked, the man with the crushed chest was dead. He hadn't said anything about the incident, despite repeated questioning by George.

The authorities took all the workers on the ferryboat as well as some of the passengers up to one of the offices. Matthew tried to keep calm, but with a twenty-five-pound gold bar in his back pack, paranoia started to creep into his thinking. He just knew that the police were going search everyone's belongings and he would be revealed as the master-mind of the robbery! But miraculously they paid no attention to his pack.

The only thing everyone could say for sure was that the as yet unidentified wagon driver shot Andy, the captain shot him, Sam shot Frank and jumped overboard and the other unidentified man was crushed, probably by the wagon. The load was a total loss with several passengers seeing it fall overboard. But no one mentioned anything about gold bars!

It was after midnight before the police were satisfied with the stories and let everyone go. By that time, the papers had gotten wind of the crime and reporters were swarming everywhere. Matthew was a little embarrassed with himself when he didn't volunteer that he knew Andy. But he rationalized that bringing up anything that tied him to the attempted robbery and the murders would cast doubt on his story, and maybe even reveal the real cargo! Matthew did not want to face the reporter's prying questions with 400 ounces of gold on his back, so he headed down the cavernous hallway to the south end of the ferry building, and dissolved into the misty night.

Anthony Colburn

Chapter 19

A MORAL DILEMMA

—————⊗⊗—————

Matthew's pace quickened. This was not the best part of town to be walking in after midnight, especially with twenty-five pounds of gold on his back! He paralleled Market continuing down Mission Street, with visions of what that gold bar could mean to Matthew's life, dancing through his head. But he had to concentrate on his feet, to keep putting one in front of the other in a constant beat against the bricks. Reaching in his pocket, he slid the lever on his watch. The faint chime rang out 12:37.

All of a sudden, some unnamed instinctual feeling forced him to look up. On the corner at Freemont, music drifted into the stillness. A street light created a misty cone, illuminating two men leaning on a fence next to the entrance of a bar. They seemed to take an interest in Matthew's progress as he paused. His heart began to race, in preparation to fight or run and he quickly crossed to the opposite side of Mission. The men left their posts, slowly at first, but with quickening steps, keeping up with Matthew.

He couldn't believe his bad luck! To be handed a small fortune only to lose it to a stupid choice of streets! Matthew did an about face and headed back toward the docks. He dared not look back for fear of revealing his hand but he could hear the men's footsteps quickening into a run. He had to look now to assess his options. They were big, but didn't seem to be running all that fast so Matthew just kept his distance, matching their speed.

From out of the corner of his eye, Matthew noticed another man coming out of an alley, converging on him. He crossed to the south side of the street and picked up his pace. His mind inexplicably recalled a book on Africa he had read on a cold night at the Tahoe Inn. It seemed to Matthew that he was like an antelope on the Serengeti, being pursued by a pack of Hyenas. He darted once more to the north side of the street when he spied yet another man. Matthew shifted into a full sprint now, up Main Street and back toward Market. His only hope was to find other people, but at this time of night!? Matthew burst out between two wagons and onto the broad boulevard. With two men still tailing him, Matthew turned back toward the ferry building, three blocks away.

As he maintained a break neck pace, he felt the weight of the ingot digging into his shoulders. Gradually through the mist, Mathew could see a light approaching. It was a cable car! Continuing until the two met, he took one final leap and caught the front of the car and hung on. The two men slowing to a walk now, waited and jumped on at the back.

"What are you in such a hurry for?" inquired the operator, amused with the show. Matthew moved up to the operator, sat next to him and paid his fare.

"Just need to get home in one piece." He replied breathlessly.

"Hey, what about you two! Pay up or get off!"

The two men scowled and jumped off at Freemont without a word.

So, this is what it feels like to be the prey, Matthew thought to himself.

He took off his pack sack and cradled his future in his lap like a new born lamb.

Matthew did not sleep well that night. First there was the matter of a 400-ounce bar of gold under his pillow, then there were the questions. Why did Andy have to die? Did anyone else see the gold? Were there really twenty-four more bars? and, what am I going to do with my bar? The last question almost answered itself. His fitful dreams were an amalgamation of dark figures chasing him down misty streets and Andy imploring him to return the gold and sliding a ring on Julia's finger.

Finally, the dull gray light of day asserted itself and stirred Matthew from his tortured slumber. He didn't have to check on his new found wealth, his aching neck confirmed its presence. As he rolled over, he thought of Julia and her disapproving father. What protest could he mount in the face of this new found wealth? The only problem was that he would attract quite a crowd and a lot of interest from the mint if he just waltzed into a bank requesting it be changed into coin or other currency.

Then it hit him. Matthew had heard about old timers taking gold nuggets and pounding them into a roughly round shape, trading them as coins of different denominations. He could do the same by cutting off a piece of the soft metal with a knife or maybe a chisel and pounding it flat. No one would then be able to tell the origin of the piece!

Still, something gnawed at his conscience; whose gold was it? The mine workers got paid. The mines got their money from the assay office. The mint in San Francisco hadn't lost anything because the gold was never delivered, and besides it was probably insured... and the insurance companies will just write it off...And besides, Matthew fully expected to treat this as a loan he would pay back, with interest.

So, it was settled, at least in Matthew's mind. He would work hard and invest his wealth wisely and prudently. He would do good by the less fortunate and repay it in the end.

With this dilemma settled, Matthew rolled back over and slept soundly 'till 10:00. When he finally arose, Matthew was consumed with what the newspapers might have written about the incident.

He walked down to a corner market and picked up the 'Call'. Taking up almost half of the front page was the article with the heading- *'Card Game Goes Bad, Four Dead on Ferry, One Murderer Fished Out of Bay.'*

The report concluded just what the police were told the night before, but they made Captain Turner out to be more of a hero than he really was. Matthew read on; *One passenger stated, "We might have all been in peril if it had not been for the quick thinking and heroic efforts of the captain."* The report continued, *'One murderer who was seen gunning down another of his own kind, jumped from the ferry, but not before being wounded by the heroic captain. Not long after, authorities pulled him from the bay along the Broadway Street wharf.'*

Matthew stopped short. He racked his mind trying to think if the man had seen him with Andy. How could he have while he was wrestling for the gun? Suddenly, his blood ran cold. The suppressed image of a figure in the water, watching, as Mathew leaned over the gold bar was indelibly etched in his mind.

The police have him now. He'll never tell them about the gold and he'll never get off with that murder charge over him. The logic of this scenario comforted Matthew. As he skimmed the article, he noticed there was no mention of the men being U.S. Mint workers and certainly nothing about any gold. Was no one aware of the gold, or were they keeping it secret until it was located?

Anthony Colburn

Chapter 20

THE OVERTURE

‑‑‑‑‑◦⊗⊗◦‑‑‑‑‑

Tomorrow would be Easter Sunday, but Matthew didn't have a 'Sunday suit', only the clothes he used for work. He was given Friday and Saturday off because of the incident on the ferry, so Matthew still had one more day and now the means to get himself a suit befitting his newfound wealth and rightful stature in the community.

He pulled out the bottom drawer of his dresser, revealing a newspaper. Under it was a metal box with a substantial lock protecting its contents. He bought the box and had it engraved the day before; Matthew Robert Donohue, Esq.

"A name to be proud of," he whispered.

He took a key from his pocket and released the lock from its duties. Inside, still glowing like that first night, the bar lay motionless with the words 'Mizpah Mine' embossed on it. He lifted it with care and producing his knife, slowly scrapped it across a corner. A thick sliver of the precious metal curled up until Matthew estimated he had enough for his foray into fashion. He split it in two and pounded the fragments into roughly rounded shapes.

Matthew had often passed a men's clothing and tailor store at the corner of Geary and Market Streets that looked to be of the highest caliber. On the window the arched letters painted in gold leaf spelled out: 'C.H. Rehnstrom & Co., Tailors and Importers.' Matthew gave himself over to the expertise of the tailors and they did not disappoint. By noon, a new person walked out onto the great thoroughfare, any gentleman's equal. As he strolled past Lotta's fountain, he politely bowed and tipped his bowler at each lady he passed, receiving the recognition a man of his station should be afforded. Matthew even secured a flower for his lapel from one of the vendors.

Turning up Geary, Matthew found himself passing by a women's hat store. Remembering the fine lady in the carriage leaving the ferry that one night, he decided to take his first stab at women's fashion. The lady store keeper greeted Matthew warmly, seeing that he was a young man of some means.

"How may I be of assistance, sir?"

"I was wondering," he said, being careful to enunciate correctly, "what you have in red with an ostrich feather."

"Just one moment. I'm sure we have some styles to impress your lady friend."

The woman hurried to the back of the store and through a curtain. In a short while, she emerged with four boxes stacked above her head, peering around the second one to navigate. As she made her way closer, Matthew could see that the stack was teetering, so he grabbed the top two.

"Oh! Thank you! Maybe one too many at a time!" she said with a sheepish grin.

"Don't think of it." Matthew replied in his best patrician manner.

All the hats were stylish and quite well made, but the third one struck Matthew's fancy because it reminded him most of that other hat. Also, Matthew could imagine Julia's raven hair set off by the deep crimson ribbon.

"That is an excellent choice, sir!" The woman declared a little too approvingly. It was also the most expensive one of the lot. It didn't faze Matthew though, and as he produced another shaving off the gold bar the shop keeper beamed.

"Thank you so much! Have a wonderful day!" she gushed.

As he walked out the door, Matthew got the feeling that he had miscalculated the value of that sliver of gold.

But no matter. He walked back down to Market and confidently strolled into the Palace Hotel's lobby and inquired as to the cost of retaining the Grand Courtyard and a pianist for the evening of the eighteenth. Having done so, he retired to the courtyard and sat in one of the high-backed chairs for a few minutes, observing his peers.

Matthew was poised for great things. All he had to do now was seal his good fortune after the opera and subsequent feast. He would then ask for Julia's hand in marriage. How could Mr. Thomas resist such a well-placed gentleman as himself!?

Chapter 21

INVESTING IN THE FUTURE

—⋯⋯⋯⋯⋯◦⊰⊱◦⋯⋯⋯⋯⋯—

Easter Sunday morning. Matthew lay propped up by his pillow in his room, imagining all that was about to come to pass. Then it occurred to him again, why was that piece of crate wedged in the coal cute hatch? He had been unconsciously ruminating on this for the last three days and suddenly it became clear to him. The men on the wagon and the one who jumped overboard must have planned to put the bars into the coal bunker for safe keeping until they could get them out at a later time! And Frank, in his dying gesture, pointed to the hatch! That was it! The rest of the gold must be in the coal bunker of the 'Golden City'! Never before had that name rung so true for Matthew!

He got out the bar again and with his knife, scratched on the back: 'The rest is in the Golden City'. "Just in case…" Matthew chuckled, "as if anything could keep me from remembering that!" His mind swirled with plans to retrieve the other bars when the vessel went to drydock.

Next, Matthew took out a pencil and began to write down some figures. $20.64 (The price of gold per ounce), multiplied by 400 (The weight of the bar in ounces). Matthew did the calculations once more and then again. Each time it came out the same; $8,256.00. If he retrieved all the bars, the total would be $206,400.00! He sat for a second, dazed by the enormity of the figure and all its possibilities but he stopped and deliberately said out loud, "A bird in the hand…" something his mother always used to say whenever Matthew's dreams outstripped his reality.

Finally, he said, "Eight thousand dollars is a lot of money. I can do an awful lot with that and I can turn it into a lot more with the right investments."

"Signore Matthew!" His heart skipped a beat. It was Signora Marinelli's voice. "Time for church! You OK?"

"Si, nonna. I'm getting ready now!" He let out a breath of relief. The Signora could not have heard…

Matthew enjoyed the church service with all its color and flowers. Little girls were all dressed in white and the women wore fancy hats. He felt good in his tailored suit and attracted approving looks from many a young lady.

On their way back, Signora Marinelli said, "How is it you have such nice clothes?"

"I've been saving and I got some money from my mother." He felt bad lying about it, but what could he do?

"Well, you need more than church to go to with that nice suit!"

"Don't worry. I have a special event I am going to use it at. And you'll be invited!"

Signora's eyes widened, "Matrimonio?!" He nodded. She clapped her hands and twirled around, holding up her long skirt.

Later that afternoon, Matthew walked down to the Palace Hotel and reserved a room for Tuesday and Wednesday night, the seventeenth and eighteenth, with another shaving from the gold bar.

As he paid, the manager was called to the front desk. He examined the hammered gold with a raised eyebrow.

"I won it in a card game just last month in the bar." Matthew overconfidently asserted.

"It's authentic," the manager replied. "This will cover the room and all tips."

He did it again. I'm going to have to start weighing it out, Matthew said to himself.

When Mr. and Mrs. Thomas find out about the reservation, that would be the icing on the cake…The 'coup de gras!' He wanted everyone to know that he had arrived!… and his new address, (for the time being anyway), would be THE hotel in the city, maybe even in the whole West!

Matthew went to work Monday looking forward to seeing the 'Golden City' again, for in its coal bunker, unknown to anyone except Matthew… (and that other man, who would probably be swinging from the end of a rope by month's end), was enough in gold to buy her a couple of times over!

Part way to the Oakland Mole, George called Matthew over to the starboard railing.

"Looks like they're still searching for those machine parts."

"Yeh," He felt like he was being interrogated and coerced into a confession, but his guilty feelings faded as they passed the salvage barge.

"How you feeling, Matthew? I just thought if you wanted to say anything…"

"No. I'm OK, just a little under the weather."

By the end of his day, Matthew had successfully laid the ground work for calling in sick the next day. He feigned sea sickness leaning over the railing in view of George and did his duties at an increasingly slower pace.

Finally, George said, "I'm going to tell Captain Turner. You're not fit for tomorrow."

Matthew managed a feeble, "Thanks."

So, his day was set! Matthew would happen by the music store just before closing and nonchalantly mention, (with Julia's father within earshot), that he was going to get a haircut and a shave in preparation for the opera that night. Matthew could hardly wait to see the look on his face! He would present Julia with the hat for her to wear that night, and then at the restaurant, he would ask for Julia's hand in marriage and present her with the ring…The RING!

Matthew, in all his planning and scheming, had forgotten the engagement ring! His face turned pale, trying to think of what to do. He stumbled back and plopped down on a sack.

Anthony Colburn

Palace Hotel Balcony

Chapter 22

CARMEN & CARUSO

The big day was here! Matthew checked his suit and decided that having it cleaned would be a waste of money and it might take away the sharp creases of the pants and cuffs. All he really needed was a good bath and a shave.

Matthew's first order of the day though, was to find a suitable ring. He pulled out his gold and shaved a couple of pieces off the end. I can always pay more, he said to himself, not wanting to repeat his extravagancies with the hat. Besides, a jeweler will have a scale and I can be sure of how much I am paying. With that, he cut off two more pieces.

He decided to stroll down Market and window shop then turn back around Union Square. By the time he got to the Palace Hotel, Matthew was a little warm in his suit, so he decided to get himself a beer at the bar. Once again, the manager was called to verify the authenticity of his preferred mode of payment and this time he was given change. After his refreshments, Matthew crossed Market and went up Kearney past Lotta's Fountain to Post. He had recalled a very nice jewelry store on the corner of Grant and was soon gazing through the window of 'Shreve & Co., Jewelers.' As he entered, an older salesman of small stature approached. Matthew felt a little awkward looking down on this man who could not have been much more than five feet tall.

"I am George Shreve," he announced. "May I help you find something?"

"You are the owner?"

The man had seen this reaction before but it was evident he didn't let it bother him. "Yes, that's my son over there." He pointed to a man in his thirties about two inches taller than Matthew.

Matthew appreciated the comeback and smiled.

"Now, may I help you find something?"

"Oh. Yes. I am looking for an engagement ring… not for myself."

"That's good." Both men smiled.

"Let me show you some wonderful examples of platinum rings. These rings never lose their metal when polished and they set off colored stones exquisitely. You know, it is the choice of kings." and as the jeweler set out a tray he said, "That's because platinum is about four times more valuable than gold."

Matthew was a little taken aback as he scanned the rings.

"How much is this one."

"One hundred fifty dollars. But you can see the fine two carat diamond and the smaller diamonds down the side.

"Carrot?"

"Yes, Carat." Mr. Shreve could see that Matthew was a novice at the ring buying business and continued. "A carat is a way of measuring the weight and by comparison, also the size of a precious stone. There are many other factors such as clarity and cut to consider also."

Matthew's head was swimming. He thought he would find a ring he liked, pay for it and go home, but there was so much to consider.

"Now 'karat' also refers to the purity of gold such as twenty-four karat gold." The jeweler could see that Matthew had gotten too much information too soon. "Sometimes," he continued, "you just have to pick what you like and not worry about those other things. That's why you come to a reputable jeweler like myself. I've been in the business over fifty years and plan on another twenty, Lord willing. With Shreve and Company, you can be assured you will get the best ring for your money."

Matthew could tell this man was the type you could do an honest business with. "Do you take gold?"

The man smiled and said, "Of course. We deal in gold every day."

The third tray of rings had one that immediately stood out. It had a very large pale ice blue stone set in platinum with small diamonds down the sides.

"What is this?"

"Ah, yes. This is an Aquamarine. Such a delicate color. I prefer them over diamonds though they are considered less valuable. The mineral is actually called Beryl. The green form is the Emerald. The best Aquamarines like this one, come from Russia."

"It seems so pure…"

"Actually, it is the impurities that give it the color."

Without thinking Matthew said, "How much is it?"

"Two-hundred-dollars."

Matthew was hooked. He couldn't stop looking at the stone in the same way he looked into Julia's eyes.

"You were going to pay with gold?" The jeweler got out a scale.

Matthew reached in his pocket and produced the shavings of gold.

Mr. Shreve raised an eyebrow. "What nugget did you get that off of?"

"This is from a years' work paid out in one lump."

"Yes, I've seen that before." The jeweler was a little skeptical but judged Matthew as believable.

The ring took most of the shavings, nearly ten ounces, but he would gladly exchange again what now seemed to be a rather ordinary gold colored rock for this scintillating creation. Matthew slipped the small box in his pocket and patted it.

"You can't go wrong with a ring like that," said the jeweler as Matthew made his way to the door.

"Thank you for all your help. This is perfect."

It was late afternoon and that meant pasta. Matthew had to tell Signora Marinelli another lie about why he wasn't at work that day and he could tell she wasn't completely convinced either, but she didn't question it.

And now, the time had come. Matthew, in all his tailored grandeur, quickly walked up Fifth Street so he could stroll down Market on the 'right' side of the 'slot' for a couple of blocks before O'Farrell. He decided to go one more block to Lotta's fountain to get a ceremonial drink of water and a flower for his lapel. He then doubled back and up O'Farrell towards the music store whistling 'Red Haired Boy'. Just as planned, he arrived a little before closing and was greeted by Mrs. Thomas.

"Why, Mr. Donohue! What a fine suit! Julia, Dear! You have a visitor!"

As Julia glided down the stairs, she paused, letting a smile overtake her.

"Why, Mr. Donohue!" she said, mimicking her mother, "What a fine suit! What do you have planned, or is this just your usual Tuesday attire!"

"No. I was just going out for a haircut and an early light supper before the performance."

"Performance?"

"Yes, you know, the opera tonight, 'Carmen'. Signore Caruso will be playing Don Jose."

Julia took a step back. "You are going to the opera, *tonight*!?"

"Yes," Matthew responded matter-of-factly. "A friend owed me a favor. I wish I had another ticket so I could take you too."

"*We're* going, too!"

"Well, good! I'll see you there! Maybe you would like to wear this hat. I thought it complemented your hair."

Julia was practically dumbfounded and her eyes widened as she took it out of the round box. "It's beautiful! Where did you get it?!"

"I just saw it in a shop as I was walking down Geary and I thought of you." Matthew said as coolly as he could.

"I know the place! Those are nice hats they sell!" Mrs. Thomas smiled approvingly and Katy giggled.

"I'll be staying at the Palace Hotel, so maybe I could accompany you to the opera house." Julia's mouth dropped open.

Matthew looked around for Mr. Thomas. "Would you like to go out to the Oyster Grotto up the street for a late dinner after the performance?"

"That would be great!" said Katy, as she slid halfway down the railing.

"Will Mr. Thomas be joining you?" Matthew asked as he scanned the upper floor again.

"Yes. He is in Oakland right now, but he will be back in time."

"Good, good." returned Matthew, somewhat less enthusiastically now. "The Palace Hotel!?" Julia said, examining the hat's Ostrich feather

"Well, I'll see you there!"

"Meet us in the lobby after the performance." said Mrs. Thomas.

"Alright. Well, until then…"

"See you tonight!" called Julia, trying on the hat as he left the store. "The Palace?!" she said again to her reflection in the hall mirror.

"Well! Mr. Donohue certainly knows how to present himself!" said Mrs. Thomas as she watched him head toward Market Street.

"Yes, he does…" whispered Julia.

Matthew went back to his room at the boarding house to get his box and then walked to the Palace Hotel and asked the manager to take all his hopes and dreams for the future for safe keeping. Matthew couldn't conceal his excitement as he took the 'moving room' elevator to the fifth floor.

#534. His room was richly appointed with wall hangings and textured rugs. The heavily carved walnut and mahogany chest of drawers and armoire oozed 'class'. He plopped down on the soft bed and stared up at the ornate chandelier. Going over to the large bay window, he gazed down at the people walking along Market and then an automobile caught his attention moving westbound up Geary.

"I think I'll get one of those to take to the beach on Sundays."

With a lot of time to kill before the opera, Matthew decided to explore the hotel. He took the elevator up to the seventh floor that looked down on his future wedding venue, the Grand Court. The tropical plants and statuary were softly illuminated from above by the glass domed ceiling. Back down again on the main floor, Mathew entered the billiard room from which he had been evicted six months before. He stood by the fireplace and watched two gentlemen of questionable skill play a game, trading off shots and glasses of beer. Over at the bar, Matthew ordered a beer of his own and took a long cool drink. As he stared into the mirror, he noticed the foam had covered his moustache and he would have wiped it on his sleeve if not for the quick actions of an observant bar tender.

"Towel, sir?"

"Yes, thank you." Matthew pulled out his watch and opened the case. 6:00.

Next, he entered the barber shop and got the full treatment. As he lay back in the chair with a steaming towel wrapped around his face, Matthew imagined his wedding night and his future, commanding the 'Tahoe'. I don't need any 'vision' to tell *my* future. he thought, I'll make it myself!

Finally, Matthew strolled out to the Grand Court, found a chair with a paper left on its seat, and sat down to read it. On the second page, was another account of the botched ferry robbery and near the end of the article, it described the lone surviving robber- *'Sam Cleveland, lately of Denver and employed by the U.S. Mint in that city...'* Still, there was no mention of any gold, but that a cargo of machine parts was lost in the bay.

Getting a little restless, he decided to head over to the opera house and talk to some of the workers he had gotten to know. The head usher, Mr. Doran greeted Matthew with a smile at the side door. Employees of the Metropolitan Opera Company were still moving props and costumes backstage.

"Best not get in the way! These guys are on a pretty tight schedule! Will you be entertaining a companion tonight?"

"Not for the opera," replied Matthew. "Julia's family will be sitting in the balcony on the right."

"Oh, Julia is her name! Sounds nice!" He pointed to Matthew's seat.

"You'll be sitting there." Matthew frowned, looking at the second to the last row. "Don't worry, there's not a bad seat in the house! Besides, you'll be one of the first ones out for intermission and at the end of the performance by the side door. There's always such a crush in the crowd to leave!"

Matthew looked on the rosy side of it. He would be sure not to miss Julia at the end of the opera. They would most likely turn up Mission to the left and Matthew would be there to meet them.

"But...," he started as he looked at the play's synopsis.

"But what?"

"I can't... That is, I've never spoken French." Matthew said sheepishly.

Mr. Doran laughed, "At least you recognized it *was* in French! Most of these people wouldn't know French from Italian!"

Thinking about Signora Marinelli and her speaking in Italian half the time, Matthew was pretty sure he would be able to tell.

"Most of the time you'll know what's happening just from the acting, but let me tell you what the story is about."

Mr. Doran went on to tell Matthew about the simple-minded Spanish soldier, Don Jose and the character of Carmen. "She was a hot-blooded Gypsy who said she loved Don Jose, but she just couldn't seem to keep from straying. Well, she gets poor Don Jose involved with some smugglers and disgraces him when she dumps him for the flashy bull fighter. Finally, Don Jose, in a fit of jealousy and rage, stabs Carmen and falls down sobbing, his life ruined and his love, dead."

"What a sad story! Why would people want to see something like that?"

"I don't know, I guess it kind of grows on you."

"And why don't they speak Spanish if the characters are all Spanish and it takes place in Spain!?"

"Probably because Bizet was French!" replied the usher, chuckling. "Never mind trying to figure that out, just enjoy the show. I have some couples coming in now…" He took off up the aisle. "And good luck with the girl…Nice suit!"

Matthew took the stairway to the balcony that seemed to be perched over the stage. "Wow, this is like peeking over their shoulders!" He descended again, noticing now, more and more people coming in. There were some pretty fancy gowns and a lot of jewelry being worn by the women and most of the men had top hats. Matthew took off his bowler and held it by his side and tapped the pocket to ensure the ring was still there. As he milled around the lobby, he even noticed Mayor Schmitz among the distinguished guests.

From the outside came a familiar laugh. It was Katy Thomas. Matthew strained to see around the other patrons when Mr. and Mrs. Thomas entered with Julia at their side. Matthew's heart raced. Julia fairly glided in her flowing white dress topped off by her red hat with the Ostrich feather. Matthew glanced at the playbill and then back up at Julia. He thought he was seeing double. The angelic figure in white on the cover had the same raven hair and blue eyes! His hands were getting sweaty.

Mrs. Thomas spotted him and waved. Mr. Thomas had a look of surprise mixed with wonderment.

"Nice to see you, Mr. Donohue," as he extended his hand. Matthew had years of working with his hands already and he had a good grip, so he was up to the challenge.

"I hear you enjoy 'Carmen'." Mr. Thomas said, attempting to reveal Matthew's naiveté and ignorance.

"Yes, even though I don't approve of Carmen's actions or Gypsies in general, and especially taking advantage of a simple man like Don Jose. It's a good character lesson, though. And the music! I come for the music."

Mr. Thomas was caught back on his heels.

"It's a shame you can't sit with us," said Mrs. Thomas. "Maybe we'll talk at the intermission."

"See you then, Matthew. You look nice." said Julia in an admiring tone.

As the curtain rose, Mathew could not believe his eyes and ears! How could a group of actors transport an audience from the streets of San Francisco to a bull fight in Seville? And how could they weave speech and song into such a compelling story? It was enchanting. He was nudged by the man sitting on his left when he started humming along with the bull fighter's song. By the time the actors took their final bows, Matthew's hands were sore from several standing ovations and his eyes were damp.

He sat back down, thinking of Don Jose's plight and the tragic death of Carmen, even though she deserved it. As a result, Matthew didn't get the jump on the crowd he should have, so he wasn't sure if he had missed Julia. Hurrying out to Market Street, he searched for the flowing white dress and the red hat. He thought he spied her turning up O'Farrell so he ran across the street toward the music shop.

"Julia!" Matthew yelled, almost out of breath, as the family was just entering the door to the music store.

Julia looked back and waved. "Matthew!"

As he caught up, Mr. Thomas said, "I hope you enjoyed the performance. Well, good night."

"But what about the oyster grotto?" Matthew protested. His plans were all evaporating. How would he be able to ask for Julia's hand?

"Sorry, we're turning in for the night."

"Father! You promised!" protested Julia.

"Your mother and I have had a long day. This can wait. Maybe tomorrow."

"Sorry, Matthew. See you tomorrow?"

"Yeah, sure." A dejected Mathew fumbled with the box in his pocket, holding the key to his dreams, and turned back toward Market Street.

Matthew's head was spinning as he walked into the lobby of the Palace Hotel. What use did he have for this high-priced room now? He asked for his metal box from the safe and slowly walked up the stairs, not wanting any company in the elevator. He threw the box on the bed and leaned against the window, blankly staring out on a still vigorous city alive with lights and activity.

Eventually, he summoned a waiter via the electronic call button and ordered the very best champagne. After a few sips, he ceremoniously dashed the champagne flute in the fireplace and yelled, "Au revoir, mon amour!" He sat on the bed and drank directly from the bottle while holding the gold bar in his lap. Then he suddenly remembered the ring.

Matthew searched through the pockets of his coat and finally produced the small box. He opened it, revealing the icy-blue treasure meant for Julia's finger. With mock pomp and ceremony, he lowered it into the metal box along with the gold bar. Halfway through the bottle, he got out some writing paper and a pen and wrote a note:

April 17, 1906
To Miss Julia Thomas,
Thomas Music Store, 245 O'Farrell St.

Dearest Julia,

Meet me tomorrow at Lotta's Fountain at 10 a.m. Wear your
red hat, the one with the ostrich feather. I will be wearing my
bowler. We will be married at the Palace Hotel and there we
will spend our first night together.

Love forever, Matthew

He put the letter in the box for safekeeping until morning when he
would send a courier to deliver the note. But after reconsidering and
a few more swallows of champagne, he decided to write another
note, this time not so revealing of his feelings in case it fell into
the wrong hands.

He wrote:

Dear Julia,

Please meet me at Lotta's fountain at 10:00 a.m. tomorrow.
Wear your red hat, the one with the ostrich feather. I will be
wearing my bowler. I would like to have an early lunch with
you at the Palace Hotel to discuss our future.

Love, Matthew

Again, he addressed it on the outside and called for a boy to deliver
it that night. He also instructed the boy to confirm to him that it
had been received. Matthew paid the boy with a sliver of the gold,
promising another when he returned. Sometime before midnight,
there was a knock on the door. Matthew was just barely able to
make it over and open it. The boy had tried to deliver the letter, but

no one answered at the music store.

"I'm sorry sir," the boy said, "I put the letter in the safe for the night and I will deliver it personally tomorrow."

"That's alright." Matthew was already awash in self-pity and the bubbly wine. This just enhanced it so there wasn't much left for him to do but finish off the bottle and hit the sack.

Sometime after 1 a.m., Matthew was roused from his drunken stupor by a group of people partying across the balcony. He stumbled to the door and peered across to the revelers. They were all very well dressed, spilling out of the room and onto the balcony.

Was that the cast of 'Carmen'? He blinked and looked again, trying to focus and thought he saw the great Caruso walking toward the elevator. Waving back to the group, he shouted, "Bravo!"

"Bravo for me!" Matthew yelled, as he slammed the door and stumbled back to his bed, falling on the box, out cold.

Fire Spreading Through Downtown

Chapter 23

THE NIGHTMARE

ometime before sunrise, Matthew stirred, his body used to waking at this early hour for the last six months. Matthew searched his pockets for his prized pocket watch. Without looking, he pulled the lever and it faithfully chimed the time to the minute; 5:12 a.m., two minutes fast.

Matthew was a mess, having fallen asleep on top of his metal box and its valuable contents. His pants and shirt were wrinkled and his coat lay in a pile on the floor with the empty bottle of champagne. His new hat was smashed beside him. Matthew stumbled to the window and gazed out once more, this time on a sleeping city. He looked down and to the left at Lotta's fountain and cursed the day he first set eyes on it. A glow coming from the east, heralded a new day and it illuminated the buildings along Geary Street with a faint glimmer.

Then, in the distant beginnings of the day, Matthew thought he saw a slight disturbance in the air, like heat waves on summer pavement. A flock of pigeons took flight from the ledge of the building across the street. Suddenly, coming from over the hill and down Geary St., Matthew witnessed what could only be described as a wave. Not an ocean wave, but the earth itself, rising and falling, like the swells in the ocean before they break on the shore. He thought it odd that he also heard church bells ringing, not like a call to services, but wild and out of control. "Is this another one of my visions?" He thought out loud. It raced toward him at lightning speed, lifting and dropping buildings in its wake. In his impaired state, Matthew could hardly move from the window before it was upon him. The force of the juggernaut shattered the window as the very walls of the hotel groaned.

He was thrown back against his bed, clutching his precious metal box as everything on the walls and tables fell to the floor in shambles. The chandelier swayed wildly, finally breaking off and striking Matthew on the side of his head. His vision blurred, and in a second, he was unconscious.

The furniture careened across the room as if possessed, while the wave took hold of the entire hotel. The huge, heavy chest of drawers pinned Matthew's arm between the bed rail and its corner, with an audible crack. Matthew had already mercifully, passed out. Ten seconds passed and another shock gripped the earth. Once more, the furniture danced across the room, the dresser releasing Matthew in the bargain. Then, an eerie, uneasy quietness ensued. Sometime later, in a haze of semi consciousness, Matthew thought he heard the great Caruso singing, but soon, he slipped back into limbo.

While Matthew lay motionless, the stage was being set for the greatest conflagration the West had ever seen.

The employees of the hotel were racing from room to room

looking for injured and missing guests. By the time they reached the fifth floor, the scene outside was already grim. Buildings up and down Market Street had lost their cornices and chimneys with many missing their entire façades. People were wandering aimlessly down the street in their night gowns and there was the smell of gas in the air. Already, south of the hotel, a thread of smoke rose languidly in the early morning sky.

When the workers finally found Matthew in his room, they gingerly carried him down the five flights of stairs, his hand still clutching the box, and laid him on a table to await medical aid. A few minutes later, a milk wagon that had been pressed into service as an ambulance, came rumbling down what was left of the street. The once great thoroughfare had been contorted into small hills and valleys with great gaps in the pavement. There was rubble everywhere, and the cable car tracks were twisted like pieces of spaghetti, making the street almost impassable.

As the rescue personnel lifted Matthew from the table, his grip loosened on the box and it fell among some bricks, unnoticed. Matthew was loaded in the wagon with five other injured souls and as it went bouncing west down Market, he finally started to come to. He screamed in excruciating pain, prompting one man to put something over his face and he once again slipped into unconsciousness.

When he gained his senses again, Matthew was looking up at the ceiling of a great, cavernous wooden structure. He recognized it as the 'MechanicsPavilion' where he and Julia had once roller skated. Moans and screams rose from every corner of the building. Matthew felt for his box, but when he tried to reach out with his right hand, a stabbing pain stopped him. He looked at the bandaged arm and felt the throbbing near his elbow. Matthew lifted his head to view row upon row of bodies, some being worked on and some with sheets drawn over them. The floor was splattered with blood.

Suddenly, Matthew understood the magnitude of the situation. He sat upright and immediately felt faint.

"Best take it easy at first!" A middle-aged nurse said.

"I've got to go!" Mathew cried out, needing to see if any harm had come to Julia… and to find his box. When he tried to get up, his legs would not support him, so he fell to his knees and was helped up by a priest.

"We could all use a little help from above!" he said jokingly. He then continued his rounds, administering last rights to the dead and dying.

Before Matthew could make another attempt, a man hurried down the rows. "We've got to get the wounded loaded in the wagons! Help the wounded!"

One nurse stopped him near Matthew and the man whispered, "The fire is one block away and gaining fast!"

"What about the dead?" the nurse asked.

"Leave them! We have to save the living!"

Everyone who could walk under their own power left, followed by stretchers of the more seriously wounded.

Matthew could see the folly of trying to go back towards downtown- fires were spreading on two fronts from the direction of the bay and from the north and south toward their location. Their only hope was to head up Oak Street towards the park. The priest took Matthew under his good arm and led him to a wagon.

About thirty minutes up the street, the refugees witnessed the pavilion go up like match sticks. The disheveled convoy had to make their way around block after block of collapsed houses and twisted track, but they finally decided to turn up Steiner.

"We can rest at Alamo Square." said a doctor.

As plumes of smoke rose over downtown, Matthew was laid on the grass, exhausted, and he slept.

Crowd Watching the Fire

Chapter 24

THE MUSIC STORE

At the instant of the earthquake, Julia's family was still asleep. Julia was literally thrown out of her bed and was stopped only when a shelf rained books down on her. But she immediately sprang to her feet only to be knocked back on to the bed. She held on, screaming while the building swayed and creaked. At a pause in the terrifying shaking, her father yelled and both Julia and Katy ran into their parent's room. Then came the second jolt. In an instant, the whole front of the music store parted from the rest and came crashing down onto the street. Julia's room did not exist except as a jumble of wood and bricks below. The petrified family huddled on the bed, looking out on a decimated city, the view unobstructed now by the nonexistent west facing wall.

After a few minutes of calm, Mr. Thomas decided it was safe enough to lead his family down the stairs, now exposed at the edge of the stripped building, and out onto the street. Shivering in their night gowns, Julia and Katy searched through the rubble for a blanket. In a crushed chest of drawers, Julia found more clothes, then she touched something coarse. Among the clothes was the Indian basket Matthew had given her. She held it close and worried about what had happened to her love. She looked in the direction of Market Street and saw smoke rising some distance south of the Palace Hotel.

"Hurry!" said Mr. Thomas. "We need to get away from these buildings. It's too dangerous here!"

"But my china!" screamed Mrs. Thomas.

As if on cue, the back wall of the music store building folded and the whole place imploded on itself. She screamed again and fainted.

Julia got some water from a pipe that was spraying in a graceful arc across the street and revived her mother.

"We need to move, mother. We still have each other."

"Where can we go?" Mrs. Thomas sobbed.

"We'll head for the ferries," Mr. Thomas replied in a confident tone, though his hands were shaking. "Maybe Oakland wasn't hit as hard. We can stay with your sister."

So, they headed toward Market Street with little more than the clothes on their backs. As they passed a collapsed building, a faint moan drifted up from somewhere deep in the wreckage.

"We need to help!" Katy yelled.

They moved a few boards from over the sound and could see a man hopelessly pinned under a large timber. The space he was trapped in was quickly filling from a broken water line. Soon he would drown.

Mr. Thomas said reluctantly, "There's nothing we can do. We need to move on." Katy screamed in protest as Julia dragged her away.

Coming upon Market, Julia saw that the Palace Hotel had appeared to have sustained only minor damage. She glanced up at the broken windows, wondering if Matthew was inside. A shriek erupted from some hapless soul as a milk wagon full of injured people pulled away from the hotel.

"We need to look for Matthew!" Julia pleaded to her father. "Let me ask at the hotel!"

"We can't! What if there is another shock? The whole building could come down on top of us!"

Mr. Thomas kept his family to the middle of the street, warily eyeing each structure they passed.

The ferry building clock tower was like a beacon for the dazed population who were still able to walk. The Thomas family joined hundreds of refugees moving at a steady pace toward the bay. Julia saw a mother carrying a baby who was not crying like all the others. She looked at its pale face and could tell it was already dead.

As they hurried toward their goal, they encountered many sickening sights. One woman sat on the side of the street holding a man's hand, his head leaning at a strange angle against a lamp post. She repeated over and over, "My husband's alright, he just needs to rest…"

Up ahead somewhere in the crowd, there were more screams and shouting. Julia looked down Market and saw people inexplicably running toward the buildings. It suddenly became apparent what was happening- as the people parted, she could see a herd of eight to ten crazed cattle running full speed toward them. As they rumbled closer, the cattle suddenly disappeared. It was as if the earth had swallowed them up. Once Julia and her family had regained their composure, they continued. Peeking into the chasm, Julia could see only a few legs kicking the air.

Finally, they made their way to the ferry building along with hundreds of other pushing and shoving people. It was almost like a horde of rats fleeing a sinking ship, but the land was now the ship and the boats, the only secure place.

The Thomas family was one of the first to get to the safety of Oakland. They were the lucky ones- Mr. Thomas had lost everything in the store, but no one was hurt and the family had a place to stay. As they crossed the bay on the overcrowded ferry, everyone looked back to the city, now being consumed by flames. The bright morning sun was little consolation as thick black smoke billowed miles into the air.

Anthony Colburn

Chapter 25

THE WITNESS

At the Hall of Justice on Portsmouth Square, the earthquake did its share of damage. It had rocked the structure and its walls groaned under the strain, but incredibly, the building stood, including its ornate cupola.

All the prisoners in the hall's basement jail were screaming to be let go. The din continued until finally, Judge Hunt released the minor offenders. The rest were marched out into the square by military guards and given shovels.

"Dig!" Was the order at the point of a bayonet.

In front of the prisoners were over fifty sheet-draped bodies. The inmates dug a long shallow trench, threw the bodies in and covered them up.

Among the prisoners was one Sam Cleveland. He and another prisoner, Wade Collins, had been planning an escape ever since the earthquake hit that morning. Now that they were on the outside in all the chaos, they were confident their chances were even better.

Late that afternoon, all the prisoners were put in hand cuffs and leg irons in pairs and marched through the streets of North Beach toward Fort Mason and the waterfront.

As they were trudging along, Sam said, "There's someone I'm really looking forward to seeing!"

"Who, your mother?" Wade snickered.

"Someone even closer to my heart. His name is Matthew, Matthew Donohue!"

"That's a pretty powerful family! I would be careful about settling scores with them!"

"He's not one 'a them ship builder Donahues. Least he don't act like 'em! I got him made out to be fresh off the boat from Ireland an' I'm gonna' make him wish he'd never left when I get through with him!"

In jail, Sam had gotten a hold of a newspaper that listed the workers on the ferry that night. By deduction, Sam figured out who he must have seen grab that bar on the deck that night as he bobbed in the bay. Ever since, he had thought up scenarios and contingency plans to somehow catch up to Matthew.

Even these hard-boiled criminals on a forced march witnessed things that would make them flinch. They passed a man pinned under some rubble and massive steel beams, unable to be moved.

"Just shoot me!" he pleaded as the prisoners and guards passed by. A fire in the building had slowly progressed to his location and was starting to lap at his feet as he screamed in fear and pain.

There was no hope for him, so a guard walked up, spoke with him for a few seconds, wrote something in a note book, and shot his brains out.

Later, they saw rats scurrying under a partially collapsed home. On the other side, they could see the vermin had found a man and woman killed in the initial carnage. Their noses, lips and ears had been nibbled off. The guards skewered a few of them with their bayonets, but there were too many to make a difference.

The line of prisoners marched past one of the demolition squads preparing to blow up a house along Powell St.

"Here's our chance!" Sam whispered to Collins. "When they blow that house, we'll make a run for it around the corner. Take care to start with our chained foot first; if you don't, we're goners." Collins looked down at his right foot and rehearsed in his mind. "They'll be a starin' at the blast and it'll be hard to take a quick aim with those big heavy rifles!"

The two anticipated the blast, watching the fuse race up the steps of the doomed structure. Everyone was transfixed in anticipation of the blast when the men made their break.

The plan worked just as they had hoped. As wood, glass and stone cascaded through the air, the pair sprinted down the street and around the corner. The guards were only able to get off three or four shots before the pair disappeared in the dust of the explosion. Unable to leave the rest of the prisoners, the guards reluctantly had to call off the chase.

The pair ran 'till their sides hurt. When they were sure there was no one to catch them, they sat on the steps of an abandoned house and collapsed in laughter. This part of town hadn't seen the ravages of the fire yet, so when they found a hardware store, they looked around for a file or hammer.

Finally, the two were parted and Collins said, "I'm headed for the bay! I got a friend over in Oakland an' I'll lay low for a while, then I'm leavin' with all the others back East!"

"Good luck! I'm gonna settle a score with my new friend!" Sam had a single mindedness to his actions and started toward where he figured most refugees would end up- Golden Gate Park.

Sam wandered the streets, looking for a clothing store so he could shed his prison stripes. Finally, he ducked down an alley and entered a department store through a shattered window and found work clothes and boots.

He was careful to stay away from soldiers stationed around larger buildings and found himself near Lafayette Square around nightfall. He huddled with the other refugees on the grass for the night and planed Matthew's fate.

That kid's the only one who knows about the gold. Sam thought to himself. If I can get to him, I'll be free and clear! With everyone else dead, it'll all be mine! The next morning, Sam noticed a group of bedraggled souls trudging up Sacramento Street. He stepped in with a woman and her two small children.

"Let me help you with that." He said as he took the heavy bag off her slumped shoulders.

The woman was visibly relieved. "We're going to the park. My husband is there." Sam could sense the desperation in her voice as they made their way past the police lines headed for the park.

City Hall

Chapter 26

THE AFTERMATH

M atthew awoke to a girl making the rounds, giving sips of water to the sick and wounded.

"Is it still night?" He inquired.

"It's morning, Thursday." Matthew scanned the sky for the sun but saw only the pall of black smoke. "You've had a good rest. Try not to move that arm."

He didn't need to be reminded about that. The pain seemed to have subsided a little, but the slightest movement made it almost unbearable. He inspected the wound. A long cut in his arm had been crudely closed with sewing thread. Blood started to ooze out between the stitches, so Matthew wrapped a new bandage back around the swollen arm.

He moved between people lying all over the grass to a spot between the trees with a better view. The whole of downtown was being consumed by the inferno. He could see flames leaping up hundreds of feet into the dark, smoke choked air. A dark reddish orb he could just make out must have been the sun, but it shed no light on the hellish scene. He knew that if Julia and her family had not escaped the day before, they surely must have been incinerated. Then Matthew's thoughts turned to Signora Marinelli and her grandchildren. He bowed his head and made the sign of the cross with his good hand and whispered, "Amen."

Later that morning, soldiers came to the square and directed everyone to go to Golden Gate Park. A captain stood on a box and announced- "We have set up a camp in the park with accommodations for your basic needs. There is water and we will be getting tents this afternoon. We will escort you there." With that, everyone who could walk picked up what little they had and followed the soldiers.

Matthew decided that the balance of the day should be devoted to rest if he was to be of any use later. That didn't keep him from helping with water for the less fortunate and doing errands for the few doctors attending the injured. In the middle of the day, a cart filled with bread arrived and he joined with military personnel who had come from the Presidio to ration it out. He was happy to see the soldiers as they gave a sense of order and calm to an otherwise terrible situation.

At least they were out of the way of the inferno, but no one could be sure where the flames would turn their attention next. Finally, as the sun was near setting, it broke through the oppressive smoke and cast weird fanciful shadows on the great billowing mass, making it seem almost alive.

The night was cold but almost everyone had at least one blanket, provided by the military. There were only a few tents put up for the most seriously injured, so Matthew huddled under a bush and spent the night in a fitful sleep punctuated by sporadic explosions. The next morning, Matthew inquired about the sounds and was told that the military had started to dynamite buildings in front of the advancing flames in hopes of denying fuel to the inferno. The line was being formed along Van Ness Avenue and for now, it was holding.

All Friday morning, Matthew walked among the refugees, trying to find people from Julia's part of town. He found one family from Sutter Street who said they didn't have to evacuate until early Thursday, so it was possible Julia's family had time, if they hadn't been one of the casualties of the many collapsed buildings.

Matthew could tell the fire had done its work from the area south of the 'slot'. It then had turned toward the Mission District and also out beyond Nob Hill to the North, so he decided to try to make his way back toward the music store and the Palace Hotel.

The next day, fortified with a small canteen of water and half a loaf of bread, Matthew headed down Fulton toward City Hall. By the time he reached Gough, he was beginning his descent into hell on earth. Everything that could burn, had and if it didn't burn, it had been melted. Street signs and cable car rails he had ridden on just a month ago were twisted beyond recognition. He could tell the fire had advanced so fast in some places that it merely singed everything in its path. There was a bloated carcass of a horse, smoldering in the middle of the street. He was somewhat comforted by the appearance that it might have met its fate from the fallen brick building partly covering it and not the flames.

As Matthew advanced, there was the awful, undeniable smell of burnt flesh from three indistinguishable black forms in the street. They must have been people at one time but he didn't pause to investigate.

When he finally approached City Hall, he witnessed what might be what the end of the world would look like. The beautiful arching dome was precariously perched on the skeleton of a burned-out metal framework and the rock foundation the cable car operator was so proud of was crumbling into dust.

From here on, he found regular detachments of soldiers patrolling the area. At every encounter, the soldiers kept Matthew moving, promising to shoot anyone caught looting the burned-out shells. He would have laughed at the folly of the orders had they not been so serious in their demeanor. Then, there were the occasional rifle shots that kept him on his toes.

Making his way down Market Street, Matthew could finally see landmark buildings coming into view. They were still standing, but the occasional wisp of smoke from a window or door let him know that they all had been consumed. A sudden zephyr of fresh air turned his attention to the sky. Matthew felt dizzy as the reflection of a thousand windows in a canyon of gleaming white buildings flashed in his eyes. He saw people inside the glass walls sitting at desks. He covered his eyes for a long moment, shielding against the reflections, then everything went dark again. The smoke once again was denying the sun and as Matthew looked down Market, everything was back to the way it was.

Turning up O'Farrell, he could see in an instant that there was virtually nothing left of the music shop. In fact, he had a hard time finding the exact spot where it should have been. Matthew reluctantly headed back toward the Palace Hotel. Curiously, Lotta's Fountain seemed little worse for wear, but just down the street, the hotel was just a shell, with its rows of bay windows darkened by the gutted interior. Matthew got as close as he could before the soldiers turned him back. He could see piles of bricks and rubble pouring out of the entrance, making it almost impossible to enter anyway.

Looking on toward the bay, the ferry terminal clock tower rose like a phoenix above the smoldering city. He asked to confirm that it had not been destroyed and when he was told it survived, gave out a loud hoot.

People were streaming down Market, headed toward the bay to escape by way of the ferries. The exodus was not at all joyous or even upbeat. The masses just trudged toward the bay like they were in a trance.

Matthew made a decision that would change the trajectory of his life that day. Instead of heading to the ferry building and Oakland, he turned back toward the park, satisfied that he had done what he could for now to find Julia. For all he knew, she might have been evacuated to the Presidio or the park just as he was, especially if she was injured.

It took the rest of the day for Matthew to make his way out of the burned zone and back toward the park. This time he headed down Market past City Hall to Fell Street.

Not too far up Fell, Matthew found families camped out in the street using all the resources of what were once their homes, to fashion shelters. There were bricks stacked up to make cooking stoves and pieces of metal and boards covered with canvas. One man stopped him.

"Have you been downtown?"

"Yes," Matthew replied unenthusiastically.

"How did the Phelan Building fare? I work in the Phelan Building." The man was hoping for a miracle but expecting the answer he got.

"It's gone, they're all gone."

He still asked Mathew to share what little they had to eat. He declined but accepted a cup of coffee. Back at the park, he finally found the comfort of a cot and blanket, and fell asleep once more.

Saturday dawned dark and dreary. There was a chill in the air, but not the crisp bighting kind that is a harbinger of a clear spring day. This chill was the bone chilling type that foretold of rain. Rain! Later that morning, it started to rain, a steady spring rain that feeds the flowers and renews the land. It just came four days too late.

Chapter 27

THE SEARCH

⸺∞⸺

After a week in his tent city, with bread lines and latrine lines, Matthew got restless again. His arm was healing nicely, although slightly bent where it should be straight. He heard that messages were being left for missing relatives at Lotta's Fountain, so he hitched a ride back down town on a wagon headed for the ferry to pick up more medical supplies. Matthew hopped off at O'Farrell and made the walk a couple of blocks up to the music store site again. There was nothing worth picking over. In a corner lay a row of white ivory keys sitting in a pillow of ash; a little further, a tangled mess of wire that once was some kind of stringed instrument.

At the fountain, there was a small crowd peering at scraps of paper and leaving others, some taped, some wedged in cracks. There was also a more official looking list tied to the fountain with string. As Matthew jockeyed for position, he realized it was a list of the dead. Skipping down to the 'T's, Matthew saw two Thomases, but he had never heard of the first names. After all, it was a pretty common name. He was relieved not finding Julia's name or any of her family, so with this optimism, he left a note:

To Julia Thomas,

I'm OK. Staying at the Golden Gate Park camp.

Love, Matthew Donohue.
April 26th

He reached up high by the lion's head, wedging it in a crack and pointed it to the north, thinking they also might have gone to the Presidio.

Matthew milled around for some time hoping against hope that Julia might coincidentally show up. After an hour or so, he wandered down Market, meaning to go to the ferry terminal to find out about his job. Passing the shell of the Palace Hotel, he wondered where the box and gold might be. He knew he wouldn't be able to do anything until his arm was completely mended, so he gave up and eventually got another ride back toward the park.

Sam was also searching. He walked up and down the tent city inquiring about his 'nephew', looking worried. Eventually, he got the lead he was hoping for. A nurse described Matthew and pointed Sam toward the row where his tent was. Sam found the right one and then backed off, taking it easy leaning up against a tree. Hours passed and a few men came and went from the six-man tent. Sam was thinking he might have gotten the wrong one but he finally spied Matthew slowly walking up the long row.

Sam turned away, not knowing if Matthew would remember his face. He decided to wait until night fall and then he planned to cut a hole in the tent and do the deed. First, he would have to find a knife. A logical place to find a sharp one would be the surgery tent so, after the sun had set, he strolled past and found his weapon. There was no activity there, since most in need had been helped days before so Sam slipped in unnoticed and groped around for a scalpel. Once he found his weapon, he snuck around to the back of Matthew's tent. He slit the heavy canvas just enough to crawl in and stood over the cots, trying to let his eyes adjust to the dim interior.

Finally, he spied Matthew's cap next to one of them. He carefully leaned over the form and quickly thrust the razor-sharp weapon through the covers and deep into the chest area.

Instantly, the cot was upended, throwing the surprised assailant back against the wall of the tent. A soldier holding a lantern immediately burst in and another pointed a rifle at Sam's head.

"Looking for me?" Matthew said confidently from the front of the tent.

"This man stole something that belongs to me!" Sam protested.

"And just what would that be?" replied the soldier coolly.

"It's very valuable!"

"Well how will we know if you won't tell us!? And is it really worth killing for?" the other soldier returned.

Sam was led off at gun point, glaring at Matthew. "You haven't seen the last of me! Mark my words!"

The nurse had stopped Matthew earlier when he returned, and told him that his uncle was looking for him. Since his uncle had died before he was born, his suspicion proved to be well founded. So, the other tent's occupants were moved while Matthew and the soldiers waited for Sam to attack.

Matthew thought he would sleep better from now on, but the incident only reinforced his anxiety about the gold and his would-be assassin.

Chapter 28

FINDING WORK

⊹⟢⟁⟣⊹

t was early June. San Francisco was well underway reinventing itself once again. Matthew's arm had healed with a scar to remind him of his experience the rest of his life. He had found a few odd jobs, helping some well-off home owners clear away rubble from their quake damaged homes. They were the lucky ones, living far enough out to be beyond the reach of the great conflagration.

This gave Matthew an idea. Maybe there would be work clearing out destroyed buildings downtown. He had heard there were plans to rebuild the Place Hotel. Maybe someone would find the box, maybe he would…

The work to clear debris along Market Street started early. Railroad tracks had started to be laid down by the ferry building so rubble could be hauled to barges. Rebuilding was already underway in some quarters. Matthew wandered Market until he reached the burned-out shell of the Palace Hotel.

He approached a man who was giving directions to a small army of men digging and throwing bricks toward a waiting wagon.

The boss pointed to one of the workers. "You there! Take two men and work in the office area! We still need to find that safe!"

Matthew cringed. If he had only left his box in the safe that night, they might soon be pulling out his treasure right in front of him.

He watched the men work for some time, then approached the foreman.

"Can you use another hand?"

"We can always use another hand, if you don't mind just $2 a day!"

"OK. When can I start?"

"How about now? You got gloves?"

"Yes, sir!" Matthew was good at anticipating what was needed.

After a few hours of sorting over bricks and other rubble, an older, quite rotund man pulled up in an automobile. The foreman halted work and walked over to him to talk. The big man gesticulated toward the north and pointed to three wagons and their teams of horses that had pulled up behind his vehicle. The foreman shook his head in reluctant agreement and turned back toward the crew.

"OK, boys. This is what we're gonna' do." He went on to explain that the man was in charge of the demolition of the hotel to prepare for reconstruction, but he also had some land over in Harbor View he wanted to fill in because it was low and swampy. So, the workers were to load the wagons with any and all debris that would make good fill for the swampy land.

"You know," said the foreman to one of the men as the fat man drove away, "He has a lot more money than sense. It'll take a thousand wagon loads to get done what he wants! But, a dollar's a dollar! Let's get to work!"

So, Matthew and the rest set out loading the first wagon. When it left, it headed up Geary toward Van Ness.

"That's gonna be a hard pull for that team, even with four horses! Then it'll be hard on the breaks the rest of the way." In another hour and a half, the other wagons were off to the dump site. The wagons did not return until almost sun set, so work was halted until the next day.

The day started early and Matthew was glad to be doing manual labor just to keep warm. The wagons took off once more, this time down Market.

"I told Mr. Herman those horses wouldn't last goin' up an' over the hill. I sent them down to Battery, then they'll follow the bay around. It's longer but it's mostly flat."

"What's he want to do out there, Jack?" asked one of the workers.

"He thinks he's gonna' have some sort a' resort or something."

With that, Matthew and the rest continued to load wagons, managing only nine or ten a day. The work was hard and dirty, but Matthew was intent on finding his precious box. He knew it must be there somewhere...

The workers traded off shoveling and hauling the rubble in wheel barrows up a ramp and into the wagons. The work became rather tedious and monotonous, so the men took to singing. The rhythm of the songs kept them at an even pace so they could work through the day. On the fourth day, Matthew was working with another man only slightly older than him. Matthew stopped to wipe his brow while Fred kept shoveling.

"I got me a mule an' her name is Sal," One shovel full went into the wheel barrow. "Fifteen miles on the Erie Canal." Another shovel full went flying. "She's a good ol' worker, an' a good ol' pal," This time, along with the broken bricks and tile flew undetected, a small metal box, about the same size as the bricks, "Fifteen miles on the Erie Canal."

Matthew dutifully ran the load up the ramp, upended the wheelbarrow and off the wagon went to Harbor View.

On the seventh day, Mr. Herman came by once more in his automobile. He took Jack, the foreman aside and they talked for a few minutes. Mr. Herman raised his voice a few times, but in the end, it was he who slowly shook his head in affirmation of Jack's words. He drove away down Market, the empty wagons following.

"Well, that's it for today, boys!"

"What's going on?" inquired Matthew.

"Mr. Herman finally saw the writing on the wall. We got less than a hundred loads an' the horses are beat an' it hardly made a dent in that marshy place! Besides, the railroad is getting close to finishin' laying the tracks. Pretty soon, we'll be loading gondolas fifty tons at a time!" He continued, "Come back in three days an' I'll have more work than you can shake a stick at!"

Most of the workers consented, but Matthew had had enough.

What am I breaking my back for? he thought. That box is gone forever.

He was paid on the spot for the balance of his work and turned back toward his camp in the park.

Matthew had thought long and hard about his job working on the ferry. His daydream of becoming captain of the 'Tahoe' really hinged on his future with Julia. Now that it seemed only a memory, Matthew decided to explore other options. After all, the 'Golden City' was still out there on the bay somewhere. Maybe he could explore the possibility of searching its coal bunker…

One day, he decided to go on down to the ferry building and see what was going on. He found out that Mr. Mulloy, the Southern Pacific Ferries manager had been killed in his sleep when a chimney collapsed onto his bed. Matthew decided to find out if there was any work for him anyway. When he entered the office with all the ferry paintings, there was no one at the front desk. In the inner office, Matthew heard the tapping of a typewriter.

Matthew shouted, "Hello? Is anyone there?"

From the inner office, a man replied, "Who wants to know?"

"My name is Matthew Donohue," still shouting through the closed door.

"So?"

"So, I was wondering if there was any work for me on the ferries."

The man slowly opened the door and poked his bald head out.

"Half the population of San Francisco is gone, there is practically no business save for demolition and the government is dictating what we do! And we have twenty-seven ferries sitting idle for lack of work!"

"What about the 'Golden City'? I used to work on her."

"She's up to Sacramento for the time being. No work now. Why don't you check back in the fall!" He slammed the door and went back to his typewriter.

Matthew returned to the park and later found part time

work along Van Ness helping merchants stock their newly created businesses. The dynamiting of buildings to stop the advancing flames was, for the most part, a disaster because the inexperienced crews didn't know how to handle the explosives. Most of the time, the detonations just launched burning scraps of wood over the streets to start a new fire. But along Van Ness, the operation was done with more precision and most of the buildings on the west side of the street were spared. These buildings were actually mostly homes of well-off merchants, so with their businesses destroyed, some turned their residences into temporary stores.

One day, Matthew got a letter from his mother through the make-shift post office in the park. She was glad he had let her know he was doing well, considering. After a halfhearted suggestion about moving back to the lake, she let Matthew know that Mr. Bliss' son Walt, had gone to the home in San Francisco. It was on Broadway, only a few blocks from the Presidio. She conveyed that he had many connections in the city and maybe he would be able to help Matthew. He appreciated his mother's common-sense advice and decided to follow it once more.

The next day, he went to see Mr. Bliss, the kid he played with back in Carson City. Matthew hoped he would find someone home, as there was no way to contact anyone beforehand. As he approached the three-story brick home, it appeared to have weathered the earthquake well. Matthew rang the doorbell and was greeted by a housekeeper.

"Hello, my name is Matthew Donohue. My mother used to work at Mr. Bliss' home in Carson City..."

"Who is it, Mary?" came a voice from the library.

"A man. He says he is Matthew Donohue. His mother—"

"Yes, yes! Show him in!" replied the voice.

Matthew entered the library as Walt rose from his comfortable leather chair. He laid down the book he had been reading and approached Matthew with outstretched arms.

"What a nice surprise! How great to see you! How are you Matt? Did you make it alright? How about that arm? What happened there?"

Matthew had a hard time keeping up with him. "I'm OK. Lost most everything. It could have been worse."

"Well, sit down and let's catch up on things! Mary, we'll have one more for dinner. You don't mind, do you?"

"No, not at all. How's your father?"

"He's still getting around, just not quite as fast."

The next two hours were a mixture of reminiscing and comparing notes about the quake and fire. The dinner was a modest stew, but satisfying.

As Walt took a second helping, he asked, "What are you doing now, I mean for work."

"Well, I've been doing some debris removal and some odd jobs… I don't think I'm going back to the ferries. It was a good job, but I don't think there's much room for advancement."

"You're probably right…" Walt looked at the shelf of books for a moment.

"What would you think about working for the Crystal Springs Water Company? They have a huge task before them and they will be taking on quite a few people."

"Well…" Mathew didn't want to seem unappreciative.

"Listen. I know the chief engineer, Mr. Schussler. He owes me a few favors. We still only have water for two hours a day. I'll try to find out where he is tomorrow and introduce you. He's been pretty busy since the quake." Walt walked Matthew to the front door.

"So, where're you staying these days?"

"I'm still up in the park. It's not so bad."

"That won't do! March right back in here! You are a guest of the Bliss family 'till you get back on your feet!"

Matthew had almost forgotten what 'normal' was. It was so nice to sleep in a real bed in a room with no one else snoring or crying out in the night from some terrible nightmare.

The next morning, Walt took Matthew over to the water company's temporary offices on Dubose in his Ford 'model C'. They were told that Mr. Schussler was out inspecting the water line that was being laid down Valencia to Market and Sansome. It continued down Bay, to the Francisco Street Reservoir.

"Well, I guess we'll just take the 'scenic route'," quipped Walt.

So, they set off, bouncing down Market, following the twenty-two-inch water line laid right up on top of the street. The once grand edifices were reduced to skeletons or heaps of blackened brick. Matthew couldn't help but glance back up O'Farrell only to find it unrecognizable. Already, workers were finishing what the quake and fires started. In all the destruction though, Lotta's Fountain looked as if it had not suffered even a scratch. To the right, the once opulent Palace Hotel was in its final stages of demolition.

"They're going to build her back, better than ever!" Walt exclaimed. "Would like to have been in on that design!"

As they turned up Sansome, Matthew was happy to see the tower clock at the ferry building. The time showed 5:14. Confused for a second, Matthew checked his trusted pocket watch, revealing a few minutes after noon and then he remembered; The great quake began at 5:12 that fateful morning, and the ferry building clock was always two minutes fast.

They were both surprised to find most of Telegraph Hill untouched by the fire but not surprisingly, the ramshackle Barbary Coast and China Town areas never had a chance. Most of the structures were wooden and they must have burned brightly.

"What a mess," remarked Walt. "Well good riddance to that place!" He said, motioning toward the bay.

They finally caught up with Mr. Schussler where Mason crossed Bay. He was checking a joint on the large pipe.

"Hey, Herman! Find any water for us?"

"That's a good one!" chuckled Mr. Schussler. "Actually, we should have this provisional line charged in just a few days!"

"That's great! Maybe I'll be able to take a bath again!"

"Well, there's a lot of water out there in the mean time!" he replied, pointing toward the bay. "How's your father, Walt? You know I still need to get up to Tahoe to catch that big one! Or better yet, get him down here and we'll go for some really big salmon up in San Pablo Bay!"

"I'll tell him. I think he's planning to come down next year." Turning to his right, Walt said, Herman, this is Matthew Donohue…"

"Oh, yes! The Donahues. How are you, son?" Matthew knew he must have thought he was related to THE Donahues with an 'a' not the 'o', but he didn't try to correct him. "What can I do for you two?"

"Well," began Walt, "Matthew could use some work, just 'till the ship building picks up again."

Mr. Schussler grinned. "It's not like things are slow around here! What can you do, son?"

Matthew began to reply, "Well"—

But Walt interrupted, "He was overseeing a couple of projects and before that he was a foreman." Matthew's disapproving look caught Walt's eye. "But he doesn't like to toot his own horn!"

"OK, Son, we can use a foreman down along Market and up Taylor and Jones. There are quite a few crews there and more being hired all the time. You come down to the office tomorrow and I'll introduce you to Victor Perry. He's my right-hand man down there."

"Thank you so much, sir! You won't be disappointed!"

Mr. Scussler laughed, "Then what will I be able to complain about next time I see you, Mr. Bliss?"

"You'll think of something!"

They waved as Walt and Matthew made their way back toward the Bliss home in Pacific Heights.

As they bounced along the uneven streets, Matthew said with some consternation, "Why did you tell Mr. Schussler I was a foreman?"

Walt looked over and said confidently, "I know that you have it in you. You just need someone to give you the chance to believe it yourself!"

The wind was brisk and bracing and Matthew looked out to the ships in the bay, cutting through the white caps, moving steadily past Alcatraz Island.

Chapter 29

BACK EAST

⸻⸙⸻

No one was allowed to return to San Francisco from Oakland for more than a month and hearing of the music store's fate, Julia's father had decided to move back East to St. Louis. Mr. Thomas had a friend from his days working for Baldwin Pianos in Cincinnati who offered him a partnership in his music business. Luckily, Mr. Thomas had insurance that was honored and he was ready to start again in a more genteel environment.

Julia was crushed at the news. As soon as she was able, she went back to the city with her father, ostensibly to survey the wreckage of the music store. Julia was somewhat encouraged by the fact that the cars were running once more down Market Street. They were different than the cable cars though, with wires overhead providing the power. Every once in a while, Julia would notice sparks spraying out from the connection between the wire and the rod protruding from the car's roof. As they passed the remnants of the Palace Hotel, Julia asked her father if they could get off there. It had been razed by dynamite blasts to make way for the new hotel. A sign in front proclaimed; 'Like a Phoenix rising from the ashes, the new Palace Hotel; Opening January, 1909'.

"That's a little optimistic," said Mr. Thomas.

As they passed Lotta's Fountain, Julia noticed the many letters and notes to loved ones. She circled, wondering if there could be any hope at all that news of Matthew might be among the many fluttering pieces of paper. Taking up more space and looking more official was a paper with the sobering title; 'Missing and Dead'.

Julia scanned down the list to the 'D's'. Davis, Darling, Dimmel, Dobbins, suddenly, Julia felt a faintness and she dropped her head not wanting to continue.

Slowly, she raised her eyes, Dimmel, Dobbins...Donohue. There were two Donohue's listed as dead or missing- A. Donohue and M. Donohue. Could it be that it was some other M. Donohue? Julia had not heard anything from Matthew all this time and also when she inquired at the ferry, they said only that Matthew hadn't worked for them since that fateful day. Mr. Thomas took Julia's hand and slowly led her away from the fountain, wiping a lone tear from her cheek.

There wasn't really much to look at where the music store once stood. Julia remembered the catastrophic destruction of that first morning, but this-this was complete and utter annihilation. Everything had burned with an intensity that left even very little ash.

The only clue that a building had once stood there were brick and mortar and unrecognizable melted objects.

"Well," said Mr. Thomas in a very detached tone, "this makes my decision a little easier." Julia began to cry, softly. They went back down to Market Street to hail a streetcar.

In the following weeks, the Thomas family finalized plans to make the move to St. Louis. When the insurance claim was settled, Mr. Thomas went out first to find a house and then he sent for the others. Julia would always remember the day she left the bay area. Sunset and the silhouette of San Francisco against the sky, softened the reality of the disaster. Julia would return only one more time.

Hetch Hetchy Valley

Chapter 30

A DIFFERENT DIRECTION

M atthew spent his days toiling alongside his co-workers and his
nights learning as much as he could about the Spring Valley
Water Company and how water was delivered to San Francisco. He managed to keep two steps ahead of his work and eventually,
was promoted to overseeing the rebuilding of the city's cisterns.

Matthew was beginning to lose interest in the gold bars-if they
were even still in the boat at all. He had read with some relief, that
Sam Cleveland had been found guilty of murder and sentenced
to life in San Quentin Prison, though Matthew hadn't even been
contacted about the attempted murder in the park.

He bought some land on Masonic Avenue near Buena Vista Park and planned to build a house once he had saved enough money. Matthew's good work got him promoted to assistant to the engineer and by 1910, he oversaw all water service to the north end of the city.

Matthew married a girl from the Napa area, Anne Yount, and they moved into their newly built house on Masonic. They met curiously, along Market street. She was visiting her aunt in the city and Matthew was helping realign a water pipe to the new Chronicle building. As he toiled in the five-foot-deep ditch getting measurements, Matthew heard a feminine voice from above and his mind instantly flew to O'Farrell Street and the window above the music store.

"Prospecting for gold?"

Matthew was at a disadvantage. He squinted up toward the voice and could only make out a silhouette against the glare of the sun. "No gold in this mess."

Realizing the angle of the sun, Anne hopped over the ditch. As she did, Matthew couldn't help but notice her under garments which revealed much more of her slender legs than a man was intended to see. With his back now to the sun, Matthew noticed her short blond hair and her boyish appearance.

"That was a good jump," Matthew observed as he recalled his ferry days.

"Good practice for the street cars. Do you do this all the time?"

"Actually, I don't do this much anymore, but sometimes if you want something done right you have to do it yourself."

"What are you doing for lunch then?"

Matthew was surprised and pleased by her directness. Little did he realize it at the time, but this would be the start of a relationship that would help Matthew heal his heart and move on.

One day, they took a wagon ride up Napa Valley to see the geysers. It was an all-day ride up and back through Saint Helena and just past Calistoga but the weather was perfect.

As the steaming water exploded against the blue sky, Anne exclaimed, "It's just incredible to think about the power of the earth so near to the surface."

"Like it's giving us a warning of things to come. Were you affected by the quake?"

"Not so much. We lost a lot of dishes and one wall cracked, but no one was hurt."

When Anne visited Matthew in the city, they often went to the park but Matthew could never seem to bring himself to visit the Japanese Tea Garden. He told Anne he was allergic to the cherry blossoms and he always seemed a little melancholy when they listened to the band play at the music concourse.

Matthew and Anne had two children. He insisted their first-born daughter be named Julia, saying it was a family name. She was born in 1910. Their son, Jonathan, tragically died soon after birth in 1913.

In 1912, Matthew quit the water company to go to work for the City of San Francisco and newly hired city engineer, Michael O'Shaughnessy. He admired O'Shaughnessy's work and reputation of not being swayed by politicians.

He was also excited about the prospect of having a hand in helping the Hetch Hetchy project come to fruition. This project would bring water to the city from the Hetch Hetchy Valley in the newly established Yosemite National Park, high in the Sierra Nevada mountains. One day, at the city engineer's office, Mr. O'Shaughnessy was talking with other engineers about taking a trip up the Tuolumne River to the Hetch Hetchy Valley to determine the best spot for the construction of a dam.

"This project is big and will provide water for our city into the next century!" he declared, "It's going to take everyone working together to determine the best way to attack this. I need someone to take a trip with me to the proposed site to get an idea of how to proceed. Maps only go so far. We need to see what we are up against." Everyone agreed that seeing the site first hand was important, but there were varying degrees of enthusiasm for going.

"What about you, Donohue? What do you say?"

"I'm not an engineer, but I'd like to be involved in the aqueduct. And besides, it would be nice to get out of the city for a while."

"Oh, that's right! You spent some time in the high country around Lake Tahoe, didn't you? Good, then! Should be an invigorating ride!"

Plans were made and on a Saturday in early September, Mr. O'Shaughnessy and Matthew set out for the mountains. After the train ride to a place called Chinese Camp, they took a stage to Groveland. The next day, the two men secured a buckboard and took off toward Hamilton's Station. They took a mid-day lunch and Matthew opted to sit under a huge pine tree to take in the fresh mountain air.

"What do you think?" Mr. O'Shaughnessy asked from the store's steps.

"This is beautiful country. I bet it's even nicer in the spring. There doesn't seem to be any major obstacles to constructing a pipe line."

"That's the attitude! Let's get going. We need to make Hog Ranch by night fall."

The duo once again departed and were soon bouncing over a primitive road.

"We'll have to lay in a railroad if we're going to get material in at any reasonable cost!"

Finally, after two days, the travelers reached a cabin owned by the city at Hog Ranch. The structure was in bad repair with a rotting foundation and sagging floor but it was shelter. That night was as quiet as Matthew had experienced since Lake Tahoe, with the exception of an occasional whinny of the horses.

On Monday, they met up with Mr. Williams who would be their guide.

"Forgot to ask," Mr. O'Shaughnessy said. "Have you ever spent much time on a horse?"

"Yes, sir, but it's been a while."

They took off for Hetch Hetchey on horseback with one pack mule. Along the way, Matthew noticed the steep canyon walls of granite and every once in a while, a peek of a deep blue-green pool or rapids of the Tuolumne river. By mid-day they were upon the valley, suddenly opening up into a broad, flat meadow filled with dry ferns and tall, brown grasses studded with stately oaks. In the distance, the faint sound of water crashing against rocks could be heard.

"That's the Wapama Falls!" said the guide. "We'll leave the horses at the cabin over in those trees an' if you want, we can explore the rest on foot."

"Good idea!" interjected Mr. O'Shaughnessy.

The valley was different shades of green and gold. The majestic pines were full of cones and the occasional lone oak's leaves were ablaze with reds and oranges. Fall was in full force and it wouldn't be much longer before winter would be asserting itself.

On the north side of the valley, water came falling from a high cliff, first in a free fall, then crashing and cascading over huge boulders until finally running out to the valley floor in numerous rivulets. Matthew thought for a moment how some of the water of San Francisco bay was from this source. On both sides of the valley were towering granite cliffs, with small trees and shrubs clinging to whatever foothold they could find. Kolona rock jutted up above the surrounding topography in a distinctive pyramid like shape. At the head of the valley, about at the confluence with Rancheria Creek, the granite constricted back into a precipitous canyon.

Matthew was having a hard time pacing himself with his picture taking, with only two unexposed frames in the camera and one more roll left.

He had a strange feeling about the valley, trying to imagine what it would look like with the oaks and pines completely submerged. He looked up the granite walls, wondering at what level the impounded waters would be lapping. He continued to photograph any and all interesting land marks that could soon be gone forever.

As they walked, Matthew asked Mr. O'Shaughnessy, "This valley is so beautiful. Isn't there another place lower down in the canyon that would be suitable?"

"Don't get all 'nature lover' on me now! I bet you've been listening to that Muir character! This valley is a mosquito ridden swamp in the spring! It'll be a blessing, taking away that annoyance and replacing it with a pristine mountain lake! Besides, we'll still have the valley of the Yosemite. It's even more scenic. You should go there some time."

They returned to the end of the valley where Mr. O'Shaughnessy explored the bedrock on the bluffs on both sides of the river. "This will make for a fine foundation! I can see a dam well over 300 feet tall at this site!" He took out his camera and snapped a number of photos from different angles.

Matthew was uneasy the rest of the day as he wandered over the golden grass and fern covered meadows. As the sun went down, shadows climbed the shear granite slopes, finally overtaking North Dome.

The next morning, the trio forded the river and followed a ravine up to McGill Meadow. Up and over a small ridge lay Lake Elanore, a beautiful natural lake created from the scouring action of glaciers many millennia before.

"I figure we can add 30 or 40 feet to this lake with little effort! See this sand and gravel? It was ground down from glacial action and will make a fine readymade concrete mixture!"

Matthew scanned the lake and the peaks around it and thought, if we're going to have a 300-foot dam down there, what's the need for thirty feet more way up here?

The night at nearly 5,000 feet was flooded with stars and Matthew felt very much like he was once again on the shores of Tahoe. Around the campfire, Mr. Williams told stories of the Paiute Indians and Joseph Screech, the first white man to explore Hetch Hetchey.

The next day, they descended back to the river and proceeded to a temporary saw mill site and scouted for the alignment of a conduit to a future power station. From there, they inspected the road building camp and finally, leaving the horses at Hamilton's, drove back to Groveland. On the sixth day out, Mr. O'Shaughnessy and Matthew drove to Chinese Camp and caught a train back to San Francisco.

As they traversed the broad San Joaquin Valley, Mr. O'Shaughnessy quipped, "We got us a good site! The citizens of San Francisco will be thanking us into the next century!"

Matthew managed a feeble smile, but he said nothing.

The next day, Mr. O'Shaughnessy gave a press interview extolling the virtues of the site and the benefits the whole bay area would realize from the project. The fate of Hetch Hetchey was sealed.

From that time on, Matthew distanced himself from the project. His ideas of progress had evolved from earlier days when he was impressed at what man was capable of. Now, just because it could be done, Matthew wasn't necessarily convinced it should.

Construction of the Panama Pacific Exposition, 1914

Chapter 31

MAKING PREPARATIONS

⸙

t the same time, another huge project was getting underway in San Francisco. The Panama Pacific International Exposition set to open in 1915, had infrastructure needs that both the private Spring Valley Water Company and the city had to address.

The PPIE world's fair was going to be San Francisco's signal to the world that it had not only risen from the ashes of the great quake, but that it had left it far behind and had literally reinvented itself. This was to be the most elaborate, ambitious and ultimately the most ostentatious world's fair ever.

Matthew gladly threw himself into the assignment of installing sewage lines with the water lines paralleling them. As a result, he worked alongside many of the employees he had gotten to know while working at the water company. The exposition grounds were literally created from some of the fill of the great quake as well as sludge and sand dredged up from the bay.

Matthew remembered the scheme that man had about using the rubble from the Palace Hotel for fill and how unworkable it really was. He knew also, that sludge and sand do not make a good foundation and he voiced his concern about it at a planning meeting one night. He was overruled however, because the engineers had already addressed the problem by planning to drive pilings down to bed rock for each building.

As construction began for the great exhibition halls, the city and the water company had to make sure the water and sewer lines kept ahead of the building activity. Because of the composition of the land, digging went smoothly and easily- almost too easily. One day at a lunch break, Matthew was comparing notes with a foreman from the water company.

"You know," said Matthew, "I was living south of the slot when the quake came. All that land was made from fill. Not a single building was spared. Of course, the fire finished it, but there wasn't much left anyway."

"Yeah," said the foreman. "I heard the buildings folded like a house of cards!"

"And you know what? This place has the same look. Notice how easy the digging is? When this fair is over, what do you think is going to be built here? I'd be willing to bet whatever it is, they won't have those pilings for foundations!"

On New Year's Day, 1914, Matthew took little Julia, then just four years old, to see the progress of the largest wood and steel building in the world. As they approached the building with its graceful steel girders and arches Julia said,

"Daddy, how big is this building going to be?"

"The biggest in the world!"

"How big is that?"

"Well, Julia, it's so big, you could pilot a ferry boat through it, if it was in the water!"

"Wow wee!"

As they walked around the west side, Julia said, "Is that an aero plane, Daddy?"

Far out in the bay the constant buzzing, like that of a huge bee caught Matthew's attention. It circled once, twice and then descended to just a few feet above the waves.

"I believe that is, Julia"

"Is he going to land?"

As the fragile looking plane kept coming closer to the shore, it didn't look like it was slowing down. "I don't know what he's doing."

It was headed directly for the partially finished Palace of Machinery.

"It'll turn away, soon." Matthew said with mounting apprehension.

But it didn't. He couldn't believe his eyes! The plane kept coming closer and suddenly disappeared inside the cavernous shell of the building! There was no jarring crash reverberating through the structure like he had expected but instead, the steady drone of the engine. In a few seconds it reappeared again on the south side and made a steep bank to the left, heading out over the bay once more.

"That was fun! Will he do it again?"

"I don't think so," replied Matthew, still stupefied over the feat.

Other people cheered and whooped wildly and threw hats into the air.

"What a way to begin the New Year!" said one man.

"Who was flying that thing?" Matthew inquired.

"Why, that's none other than Lincoln Beachy, maybe the best aviator in the world!" The man said proudly. "Gonna be doing flying tricks the whole fair!"

"It'll be a trick if he doesn't get killed!" Matthew said, watching the plane approach the air field to the west of the fair site.

This was going to be a fair to remember.

Chapter32

A NEW LIFE

⁘⋙⋘⁘

Julia Thomas would soon become Julia Bartlett, wife of Michael
Bartlett of St. Louis. At the Thomas house on Maple Avenue,
Julia's mother was fitting her for her wedding dress. From the
chair she was standing on, Julia could look over the curtains and
out to the street. Her fiancé drove up the icy street in an automobile
and parked at the curb.

"Don't let him see me in my dress!" Julia's mother hurried to the
front door, grabbed a coat and met Michael on the porch.

Michael Bartlett was the son of Fredrick Bartlett, owner of
'Bartlett and Son Shipping Company.' They ran ferry boats and
barges up and down the Mississippi and business was very good.

Michael was an immediate hit with Mr. Thomas. He had a
bright future in the business and the match was approved by both
families. He was an attractive man and was good to Julia, but that
spark just wasn't there for her. Whenever she went down to the
waterfront offices and saw the ferries docking, Julia couldn't help
but think of Matthew. She didn't have any basis in fact to believe
it, but Julia couldn't shake the feeling that her love had somehow
survived.

When she visited the piano store on Olive Street, she also felt
the pang of loss when she played that Chopin Nocturne. It had
developed a much more melancholy air about it as Julia played
more pensively than ever.

But she was about to begin a new life and it would be a comfortable one with someone who cared about her. There was one

condition she put on her betrothal. The honeymoon had to be back in San Francisco so they could see the Panama Pacific International Exposition. Julia missed the ocean breezes and did not like the raw, snowy winters of the mid-west. She was also sorry to have missed the World's Fair in St. Louis that was held in 1904. Michael had told her so much about it but she was certain San Francisco would even top that. There was much fanfare and advertising for the Panama Pacific International Exposition even back in St. Louis, and the Union Pacific Railroad was offering special express trains just for the fair.

So, the wedding was set. It would take place in the Methodist Church downtown. There would be hundreds of family and guests on the groom's side, but only her immediate family and two uncles coming down from Cincinnati on the bride's. But no matter, the wedding would be grand and the honeymoon unforgettable. The union was first set to be on New Year's Eve, but Julia postponed it until Valentine's Day to mesh better with the San Francisco Exposition which was to open on February 20th…Matthew's birthday.

When asked about accommodations while staying in San Francisco, Julia said, "why not have the best? Let's stay at the Palace Hotel."

South Gardens and Fountains

Chapter 33

PPIE

The Panama Pacific International Exposition was the world's fair
that celebrated the joining of the Pacific and Atlantic oceans
via the Panama Canal.

Beginning as a project started by a private French concern, the
canal was taken over and completed by the U.S. Government with
all its resources.

Until the Yellow Fever was identified and eradicated, 30% of the
work force had died and little progress could be made. But President
Roosevelt and the American 'can do' attitude overcame all odds at
a cost of $352 million and 5,600 lives to open the Panama Canal
in 1914. Crossing the Isthmus of Panama which almost took the

life of Matthew's benefactor, Duane Bliss years before, now could be traversed in relative comfort on a boat in just a day.

San Francisco marshaled all of its resources and called in all favors to make the fair a reality. The city faced a daunting task- They had to raise over $25 million, repeal, change and sometimes ignore numerous laws, recruit exhibitors from throughout the world, and overcome all sorts of unforeseen obstacles and finally, shrug off the fact of a world war developing across the Atlantic. But those hurdles and more came to pass and still San Francisco was ready on time and on budget.

By the time of the official opening on February 20, 1915, Matthew and his family had visited the grounds often and already knew the 'lay of the land', but they still were excited about attending.

"I want to be the first one in!" said Julia excitedly the night before.

"We might not be the *very* first, but we'll be one of them." reassured her mother, Anne as she tucked young Julia in bed. "You get to sleep now, and before you know it, it will be time to go."

Matthew passed by Julia's room a few minutes later and peeked in. "Sleep tight, don't let the bed bugs bite!" but Julia was already in another world.

Beginning half way across the country, Michael Bartlett and his new bride, Julia, had already passed through Reno on the express train bound for San Francisco, only ten more hours to go.

At last, it was here; opening day of the Panama Pacific International Exposition and, coincidentally, Matthew's birthday. Matthew, his wife and daughter set off for the fair with the sunrise. They took the cable car down to Market and then, Van Ness Avenue. Soon, the street car was bogged down by the throngs of people, all walking north toward the bay like bits of iron being drawn toward a huge magnet.

There were marching bands and dignitaries in autos too, advancing toward the entrance, all eventually being swallowed up by the ever-increasing crowds. Finally, around Broadway, they hopped off and headed west ten blocks to Scott Street, then down toward the main entrance. Because of the crush of people, the closest Matthew's family could get was the corner of Union Street. There were politicians giving speeches but Mathew could not hear anything except the cheers and clapping of the crowd. He pulled out his companion of all these years in San Francisco, the pocket watch with the image of the 'Tahoe'. 11:59, exactly. Matthew had long since reset his watch two minutes back to the correct time. He lifted Julia on his shoulders and in a few moments, cannons boomed, the crowd gave a huge cheer, and pressed forward as the gates of the fair swung open.

It took about fifteen minutes before Matthew and his family finally entered the Great South Gardens. They stood, transfixed before the spectacle, even though they had been at this very spot more than once before the opening. In front of them was the enormous Fountain of Energy, featuring a heroic figure straddling a horse with heralding angels standing on his shoulders. All around, sculptures of fish sprayed graceful arcs of water. Directly behind it, the Tower of Jewels loomed over all, its 100,000+ cut crystals shimmering in the wind. And everywhere, not a square foot of ground could be seen through all the people. Julia squealed with delight as Matthew and Anne cheered.

Somewhere among the multitudes along Van Ness, a newly married couple on their honeymoon from St. Louis, rode in a motorcar, complements of the new Palace Hotel.

The next day, Matthew, Anne and Julia went to the fair after lunch, intending to stay until after dark to watch the light show. After the experience of the previous day, Matthew decided to take advantage of the new auto trains, basically a small car towing two trailers with seats facing out. The ten-cent fare was well worth it when going from the front gates all the way to the buildings of the states. After passing through the arch under the Tower of Jewels, they entered the Court of the Universe.

"What are those statues, daddy?"

Atop two identical columns on opposite sides of the court, stood statues of figures with wings. One faced to the East, wings outstretched and one to the West, wings folding around its body.

"That's the day rising on that side and the night coming on that side. You see, the sun rises in the East and sets in the West." The term 'court' didn't do the space justice seeing as it would easily hold ten thousand people.

"Let's go to the Transportation Palace," said Matthew, "I want to see who's making automobiles these days."

There were rows of automobiles to view, some Matthew had never heard of. The Kissel Kar was large enough to carry a family of six and the Pierce Arrow was sleek and powerful, but allowing only seating for two.

On the other side of the building, came the racket of banging of rivets and hammers against steel set off by the background of humming motors. The view was obscured by the crowd but Matthew and Anne held Julia's hands and squirmed their way to the restraining ropes. Right before their eyes were automobiles being assembled as they slowly rolled down the hall. The Ford Motor Company was making beautiful, shiny black cars with white wheels and brass radiators.

"I'd like to get me one of those." said Matthew to Anne.

Julia shouted with excitement, "Can I ride in the back?"

"Sure you can. But don't tell mommy," as he winked to Anne. "I want it to be a surprise!"

Just about sunset, they made their way over to the Aeroscope, a 200-foot steel arm with what looked like a small metal and glass cabin on the end. As they watched, the arm slowly lifted the cabin higher and higher until it towered over the entire fair.

"What a fun ride! Can we go?" Julia said as she continued staring at the gigantic contraption.

"Sure, honey, but we'll have to wait in line."

The line snaked around the Chinese Village exhibit in 'The Zone', an amusement park/midway associated with the fair. It took about a half hour to get to the front and by the time they were on the ride at its zenith, it was starting to get dark. Suddenly, lights exploded from somewhere in the bay.

"Look at the colors, Daddy! Where did they come from?"

"That's what I wanted to show you! See that out at the edge of the water? That's the Scintillator!" They stood in awe along with all the others on the ride as all the colors of the rainbow magically appeared in the fog which had softly stolen in below them. The rest of the fair was bathed in soft pastel colors, complimenting the ochre, green, and orange of the buildings. The family held hands while Anne rested her head on Matthew's shoulder.

Little Julia gasped, as in the mist, the tower of jewels sparkled with all those novagems reflecting light that seemed to come from nowhere and everywhere simultaneously.

On the ground, another Julia was having her breath taken away by the same lights. She stood in the Court of Four Seasons with her husband facing the Scintillator, mesmerized by the rays that seemed to bend over their heads like a rainbow. If only Matthew could have seen this, she said to herself.

The next few days were rainy and people found other attractions to fill their time. Matthew had been working on the future sewer and water lines before the fair. He was already laying out the grid on a map for the city streets and sewers that would be created after the fair buildings were torn down.

Julia and her husband took a cab out to the Cliff House, different now after the fire in 1907, being rebuilt on a much simpler plan. They took seats facing the ocean and ate lunch while watching the seals warm themselves on the rocks.

As they were leaving, Julia looked up the hill to the Sutro Heights and thought about a different day, a lifetime away.

By the end of the week, the light drizzle had subsided and the sun finally reappeared. Julia and Michael's time in San Francisco was almost over, so she took him out to tour Golden Gate Park. Their first stop was the Conservatory of Flowers and then they went on to the Music Concourse. As the band started, she stared at the columns on the right and hummed a tune, but it wasn't what the band was playing.

Michael had heard of the Japanese Tea Garden and after some cajoling, convinced Julia to show him. They strolled along the pristine paths and shared tea but Julia seemed to be lost in thought and no matter how much Michael tried, he couldn't get her to climb the steep steps of the drum bridge.

Near the end of their time in the city, Julia decided she wanted to see the fair one more time. By now, it wouldn't be so crowded and it would be easier to get to the fair, so Julia and Michael decided to walk over to the cable cars on Van Ness. She wanted to show Michael the music store site and as they crossed Market, they stopped by Lotta's Fountain to get a drink of water. As she rose, Julia reflexively glanced across the thoroughfare looking for something, but she saw only the hustle and bustle of a vibrant city. She noticed a scrap of paper tied to the fountain, flapping in the breeze. From what she could tell, it was a remembrance of those who had lost their lives in the great quake. More than half of it was gone, but the title on top read: 'Eighth Anniversary of the Great Quake of 1906.' Under it were proclamations by the mayor and various dignitaries, and allusions to the Panama Pacific International Exposition and the rebuilding and spirit of the city. Under that was a list of the dead, but it only went to the 'B's before the tear.

What do you expect? She said to herself. There had been no word whatsoever after all those years. Turning and smiling to Michael, they walked arm in arm to O'Farrell Street. As they turned the corner, Julia could just as well have been in New York or Chicago or any other large city in the country. There was no hint of a similarity to the days before the quake. The block that contained the music store, ladies apparel shop and candy store was now one large department store. Across the street was a bank with attorney's and dentist's offices above it.

Michael warmly pulled her away from the view and they continued up O'Farrell toward Van Ness.

As they rode the cable car toward the fair, Julia showed Michael the progress of destruction from the quake and how the military stopped the fire using explosives along the broad avenue. On the east side were all newly constructed businesses and homes, while on the west side, older homes prevailed.

It was an uncharacteristically mild and windless day for the first of March.

"Let's take a ride on the 'Aeroscope'," said Michael. "We can see the whole fair from up there!"

But Julia countered, "I want to see the whole city! Let me show you."

"Alright. But first we're going to do it on a full stomach!"

They passed through courts of palms and flowers to the aptly named Court of Abundance. They had a pleasant luncheon and finally Julia led Michael to the boat harbor.

"How are we going to see the whole city from a boat? Besides, I might get seasick!"

"Not that… this!" said Julia excitedly, as she pointed to a wooden ramp that led into the water.

"What!?"

Just about that time, a craft came skimming across the waves. It was not a boat, but it was floating. As it got closer, its true form became clear. It was an aeroplane! A sign by the ramp read: 'Alco Hydro-Aeroplane Co., Loughhead Bros. Owner/Operators.'

The plane pushed itself up on the ramp and out of the water while two men moved in and took hold of the wings.

"Are you one of the log-head brothers?" Michael inquired.

"That's lock-heed, LOCK-HEED!" the man responded, shaking his head.

He shouted and motioned the pilot to cut the engine and when it was finally dead, the brothers were still yelling.

"I told you we have to change it! No one can ever say it right!"

"But what would the relatives say?" yelled the other. Suddenly, the two realized that here was no need to yell and they continued a few seconds more which could not be heard. As the brother on the ground turned to address Julia and Michael, he introduced himself.

"Good afternoon, Sir and Madame, my name is Malcom LOCK-HEED. Lock, as in that which secures a door and HEED, as in taking heed to a suggestion. Lock-heed."

"We were interested in a flight—"

"SHE was interested in a flight!" Michael was looking a little under the weather. "I'm afraid I'm not quite up to it today!"

"No problem!" Mr. Loughhead replied confidently. "We'll still take the misses up for just ten dollars!" He turned to the pilot. "Just one this flight, Allan!" he replied with a 'thumbs up'.

"But Michael," Julia said disappointedly, "I so wanted you to see San Francisco from the air."

"Don't worry. You go. I'll be fine down here watching." After paying, he took a seat on a nearby bench.

The older brother took Julia's hand and led her to the plane. She had to climb a short ladder and duck somewhat awkwardly with her long dress, under the upper wing and step over to squeeze into the narrow seat.

"Keep your dress tucked in, miss!" instructed the pilot, "and put on these goggles."

The two men on the ground helped steady the wings and pushed the plane until the floats touched the water once more, and turned it until the plane bobbed out into the bay. After a few fits, the engine finally started, belching smoke at first, then taking on a more reassuring drone. Julia waved back to Michael as the backwash of the propeller blew his hat off.

He stood up, seeing that the plane was headed straight toward a large heavy cruiser, one of several veterans of the Spanish American War anchored in the bay for the duration of the fair. It got closer and closer to the ship as Michael looked on with helpless trepidation. The plane shook as it hit the tops of wave after wave but finally, it cleared the water and as it rose, turned to the south. Sometimes distances can be deceiving because the aeroplane had become airborne many hundreds of yards in front of the cruiser. Michael sat down once more, satisfied that his bride would, most likely, come back in one piece.

As the plane gained altitude, Julia could look back down to her right and see that they were approaching the ferry building at the foot of Market. Julia's thoughts were pulled back to her long, frightening walk down that devastated street and her sad crossing of the bay to safety in Oakland. They flew straight down Market to the new City Hall and then crossed over to Golden Gate Park. Julia was surprised to see how large the park truly was. She could make out the Conservatory and Stow Lake, and coming up near the coast, the huge windmill. They turned up the beach only a hundred feet over the waves and crossed over the Cliff House and Seal Rocks, finally turning back east toward the golden gate.

Julia's heart soared. Seeing the land from above was humbling and exhilarating at the same time. Out to sea, there was a bank of low clouds, waiting for evening to gain access through the narrow entrance to the bay.

In the bay again, the plane swooped low over Alcatraz Island, stirring up a small flock of Pelicans. They circled the cruiser anchored in the bay low enough that Julia could see sailors waving. She waved back, relishing the freedom that flight provided.

At the fair outside the California Building, a little girl pointed toward the ship. "Look Daddy, that aeroplane is circling the big boat!"

"Don't worry, Julia. They know what they're doing. See how it's coming down to the water? The plane is going to land on the water."

"That's a funny way to say it, land on water!"

"I guess it is. I bet the passengers had a lot of fun!" her father said, looking enviously towards the aircraft.

Soon, the plane lightly skimmed the waves, finally pressing its full weight against the water, slowing considerably. It once again skidded up the ramp while Julia triumphantly waved to Michael with both hands. As she climbed out, she turned to the pilot and gave him an unexpected kiss on his cheek.

"That was the most wonderful, exciting thing I've ever experienced!" Julia gleefully declared, as she hopped to the ground. She had the look of a little girl.

Always thinking of business, Michael said to the elder brother, "If you ever make it out to St. Louis, look us up. You could do a good business carrying parcels up and down the Mississippi with a readymade landing strip at every city!"

"Thanks, I'll keep that in mind!"

"Could we get one of those? We could tie it up at the docks!"

"But who would we get to fly it?"

Julia said nothing, but gave a polite curtsy. "Oh no! Who would teach you!?" Again, saying nothing, she glanced back to the pilot. Trying to take charge of the situation, Michael finally said, "We'll talk."

The newly wedded couple walked off, satisfied with their experiences in San Francisco and the fair, ready to begin their life together in earnest. Julia and her father Matthew, drove off toward home in the Model 'T' Matthew had just bought, one of the 4,000 built during the fair.

Later that evening, in the Palace Hotel dining room, Michael and Julia toasted to their good fortune, their honeymoon and marriage. The next morning, they would depart for home.

Palace of Fine Arts

Chapter 34

BUILDING ON SHAKY GROUND

⎯⎯⎯⎯⎯⎯⎯⎯

The Panama Pacific International Exposition was a huge success by anyone's estimation. The fair was punctuated with many firsts and superlatives. The first trans-continental telephone call was made by Alexander Graham Bell- The first indirect lighting was used- The liberty bell was brought to the fair, leaving Philadelphia for the last time- The first plane rides for the public were given at the fair- The Palace of Machinery was the largest metal and wood building in the world. Prominent attendees included President Taft, Thomas Edison, Theodore and Franklin D. Roosevelt, Luther Burbank, John Phillip Sousa, Henry Ford, Al Jolsen,

Buffalo Bill Cody, Charlie Chaplin and Helen Keller. More than eighteen million people had attended by the time the lights went out on December fourth.

On the last day, Matthew and his family along with over 450,000 people came to say goodbye to the fair and the world. There were bands and displays all over the grounds and every corner of the fair was packed with people. Midnight approached, and the lights slowly dimmed as the aviator Art Smith did aerial acrobatics with his illuminated plane. Suddenly, a hush fell over the crowd as a bugler played taps on the tower of jewels.

Within a year, the fair was gone- not just closed, demolished or dismantled but totally gone. Almost all the buildings and sculptures were razed or hauled away. Matthew stood near the only building spared, the Palace of Fine Arts, looking east across a serene pool to a perfectly flat, blank-book of a landscape, ready for development.

The water and sewer lines for the city would be laid in before any building could start. This was quite an advantage since most cities were built up first, leaving the messy business of retrofitting utilities in and around all the buildings and streets.

Matthew looked at the plans for the new streets. Baker St. would pass right in front of the reflecting pool. Beach, North Point, and Jefferson Streets would create a neat grid with existing streets coming from the South. Other streets would come in at a diagonal to give the neighborhood some variety. The area would be known as the 'Marina' district.

"This is like a blank canvas," said a fellow engineer to Matthew as he scanned the land, "ready to paint."

"Yeah, but this canvas needs a sewer first!"

As anticipated, the work went quickly, owing to the soft fill used to claim more land from the bay. One day, as the trenches were being dug down Scott Street, the workers ran into a patch of rubble. Matthew was alerted to the situation and came down to see what could be done.

"What we need," said one worker, "is a steam shovel to clear this mess!"

Matthew got down into the ditch and began inspecting the material. There was a layer of plaster mixed with bricks and tile.

"Could this be…?" Matthew didn't dare hope, remembering that week he worked loading debris from the Palace Hotel. He thought once again of his precious box and his plans, dashed that fateful night. Maybe, just maybe could his box be among the debris? Matthew dug around for a few minutes and produced a piece of a plate with a two headed crowned eagle and the initials 'PH', stamped in gold. Rubbing off the mud and holding it up to the light, a tear appeared in the corner of Matthew's eye. "This plate could have been used at my wedding dinner."

"What?" yelled a worker from above.

"Nothing, nothing. Let's get back to work. There shouldn't be too much more of this stuff!" Matthew threw the fragment back in the trench and let the workers continue clearing the rubble. The whole project was finished in about a year, and Matthew and two other engineers were given commendations for their work by the mayor, even though Matthew had written two letters stating his concerns for the unstable nature of the land in the Marina area.

Matthew went on to help with the development of the reclaimed land south of Market as well as out in the numbered Avenues. He came to be known affectionately by the city workers as the 'king of the sewer rats'.

Chapter 35

PASSAGES

⋯⋯⋯⚬⚬⚬⋯⋯⋯

The 'war to end all wars' had been hard on everyone in the Bartlet family, half-way around the world in St. Louis.

Julia's little sister Katy married in 1917 and lost her husband the same year in a place called Flanders somewhere in Belgium. Julia volunteered to help the Red Cross and was shocked to see so many men returning with horrible, disfiguring wounds.

She became a pacifist and demonstrated against the war, much to the consternation of her husband. Julia would go down to the government buildings with her children Jack 3, and Robert, 1 and walk back and forth in front of city hall with signs reading- 'When I grow up, I want PEACE!' on the side of the baby carriage. The Methodist Women aligned with the Women's Christian Temperance Union and Julia led rallies in front of the Lemp and Anheuser-Busch breweries. Then there was suffrage for women's rights. Julia was active in the movement, speaking at their meetings.

Michael was beside himself with anger and concern. He had a wife with two small children and had come to depend on the war effort and the breweries for much of his business.

One afternoon, Michael was waiting for Julia and the children after they returned from one of the demonstrations.

"Out for a stroll?"

Julia said nothing but went straight upstairs to the nursery to put already sleeping Robert to bed.

"What are you trying to do!?" Yelled Michael up the stairs.

"Just what everyone should be doing!" came the reply as Julia leaned over the railing. "What good comes of war? What good comes from drinking alcohol? And why are women still kept from being a real part of this country!?"

"Now, wait. You women have the right to vote for president!"

"And what good does that do when the mayor and his councilmen decide the affairs of this city?!"

"They are the duly elected—"

"Elected by whom!? You men who have brought us into all this turmoil and suffering in the first place!"

Julia was not going to be reasoned with, so Michael stormed out the front door, slamming it so hard the chandelier shook. Julia sat on the top stair and stared out the window while carriages and motor cars passed by.

One day, Michael's mother came over to visit. Julia was once again out at some organizational meeting and the conversation soon reverted to her.

"Listen, dear," his mother consoled, "you have a very spirited wife who just has to get her priorities in order. It's all well and good to have concerns for the world, but she has to take care of her own!"

"I just don't know what to say to her!" an exasperated Michael replied. "I want her to be happy, but I don't know how to get through!"

"All you have to do is let her know what is really important! What you need is another child!"

"What are you saying, mother?"

"Why, with two young children and another on the way, she won't have time to think about anything else! There's nothing like a full house to keep a person occupied. I should know!"

"But how can I get her to agree?"

"It's not up to her! You're the man of the house! Take her somewhere romantic. Get her a new ring or necklace. Just make sure it's her time of month!"

"Mother!"

"I mean it! I'll help you find out and I'll take the children for a few days, then the rest will be up to you!"

Thinking for a moment, a smile came over Michael's lips. "Alright, momma. I think I know what I can do!"

The next week, Michael let Julia know about plans to go to New Orleans on business, but that he wanted her to go with him.

"You know," Michael said soothingly, "this has been a hard time for all of us, what with the war and all those other things—"

"You mean the rights of half of the people in America?" Julia was not soothed.

"You know what I mean. Listen. What you need, what we *both* need is a little time for ourselves." Julia crossed her arms and looked up at the chandelier hanging above the entry way.

Undaunted, Michael continued, "There's a meeting of shippers in New Orleans next week and I thought we could turn it into a short vacation." Julia turned and looked Michael straight in the eye, but before she could respond, Michael countered, "I know what you're thinking, but the meetings will only take two days. We can take one of the company's river boats down and the train back." Julia's mood lightened. "With all the stops along the way, it'll take four days to get there, and we'll be staying at the St. Charles Hotel…"

Julia managed a slight smile. She did enjoy the slow pace of the Mississippi. She liked the herons, gracefully taking flight from the overhanging trees, she even liked the smell of the mighty river.

"Perhaps you're right…" Julia conceded, "now that the war is over…"

Michael saw his opening. "And the Eighteenth and Nineteenth Amendments are sure to pass soon!" He was right. Both Amendments were in the process of being passed by the House and Senate and would become law by the next year.

So, Julia relented and as they made their way down river on the first night, she received a beautiful star sapphire necklace to compliment her steely blue eyes and raven hair.

Chapter 36

THE END OF A DREAM

Back in San Francisco, Matthew and Anne were very concerned. Little Julia was sick. She had a cough and high temperature and she had trouble breathing. Everyone knew what she had but no one would say it, as if not saying it would make it go away.

She had the Spanish Influenza which had already killed more people in San Francisco than the great earthquake and fire of 1906.

Matthew was terrified when one day, he passed a home and saw a small figure at a window obscured by curtains. Matthew immediately felt faint and imagined his daughter, Julia. He saw a coffin and flowers and rows of white marble head stones and his wife, Anne crying. Matthew closed his eyes tightly.

"This can't be Julia! I won't let be! I have to change the future!"

When he looked again, a man had parted the curtain just enough to peer out on the street below.

Matthew took to going to church again, something he hadn't done since before the quake. Every afternoon after work, he would stop by St. Agnes Catholic Church, just down the street from their home. Every time he knelt in front of the altar and looked up to the figure hanging on the cross, he would say; "Take me, Lord. Take me, but spare my child."

Weeks went by and young Julia slowly regained her strength. She had beaten the pandemic that killed nearly 3 million people worldwide.

It was Christmas, 1919 and things were looking up. Young Julia's ninth birthday would be next month, and Matthew had been promoted to Assistant City Engineer. Matthew had very little formal education but spent endless hours late into the night studying engineering principles. That, along with astute attention to every detail of his work and that of others, gave him the wherewithal to challenge the engineering exam given at Berkeley and he passed.

New Year's Eve was a joyous affair and the family went out to look at the fireworks over the bay. On the way home, Matthew developed a cough. Unwilling to acknowledge the worst scenario, he went to work for a week before Anne insisted he see a doctor. The inevitable bad news came quickly and Matthew was confined to bed rest. He became weaker with each passing day until he developed pneumonia. Another week later, Matthew Donohue was the 2,023rd San Franciscan to fall victim to the Spanish Influenza. 600,000 Americans would eventually succumb to the deadly disease.

He was laid to rest in the Catholic Cemetery which he had first passed those years before on the street car, and to which he had donated the somewhat curious amount of $8,256.00 for the upkeep of the graves of the people who had died in the great quake.

His headstone made of Sierra Nevada Granite read:

Matthew Robert Donohue
Born, Feb. 20, 1885
Died, Jan. 15, 1920
Loving Husband & Father

And on the back side was the inscription:

"He helped rebuild our fair city"

The funeral and burial was a public event with many city employees in attendance and Matthew's name was added to a plaque at City Hall, commemorating public employees who helped in the reconstruction of the city.

The summer of 1920 in St. Louis had been particularly hot and humid, so it was not the best time of year to be expecting, but Julia was pregnant with her third child. Her other two pregnancies had progressed normally, but this time, there seemed to be one small emergency after another. There was bleeding and false labor and by August, Julia's doctor prescribed bed rest for her at the hospital.

Michael would visit each day, sometimes bringing fresh flowers from their garden.

One day in early September, Michael was called to her side. Julia had had a tough night and was feeling weak. Julia motioned for Michael to come next to the bed and she spoke in a soft voice. "Michael, I have always been supportive of you and I have always done what you have asked of me, at least most of the time..." They both smiled.

"This time, I am asking you to do something for me."

"Anything you want. Just tell me."

"This child. If it is another boy, I want him to be named Matthew."

"Alright, replied Michael. "Is that a family name?"

"No," said Julia as she turned to look out the window. "I have just always liked that name."

One evening, as Michael was about to visit, Julia's doctor called and told him to come to the hospital quickly. Filled with apprehension, he raced to Julia's side. She was laying in her sweat dampened bed, in obvious discomfort.

She didn't seem to notice Michael's presence at first. "Julia, I'm here," he said as confidently as he could.

"Come closer, Michael. It's time. Remember, if he's a boy, he will be named Matthew."

"Yes. Matthew. Everything will be alright. Don't worry."

The doctor and nurses came in with a gurney and spirited Julia away down the hall. Another nurse took Michael to a waiting room, assuring him that everything was under control. Hours passed and all the family had gathered in the waiting room. Finally, around four in the morning, a noticeably tired doctor came striding slowly down the hall. Michael was first to notice and jumped to his feet.

"How did it go, doctor? Has the baby come? How is Julia?"

The doctor managed a slight smile and said, "The baby is fine. You have a healthy boy."

"And Julia? How is she doing?"

The doctor's expression changed. "It was a difficult labor. Julia lost a lot of blood. She was just too weak…"

Michael was trembling. "She'll be OK though…"

The doctor put his hand on Michael's shoulder. "No. We lost her. She was just too weak."

Michael turned to his mother and collapsed in her arms.

He brought baby Matthew home from the hospital just two days later. His family hired a wet nurse to help Matthew gain strength. He grew to be a fun-loving boy, adventurous and curious, often asking his father and grandfather to tell him stories about his mother.

Chapter 37

GENERATIONS

⸻⸺⸻

ulia Donohue grew up and married Thomas Franklin, a San
Francisco City policeman, in 1929. She had four children;
Thomas Jr., Mary, Joyce and Alan.

Because of his Grandfather Matthew's reputation, Thomas Jr.
got a job with the city in the water and sewer department. He married in 1956 and had twin boys, Timothy and Thomas III. Tripp, as
he was called, married and had one child in 1982; a boy named after
his great-great grandfather, Matthew. Matthew had flaming red
hair and deep green eyes. As a small child, he would enjoy hearing
stories about his namesake from great nana, Julia. She would sit on
her porch at her home near Buena Vista Park and tell little Matthew
about the great world's fair and all the wonderful things she and
her father would do. Before she died in 1993, she gave Matthew a
novagem from the fair's Tower of Jewels. Her father had given it
to little Julia because he loved the beautiful aquamarine blue color
of the crystal. All generations remained in the San Francisco Bay
Area and had occasional reunions in Golden Gate Park.

Matthew Bartlett was twenty-one and enlisted in the Navy at the
outbreak of WWII. He left St. Louis and was stationed at Treasure
Island in San Francisco Bay before being shipped out to the war in the
South Pacific. Matthew was a medical corpsman with the Marines
and saw action at Guadal Canal and the Philippines. He met a girl
from Napa at a USO dance while on leave and married her in 1944.
When he returned, Matthew settled in San Jose, working as a mortician. He never mentioned his experiences in the war to anyone.

Matthew's brother, Robert was drafted into the Army and died in France two weeks after 'D' day. Matthew had two daughters; Janet and Dianne. Dianne was a defiant girl and frequently clashed with her parents. She had a baby girl out of wedlock in 1967 she named Alice, after the Jefferson Airplane's song 'White Rabbit'. Dianne moved to San Francisco and lived near the 'Panhandle' of Golden Gate Park during the 'Summer of Love'. Alice also had a daughter out of wedlock in 1985. Julia was named after her great-great grandmother because she had beautiful black hair and cold, steely-blue eyes, too.

Fire Fighters at the Marina District
(Palace of Fine Arts in the distance)

Chapter 38

LOMA PRIETA

t was a warm October afternoon with barely a breeze to cool off
the sweating citizens of San Francisco jogging along the Marina
Green. Tourists crowded Fisherman's Wharf and Chinatown.
Lovers lay on a blanket in front of The Palace of Fine Arts, the only
survivor of the 1915 Panama Pacific International Exposition. The
third game of the 1989 World Series was about to start at Candlestick Park.

Down the peninsula southeast of Santa Cruz near Loma Prieta
Peak, something was about to happen eleven miles below the ground
that would once again change the lives of the people in the bay area.

The San Andreas Fault is perhaps the most famous of those sites where plates of the earth meet and grind against each other. This fault runs along the Santa Cruz Mountains and out under the Pacific Ocean just south of San Francisco then continues on up the coast. The great quake of 1906 traveled along this fault from the north but this time the jolt would begin seventy-five miles to the south. Moving at thousands of miles per hour, it would not be denied. Santa Cruz was hit almost instantly. The city's mall was severely damaged and homes throughout the mountainous area were shaken off their foundations. Hurtling north, the earth rippled under the 7.1 magnitude of the temblor.

The first hints of what was to come for San Francisco were seen live on network TV as Candlestick Park rocked and rolled. The players emptied the dugouts and stood in the infield, and the crowd, when they saw the stadium wasn't going to collapse, began to cheer.

A split second later, the bay bridge sustained relatively minor, but spectacular damage. A seventy-five-foot section of the upper deck fell like a trapdoor as motorists drove over the edge, killing one.

On the I-880/Cyprus Viaduct in Oakland, the most tragic damage was done. A one and a quarter mile of the upper section of the two-level freeway collapsed and sandwiched the lower level, smashing any vehicle under it. Forty-one people died instantly. In some places, there was less than one foot of clearance between the two levels. Smoke escaping from various spots in the deadly sandwich indicated the location of the crushed vehicles

Across the bay, glass from store windows around Union Square rained down on pedestrians, as the buildings swayed in unison, causing many injuries.

The land under the Marina District, composed almost entirely of fill, liquefied from the intense shaking. Many buildings simply collapsed like an accordion, turning three story structures into single story wrecks.

Some homes slid into the streets leaving water and gas lines broken, with a frightening and strangely reminiscent odor permeating the air.

Then came the inevitable. Somewhere an electrical short or a spark from metal scraping cement set the gas off. Suddenly, it seemed like it might be 1906 all over again. The fire department responded quickly, but found fire hydrants dry from the ruptures.

The fire soon gained the upper hand. As a column of smoke rose from the Marina, it must have been an eerie sight for any survivor of that earlier cataclysm.

But the department countered by laying hose from far away hydrants that were not affected by the quake. Also, water pumped from the fireboat 'Phoenix' to engines on the shore provided an unlimited source of salt water.

Thanks to stringent building codes, actual structural damage was much less than eighty-three years earlier.

Fire and medical personnel, much better prepared and organized than eight decades earlier were up to the task. The result; just 63 people died, two-thirds of them on that one section of I-880 in Oakland. But the trauma was just as real for those who experienced it. There were emergency shelters set up in schools but some, fearful of the numerous aftershocks, camped out on the streets or in parks.

Eventually, people got back to a sense of normalcy. After everyone told their stories of 'if I had been just a few seconds earlier or later', people got back to their pre-quake lives. Network TV and print media thoroughly examined and re-examined the phenomenon ad nauseum, until they finally moved on to other tragedies and natural disasters. The local news reverted to traffic problems and political wrangling as headline topics. Eventually, the experience of the Loma Prieta earthquake was reduced to scrapbooks and personal journals until it seemed just a bad dream. San Franciscans were once again lulled into a 'it could never happen again in my lifetime' attitude. But in the back of everyone's mind, they were just whistling in the dark.

Thomas Franklin, Jr. had just retired the year before from the San Francisco public works department. He had been in charge of sewer systems, like his grandfather before him and the city called him in as a consultant to get his expertise in finding and repairing the broken lines in the Marina area.

The weather had taken a turn toward winter with cold rains and wind, but when the debris of destroyed homes was finally cleared away, Thomas came in to assess the job. Crews got to work exposing the water and sewer pipes at their rupture sites and the gas company mended their lines. Work was sloppy and slow. Water had to be removed from the ditches with pumps and giant suction hoses.

One such operation at the corner of Beach and Divisadero hit a lot of rubble that had to be removed by hand. Bricks and mortar, rusted metal and rotten pieces of wood were all thrown in a pile. Then, a man working knee deep in the muck, hit a piece of metal that had a hollow sound to it. After digging around under the object, it plopped in the water hitting his foot.

"Hey!" he yelped with surprise. "What the…" He lifted up a small box much heavier than he expected and set it on the pavement. Other workers gathered around to see what the commotion was about.

"Looks like that thing got the best of you, Fred!" The other worker wiped off the box, revealing a rusted lock and words engraved on the lid.

"What's it say?"

"Can't quite make it out…Looks like M-A-T-T something, something, something, then R-O-B-E-R-T, then D-O-N something-something, then U-E, E-S-Q?"

"MATT--- ROBERT DON—UE, E-S-Q? Matthew Robert Donahue!" Fred said excitedly. "You know, Matthew Donahue, the 'king of the sewer rats'! He worked for the sewer department back after the '06 quake. He helped lay these lines after the world's fair in 1915!"

"What are you, the resident sewer historian?" quipped the foreman.

"Wow! I wonder how this thing got here! Did he drop it in here?"

"That doesn't make much sense," returned Fred.

"You got a better guess? It's awfully heavy for its size."

"Maybe it's a 'time capsule!'" offered another worker.

"Let's open it up and take a look."

"That wouldn't be right," Fred responded. "You know Tom Franklin? He retired just last year but they brought him back to help with the breaks in the lines. He's Matthew Donahue's grandson. He ought to be the one to open it, seein' that he's a relation. Saw him 'round here somewhere. See if you can raise him on the radio."

In a few minutes, Thomas drove up. "What's the problem? What's this about a box?"

"Take a look!" Fred gestured to the box still lying on the road next to the ditch. "It says Matthew Donohue on the lid!"

"Well, what do 'ya know…Where did it come from?" he said, inspecting the inscription.

"Down by the pipes. What d'ya think is in it?"

"I have no idea, but I think I'll take it home and clean it up first, see if I can find anymore writing on it." The workers were visibly disappointed, but Thomas was adamant. "I want my wife and sons to be the first ones to see this too."

The box bounced around on the front seat of Thomas' pickup the rest of the day. He inspected the progress all around the Marina but the box distracted him to such an extent that he decided to quit early. After all, he rationalized to himself, I'm on a retainer. I make my own hours.

There was an air of anticipation in the Franklin home. Just how the box came to be under the ground and what its contents were was on everyone's mind.

"What do you think, honey?" Thomas' wife said.

"Let's get Tripp and Tim over here for dinner. We can open it then."

Timothy lived in Petaluma, north of the city and Tripp lived down the peninsula in Sunnyvale. It took a couple of days to get everyone's schedules synchronized before an evening could be arranged. On Friday night, everyone converged on the Franklin house on Steiner in Pacific Heights. Tripp proposed that any of the contents be examined by his colleagues at Stanford. He was an associate professor teaching U.S. history, but his passion was California after the '49 gold rush.

"OK, Tripp," Thomas finally relented. "Whatever is in here, you can check out at your lab."

"Let's get to it, then."

The hasp on the lock was quite rusted and barely holding on. It was easy to pry it loose without having to cut the lock. As Thomas slowly lifted the lid, the hinges also gave way.

His eyes widened as everyone gathered around in amazement. There, cradled in its rusty bed, was a gleaming gold bar that looked like it was formed yesterday. Thomas lifted the bar with both hands like it was Moses being snatched from the Nile. Everyone gasped. There were words and numbers stamped on it signifying the origin of the precious metal- 'Mizpah Mine'

"Mizpah, Mizpah…what does that mean…" Tripp searched his memory. It was in there somewhere. "I'm going to have to look that one up," he finally conceded.

"This is fantastic!" said Mrs. Franklin breathlessly. "Is it real? What do you think it's worth?"

"Well," continued Tripp, "gold is worth…Hey, do you still have today's Chronicle?" Mrs. Franklin brought the paper from the living room. "Look in the business section. What's the price of gold?"

She fumbled with the pages. "Let's see here…Oh, here it is! *Gold at the close of trading in New York…*blah, blah, blah, *is…$604.34 an ounce!*"

"Wow! How heavy do you think this puppy is!?" exclaimed Tim.

"Most bars of this vintage were 400 ounces, twenty-five pounds. Of course, I've never held one myself!" conceded Tripp.

"Let's weigh it!" giggled Mrs. Franklin. She hurried to the bathroom and produced a scale.

"You stand on the scale, mom and we'll get your weight, then you can hold the bar and we'll get the difference!"

"Oh, no! You do it, Mr. Historian!"

Tripp climbed on the scales and pronounced his weight; "One hundred seventy-four pounds."

"Get a calculator!"

"Already on it!" said Thomas. "400 times $604.34 equals...$241,736!"

Tripp then took the bar in his hands and peered down to the scale again. "One hundred ninety-seven." After a quick calculation in his head, Trip exclaimed, "Twenty-four! The bar weighs twenty-four pounds!"

Everyone cheered as if Stanford had just won the Rose Bowl.

"What's that come to?" said Tim.

"Let's see, twenty-four times sixteen ounces equals 384...times $604.34...that comes to...$232,066.56!"

"What are we going to do with it?" said Mrs. Franklin, somewhat dazed by all the calculations.

"You know," interjected Tripp, "a bar of gold from this era is probably worth more to a museum or a private collector than just its weight..."

"You mean it could be worth even more?!" said his mother dubiously.

"Yep. And I would be willing to bet the museum in Sacramento would consider making an offer. I know a man up there. I'll put a bug in his ear and see if there is any interest without letting the cat out of the bag."

In the corner of the box was a shiny bit of something and when Tripp wiped it with his finger, something even more brilliant revealed itself. It was a beautiful pale blue cut stone.

As Tripp held it up to the light, his mother said, "That's an aquamarine!"

"And a big one, too!" he returned.

"What's a loose semi-precious stone doing in this box with

a huge chunk of gold?!" Mr. Franklin exclaimed. Everyone was dumbfounded.

The family agreed to meet again a week from Sunday after church to discuss any more ideas. Thomas gave the box to Tripp to be examined by his fellow professors the next week. They all vowed to not breathe a word of their discovery to anyone until it could be collectively decided what to do.

When Tripp got home, he called an associate and asked about the Mizpah mine. He was told that it was a gold mine around Tonopah, Nevada active at the turn of the century. Mizpah meant 'outpost'.

On Sunday, the family reconvened and shared ideas. Mr. and Mrs. Franklin stood with their arms around each other and made an announcement. "Tripp, Tim, we have come to a decision. We will take half of the proceeds and you two can split the other half. If it is worth, say $250,000, that means $125,000 for us and $62,500 for each of you. And Tripp, you keep the box and aquamarine for study. We have been dreaming about taking a cruise around the world, but we could never quite save enough and keep up with the other obligations. Now, we can pay off the mortgage and still have quite a trip! What do you think?"

Tripp and Tim were speechless for an awkward moment. Then Tripp spoke. "I think you will get a lot more than that for the gold. I spoke to my friend up in Sacramento, and he thinks it might be worth more than double that amount to a museum or collector."

"Well," said Mr. Franklin, "I won't argue with that!"

Over the next month, the gold bar was examined and weighed and found to be 363.75 ounces. It seemed to have had pieces shaved off both ends by some sharp instrument. Research by Tripp and his fellow professors revealed that the gold had been mined in Nevada and made into bullion in March, 1906, but no other evidence of its movement could be found.

How then, did it get to San Francisco to be found in a hole in the ground in the Marina District?

Scratched into the bottom of the gold ingot was the somewhat cryptic message- 'The rest is in the Golden City'.

"That would be San Francisco, but it's a big town." This gave Tripp no clue as to where to start looking, or even if there really was more gold to be found.

A jeweler friend of Tripp's examined the aquamarine and found it to be just over four carats and of perfect clarity. The cut was reminiscent of the Victorian Era. On further inspection of the box, Tripp found a ring, made of platinum with small diamonds down each side with an empty setting the same size as the stone. An envelope, ignored in the excitement of finding the gold was partially decomposed and stuck by the rust to the top of the lid. Lab technicians and conservators in the art department managed to peel the envelope off the lid and carefully unfold the paper inside.

"Good thing a pigment ink and cotton rag paper was used," said the conservator. "Only the best of places like the Palace Hotel used rag paper. That was the only reason it held together so long."

The paper yielded the partial message on a 'Palace Hotel' letterhead:

April 17.
De----- Julia,

meet -- tomorr-- --Lotta- ----tain
*   -- 10---- ---- you- red ha-, the one w--- --e ostrich feat-*
-- - w--- -- wear--- m- bowler -- ---- be married at --- Palac-
Ho--- an- ther- we will spen- --r fir-t nigh-
*   --gether.*

Lov- forever, Matt-ew.

"This is like 'Wheel of Fortune'!" declared Tripp, "but first, I'd like to buy a vowel!" Groans filled the lab.

For the next two days, they worked on it and finally, the only possible answer became clear:

April 17.
Dearest Julia,

Meet me tomorrow at Lotta's Fountain at 10a.m. Wear your red hat, the one with the ostrich feather. I will be wearing my bowler. We will be married at the Palace Hotel and there we will spend our first night together.

Love forever, Matthew.

Matthew. This was a note written by Tripp's great grandfather the day before the great earthquake of 1906!

There was no way that meeting could ever have taken place because the Palace Hotel was wrecked by the earthquake and consumed by flames early the next day.

When the note was stabilized, Tripp had it archivally mounted and framed and hung it in his living room. Tripp's son always liked the fact that the man in the letter was named Matthew, just like him.

Chapter 39

A QUID PRO QUO

⋯⋯⋯⋯⋯◦◦◦⋯⋯⋯⋯⋯

The gold bar sat in an empty shoe box under the stairs at the Franklin's home for a month until one day, Tripp came over for dinner. He was about to take a bite of green beans, but his fork stopped in mid-thought.

"I've been inquiring around back channels," then chewing, he continued, "and I found out that dealing in this kind of gold can be a little dicey, but I think I found a way. My friend in Sacramento knows someone at the 'Silver State Mint' in Vegas, a privately owned 'boutique mint' that create unique, designer coins. Being a Nevada company, they are always interested in designing coins that reflect the history of the state and they would love to make coins honoring the Mizpah Mine from Tonopah."

His parents were completely confused. "What are you trying to say? How many have you told?" whispered his mother, glancing back to her husband.

"Don't worry, what I am saying is, our gold came from the mines in Nevada and they are very interested in getting it back there to make their own coins. Did you know the price of gold was $20 an ounce in 1906?"

"Yes, you told us before," said his father.

"Well, they want to make one ounce, $20 gold coins commemorating the Mizpah Mine in Tonopah!

"I have set up a meeting with the owners of the mint to work out an agreement. I'll let you know what I find out."

Two weeks later, Tripp invited himself over for dinner again.

As he hurried in, he almost tripped on the rug in his rush to get to the dining room chair. "This is it!" he blurted out. "This is the perfect solution for our dilemma!"

"I didn't know we had a dilemma," his dad countered. "What's the problem?"

"No problem now! Take a look at this contract!" Trip handed them a paper with the 'Silver State Mint' letterhead.

"*Acknowledging the receipt of said gold...*etcetera," Mr. Franklin mumbled, "...and so on..." Then he stopped and looked up at Mrs. Franklin. "This is good..." then, looking at Tripp, "It's good, isn't it?"

"Better than good!" The gold will be turned into commemorative twenty-dollar gold coins and will be offered for sale by the mint at $2,500 apiece!"

"Who would pay that much for a coin?" both Franklin's said in unison.

"You would be surprised." Tripp continued, "There are tens of thousands of collectors as well as resellers who would pay whatever the price to own such a unique and scarce coin. There will be only 350 minted with a 'Liberty Head' on the obverse and the Mizpah Mine 'Headframe' on the reverse. This gold actually came from that very same mine over a hundred years ago.! And look at the bottom line!"

They both scanned to the bottom of the document. "This looks like they want to give us half of all proceeds from the sale of the coins!"

"Yup!" And do you know what half of 2,500 times 350 is??" Trip could hardly contain himself now. "That's 437,500...Dollars!"

All three sat staring into their thoughts and after a few moments, Tripp continued, "That's sort of an odd amount to try to divide so how about you take, say, a quarter of a million and let us split the rest. I think that would work out pretty well for all of us..."

Mrs. Franklin mumbled, "A quarter million..." with a dreamy stare.

And so, it was done. The Silver State Mint sold out the coins in less than six months and got a $437,500 shot in the arm for operating expenses and the Franklin's had their dreams realized.

Chapter 40

COINCIDENCES

⸺◈⸺

Matthew grew up loving history like his father, but he was more interested in bringing this interest to the public. Every summer during high school, Matthew volunteered at the National Park Service's facility at the Maritime Museum or Fort Point. He spent many hours helping to restore and preserve the tug boat 'Hercules' and the ferry boat 'Eureka'. He gained much knowledge about the ferries of the 1850's up until the construction of the bay bridge in 1936, which sealed their fate.

After two years of college, Matthew was hired by the park service to help restore and maintain all the vessels moored at the Hyde Street Pier. He was most happy though, when he could pause in his work to answer questions from school children on field trips.

Julia was born in 1985. With so little conventional stability in her life, the only thing that connected her to her ancestors was a beautifully woven Indian basket Alice gave her from Julia's great-great grandmother. It was said to be from the Washoe tribe in Nevada. Eventually, Alice was able to move into more responsible positions until finally, she was assistant to the reference librarian. Julia was home schooled and often accompanied her mother to the library. Left to browse most days, her favorite subject became the history of San Francisco, especially the grand old hotels.

Julia's love of history eventually led her to study at San Francisco State University. She knew everything about the famous hotels like the Fairmont, the Mark Hopkins, the St. Francis and of course, the Palace Hotel.

By 2005, Julia was doing her graduate work in history and she was given access to much of the Palace Hotel's treasure trove of artifacts from its beginning in 1875 through the rebuilding and reopening in 1909.

One day in her research, she read that the contents of the safe which survived the great quake, were preserved. The safe was retrieved from the rubble of the hotel and could not be opened for a month for fear that the interior heat might make anything made of paper spontaneously combust when exposed to the air. The safe revealed a collection of valuable papers, money, and jewelry. The money was very interesting, but just typical of the era. Some of the jewelry was truly precious but again not too unusual. The papers were a different story. There was an I.O.U. for gambling debts and a deed for property once belonging to Adolph Sutro, former mayor of San Francisco, but Julia stopped in her tracks when she saw an envelope addressed to Julia Thomas. *Julia Thomas!*

Could this be *her* great-great grandmother, *Julia Thomas Bartlett?!* Julia knew that her namesake lived through the earthquake in 1906 and then moved back to St. Louis with her family, so it was definitely possible…

She carefully opened the envelope with her cotton gloves protecting the fragile paper from the oils of her skin and her hands shook slightly as she opened the folded document and read:

April 17.

Dear Julia, Please meet me at Lotta's Fountain at 10:00 a.m. tomorrow. Wear your red hat, the one with the ostrich feather. I will be wearing my bowler. I would like to have an early lunch with you at the Palace Hotel to discuss our future.

Love, Matthew

That would be an interesting coincidence, she thought. Was this Matthew my great-great grandmother's lover? Of course, that meeting could never have taken place.

Chapter 41

A CENTURY APART

As the centennial remembrance of the great earthquake and fire of 1906 drew closer, both Matthew Franklin and Julia Bartlett got to thinking about the two notes.

Julia thought, wouldn't it be fun to go dressed up like people of the era?

Matthew considered buying a bowler just for the occasion. A couple of days before the big day, Matthew decided to rent a period suit and go dressed as a dandy in his bowler and across the city, Julia was trying to decide which dress would complement her jet-black hair and blue eyes. And then there was the hat. She scoured the boutiques on Union Street and finally found a red hat of the right era and then the ostrich feather in a retro hippie shop in the Haight.

The stage was set- April 18th, 2006 was just a few minutes old when people started to camp out around Lotta's Fountain at the intersection of Geary and Kearny as they meet Market. By 5 a.m., the streets in every direction were choked with people of all description some wore parkas, some hard hats. Others like Matthew and Julia wore period costumes, looking like they had just stepped out of the last century. There were horse drawn fire engines and centenarians in classic cars. The newly renovated Lotta's fountain glowed in the TV lights.

Matthew looked down Market Street and a strange feeling took hold of him. He saw smoke and broken glass and debris covering the people. There was a strange smell...gas! He closed his eyes tightly, trying to understand what had just happened and when he opened them everything was normal. He took a gulp of his bottled water. He had incidents like this before, seeing some sort of tragedy or misfortune from the past in his mind, but Matthew always shrugged it off as having remembered something he had read or heard.

As the time drew nearer, guests were introduced and politicians gave speeches which were mercifully short in the cold pre-dawn air. Then, at 5:12 a.m., a hush swept over the crowd as sirens wailed and church bells chimed marking the very instant, exactly one hundred years earlier, which changed the city forever.

At the end of the ceremony, the director of emergency services announced to the crowd, "Let's go out and have a good time! The bars open at six. We should give a toast to the incredible spirit of San Francisco!"

An enthusiastic cheer erupted and hats flew in the air. Many of the bystanders started an impromptu parade toward the ferry building.

Julia lingered as the sun peeked between the sky scrapers, half-heartedly expecting to see that man in the bowler. Matthew had already departed, but he still had a feeling of belonging in his costume.

Julia decided to cross over to the Palace Hotel. During her research, she had made some friends at the hotel and wanted them to see her in her period clothes. She lingered in the Palm Court, trying to imagine what it must have been like, sitting there as famous people strolled through this very spot and how all this opulence turned into a nightmare in a split second.

After a while, she made her way to the front desk and modeled her outfit for the manager.

"Don't you look stunning!" Fredrick, the manager declared. He invited Julia into the bar for a day break eye opener.

"You know," said Julia after her first sip of whisky, "my great-great grandmother was supposed to meet someone in the Palm Court one hundred years ago, today. I think it was to talk about getting married. There was a letter in your safe that was never delivered because of the earthquake."

"That's sad," replied Fredrick. "I'll tell you what. When you get married, I'll give you a great rate on the whole package."

"Thanks, Fredrick. I might hold you to it." They both laughed at the thought.

After a gratis breakfast, thanks again to Fredrick, Julia wandered out onto Market. Checking her broach-watch, she could see it was only 9:30 a.m. Could that letter hold the kind of magic to make a person appear after 100 years? Julia was just enough of a romantic to wait around to see.

Chapter 42

A MEETING AND A REUNION

Julia was a little lost out on the street. She didn't know why she expected anything special to happen. She looked enchanting in her long white dress, buttoned high up her slender neck with the red hat and ostrich feather. She wore a stunning sapphire necklace which complemented her eyes while her jet-black hair cascaded over her shoulders. She turned many a head, but none seemed to be the right one.

She was considering taking the bus back home, but the first one was totally full. She strolled up Geary to Union Square, window shopping along the way. Everywhere she went, she caught admiring glances and compliments.

Before she knew it, it was almost 10:00. Hurrying back to Lotta's Fountain, she twisted her ankle stepping off the curb. As she leaned on the fountain, bending over to rub her leg, a strange feeling gripped her. It suddenly seemed unusually warm, and for a moment, she thought she smelled the sweet scent of fresh flowers.

Matthew had joined a small group of newly made friends with similar period costumes at a bar just down Kearney. Seeing it was close to 10:00, Matthew's curiosity got the best of him and he made his way back toward Lotta's Fountain. On a whim, he decided to check out the Palace Hotel for any signs. He could imagine the hotel of a hundred years ago with men such as himself populating the court, smoking their cigars and reading the 'Call'. Then he noticed the wall clock. It began to strike one, two, three, four…Matthew counted each strike. He reached into his vest pocket to check his watch. A ferryboat gracefully adorned the cover. "Tahoe." Matthew whispered. The watch read just thirty seconds before the hour.

Matthew decided to test the power this note from one hundred years past had on him. As he stepped outside and walked up Market, he was mildly amused watching the traffic and pedestrians go by. It seemed such a blur and hurry for no good reason. He glanced across the street through the silver and red streak of a car toward Lotta's Fountain when he suddenly froze. There, across the wide thoroughfare, stood a woman leaning against the fountain. Matthew noticed only the hat and ostrich feather with long black hair, cascading over her feminine form. Then, as if drawn by an invisible force, she inexplicably turned her head fixing her eyes on the handsome man in a bowler, all the way across the street.

The hair on the back of Mathew's neck stood up as their eyes refused to turn away for what seemed to be minutes until he took a step toward her. Suddenly, a blast from an air horn broke his concentration.

He lurched back on the sidewalk as a delivery truck sped past. When Matthew looked back, the woman was gone. He sprinted across the street, oblivious of the screeching tires and blaring horns, thinking, I can't lose her again!

Julia didn't know what to do. She was so flustered by the tingling in her finger tips that she had to try to break the spell. She wandered up Kearny out of breath, though she wasn't running.

Matthew spotted her and he instinctively called out, "Julia! Julia, wait!" She froze in her tracks, afraid to believe what she had just heard. Matthew stepped around in front of her, his bowler in his hands and his red hair curling over his stiff white collar. Their eyes met again, and she drew in a short breath as they explored every feature and nuance of each other's face.

Finally, Matthew spoke again, "Julia, I've been waiting for you."

Trembling, Julia responded, "I wore my red hat with the ostrich feather."

Anthony Colburn

Matthew put his hat back on and took both of Julia's gloved hands. "And I wore my bowler." Julia's eyes were such a captivating shade of blue that Matthew could hardly think, but presently he said, "Shall we go over to the Palace Hotel and have some tea?"

Julia responded with a broad smile, "I would like that."

They spent the rest of the morning comparing notes and ancestors and gazing into each other's eyes. Julia could hardly believe her ears when she heard about the incredible set of coincidences and chance that had led to this day.

"This must be a gift."

"What?"

"You know, a gift given to us by our long-gone relatives! There must have been a powerful force at work here, bridging life and death to bring us together."

Matthew gently took her hand. "Well, all I know is this day has been coming for a long time and it never felt so right."

They slowly walked hand in hand out along Market Street once more, getting incredulous looks from all sides as they waited for the next bus back to Julia's place.

Columns at Lloyd Lake, Golden Gate Park

Chapter 43

PORTALS OF THE PAST

Spring in San Francisco brings wonderful, invigorating weather and Matthew and Julia spent every possible moment together exploring the city. They braced against the wind, arm in arm as they stood at Twin Peaks, surveying Market Street as it stretched all the way to the bay. They walked barefoot on the broad flat beach toward the rocks under the Cliff House and explored every inch of Golden Gate Park.

One morning, Matthew called Julia, "Would you like to take a drive down to Colma?"

"What for?" she mumbled, still groggy from the early Saturday wake up call.

"I need to make a courtesy call to a relative of mine."

"Oh…"

Colma is a city south of San Francisco that has the peculiar distinction of having many more dead people than alive. Matthew was curious to find out more about the man who had brought them together, even from the grave.

The original Matthew had been buried at Calvary Catholic Cemetery but his remains, along with nearly all the departed from the entire city, had been removed and re-interred in various Colma cemeteries. All the Catholic dead were placed in Holy Cross.

He had a list of the dead and their place in the 48-acre cemetery.

"Here it is…*Matthew Robert Donohue; Section 'B', Area 4, Row 15, Plot 12*…and here's my great-great grandmother, Anne next to him."

As they walked up to the graves, Matthew took Julia's hand and stopped.

"What's the matter?"

"Oh, I don't know. It's just that I have this feeling that I know more about my Great-Great Grandfather than I can readily recall. Those places we have been together like the music concourse and the Japanese Tea Garden…it's almost like I was seeing them through his eyes."

"Well, those things haven't changed all that much. It would make sense that Matthew and his Julia had gone there. I wouldn't worry. It's not so rare for people to have a déjà vu about things like that."

"But this was different. I actually felt like I was him. Matthew!"

They both fell silent as they turned to look at the final resting place of Matthew Robert Donohue.

Then slowly he continued. "My Great Nana Julia used to say that her mother Anne told her, he had a gift of seeing." Julia didn't get it. "Like he could see things in the future. But I sometimes see things in the past, things there would be no way I could know by reading history books."

"Maybe it's *your* gift like a kind of message to you."

Matthew managed a slight smile. "Maybe," as he touched his forehead, chest, left then right shoulder and clasped his hands. "Amen. Thank you, great-great grandpa."

One weekend, Matthew and Julia were in Golden Gate Park, paddling around Stow Lake as Julia pulled dandelion petals off declaring, "He found me, he found me not..." They strolled down past Lloyd Lake, with the famous 'Portals of the Past' reflected in the tranquil waters.

"Where did that come from?"

"I think it was an entrance to someone's mansion up on Nob Hill. They moved it here to the park as a remembrance of the 1906 quake and fire."

"There really aren't many monuments to that tragedy are there?"

"You know, I never really thought about it, but I guess you're right.

Although, there is a fire hydrant out in the Mission District that was the only one still delivering water that saved that part of the city. It's painted gold every April 18th. There are still lots of buildings that survived *both* the 1906 and the 1989 quakes, like the ferry building clock tower *and* the conservatory of flowers. Can you imagine something like that made almost entirely of glass and it was hardly damaged at all? Earthquakes are strange things."

Julia took Matthew's hand. "Let's go over to the Japanese Tea Garden. I've always loved it in the spring," They wandered arm in arm up JFK drive by a grove of stately redwood trees and cut over to the tea garden.

Entering the tea garden was like stepping back to into an idyllic Japan of a century ago. Every bush and tree was pruned to the most satisfying and peaceful shape- each stone, placed expertly to appear perfectly natural.

A huge brass Buddha sat placidly cross legged with a pink flower someone had placed in the palm of its hand. They had tea and smiled as they looked into a pool, their reflections disturbed every so often by feeding gold fish.

After tea, Julia opened her fortune cookie and looked at the small piece of paper. *"You will soon find your fortune."* Julia looked up. "I already have."

Then Matthew opened his. *"You will solve a puzzling question."* He looked down at the pool and then to Julia. "I didn't know I was puzzled!"

Before they left, Matthew and Julia climbed the Drum Bridge. They watched a flower petal drift under it and when it disappeared, their eyes and lips met at the same time.

Ferryboat Wreck, Carquinez Strait

Chapter 44

THE PUZZLE

The next Sunday afternoon, as they scanned the bay from the base of Coit Tower, Matthew said, "There's something I want you to see back at my place." The fog spread over the Golden Gate Bridge, and was obscuring just the tip of the Trans-America building downtown. Later that afternoon at Matthew's home, he produced a group of photographs and handed them to Julia.

"What's this?" as she shuffled through them.

"That's the puzzle we're going to solve!" replied Matthew, as he turned and gazed out the bay window of his apartment.

"What are you talking about!?"

"See that photo? That's a solid gold bar. It was found after the '89 quake in a ditch in a box at the Marina. You know the letter I had that led us to meet?" Julia shook her head, trying to follow, "well, it was found in the same box as that bar of gold! Turned out, the gold was from a mine in Nevada from 1906! No one knows how it got there, but the box had my great-great grandfather's name on it…Since my grandfather was supervising the digging there, it was given to him."

Julia was still in a daze. "Now here's the *real* puzzle; See the photo of the back of the bar? It has a message scratched on it!"

"I see!" Julia said trying to piece her thoughts together. "It says, '*The rest is in the Golden City*.' Does that mean the hotel? There was a Golden City Hotel on Ellis between Stockton and Powell… Of course, it was totally destroyed in the quake and fire in 1906."

"I looked for every shred of information I could and found out it was dynamited by the army before the fire got to it. The rubble was piled in rail cars and sent to the wharf where they loaded it on barges and dumped it in the bay. That's where the trail goes cold." Matthew glanced at his watch.

"What's that?"

"Oh, that's my great-great grandfather Matthew's watch. He showed the engraved cover to Julia. That was the ferryboat he worked on at Lake Tahoe. After that, he came down here and worked for a time on a ferryboat between San Francisco and Oakland."

Julia's eyes lit up. "They had ferryboats named after every city they could think of back then! Let's take a look on the internet and see if we can find something out!"

Matthew laced his fingers on top of his head and grimaced. "Why didn't I think of that?! Here I've been studying and preserving ferryboats all along!"

Matthew turned on his computer and searched under all the categories about ferryboats and San Francisco history. Next, he looked for anything with just the words 'Golden City' in it.

After scrolling through ten pages, Julia said, "Try just 'Golden City' ferryboat.

Matthew got hits from around the world- There was a 'Golden City' ferry in China and nine 'Golden City' restaurants around the U.S., but then on the second page was a heading; 'Golden City ferry history' on a website devoted to just ferryboat history. The site described ferries throughout the U.S., but mostly concentrated on the West Coast. There were a dizzying array of companies and fleets of ferries that once plied the waters of San Francisco Bay.

"That makes sense; After all," he explained, "the San Francisco ferry building was at one time, the second busiest ferry terminal in the world, next to London's Charing Cross Station."

Scrolling down the boats listed in alphabetical order, Matthew slowed down to a crawl, not wanting the bad news to show itself too soon, but there it was! Matthew read aloud, "'Golden City.' Built: 1879 for the 'South Pacific Coast Railroad'. Set to be overhauled in 1906, but cancelled because of the great earthquake. Acquired by the 'Southern Pacific Railroad' and retired in 1929. Bought and taken to Carquinez Strait to be used as a fishing resort. Purchased again in 1936, towed to the town of Eckley and used as a dance hall, dining room and bar. Abandoned, 1952."

"So, is it still there?" said Julia, anxiously.

"Doesn't say. I suppose. Where's Eckley?"

All they could find out from the internet was that Eckley was once a small port community along the Carquinez Strait in Contra Costa County. Because of Julia's work, she knew an employee at the county library in Walnut Creek. She gave her a call and found the approximate location.

"We'll just have to take a ride over there this weekend and check it out."

So, that Saturday, Matthew and Julia drove across the Bay Bridge and took the East Shore Freeway toward Crockett. It was another beautiful day in the bay area, with a brisk breeze funneling through the golden gate and up into the Sacramento Delta.

They drove down along the edge of the C&H sugar refinery toward their destination, then walked along the railroad tracks that parallel the south side of Carquinez Strait.

It appeared to be almost high tide, and Matthew was afraid the boat may have broken up years ago, leaving any wreckage undetectable, *if* they were even in the right place.

Partway up the tracks, a bum approached them. He wore a faded San Francisco Giants hat, a tattered suit coat over a plaid flannel shirt, with blue jeans and high-top tennis shoes. Matthew sized him up and decided he was harmless enough.

"Got a few coins for a veteran?" he pleaded.

"Maybe you can tell me a few things about Eckley and I might find some."

"Fair enough, I'm the mayor of Eckley, you know!"

Matthew and Julia looked at each other and chuckled.

"What can you tell me about the ferry boat, 'Golden City'?"

"I can tell you lots...but it'll cost 'ya."

Matthew handed him a dollar.

"All's I can say about that is that it burnt up back in '83!"

"Are you sure?" Matthew pressed.

"Sure, I'm sure!" The old man pointed up the hill. "Sat right up there and watched it go! What a sight!"

Matthew and Julia were crushed.

"Yep, big grass an' brush fire came over the hill and burnt up the town an' everything in its path, right down to the water!"

"Sorry to hear that," Julia said as they turned to go back to their car.

"Now what are you giving up so easy for? I can tell you right exactly where the 'Golden City' lies at this very moment!"

Matthew and Julia were beginning to think that they were getting squeezed.

"Not only was I mayor of Eckley, but I tended bar on the 'Golden City', before the war. You know, the big one. Lied 'bout my age. Got stationed in England an' never got to even take a single shot at no German! When I got out, they already closed the bar down an' she just sat there rustin' an' rottin' away till there wasn't much left of her. Now, for a five spot I could direct you right to her!"

Matthew had heard enough and was about to leave, but Julia said, "Matt, wait. We've come so far and found out so much. It'll be worth it even if we find out this is the end of the line. Besides, how would he have known that it was used as a bar?"

So, Matthew relented and paid the smiling 'mayor'.

"Right this way, Lady and Gentleman!" The bum walked them about another hundred yards up the tracks and pointed out to the water.

There, in about six feet of water was a twisted mass of steel with the remnants of boilers and the massive shaft that drove the paddle wheels. A steel frame delineating the dimensions of a once impressive vessel sat, rusting for the last half century.

Just a hundred feet up stream, a modern fishing pier jutted out into the strait where a handful of people were trying their luck.

"There she is!" The bum declared with pride. "May she rest in peace!"

Seeing the excitement in the couple's faces he realized there had to be something more to the story of this boat. "Say, what can this here boat offer a nice couple like you?"

"Let's just say it's of sentimental interest."

"Come on! You can do better than that!"

"OK." said Matthew. "My great-great grandfather used to be a hand on this boat in the early 1900's. "

"That's nice…Well, I'll leave you to your remembrances, then." The bum turned up the bank of the railroad right of way and disappeared into the brush.

Matthew and Julia looked at each other. He thought about the message scratched on the bar of gold- 'The rest is in the Golden City'. Could it be that simple, that the rest of the gold was *in the boat* 'Golden City'?

And how much was 'the rest'? Just one more bar would be worth hundreds of thousands of dollars! That would certainly make it worthwhile to return on a low tide to do some exploring and prospecting. It was likely that the hull was already rotted out before the fire, so whatever was below the water would probably not have been affected by the blaze.

Matthew and Julia headed back to the car to contemplate what treasure might be waiting for them.

Chapter 45

THE TREASURE HUNT

⸻◦⸻

M atthew and Julia returned to her house to do some more research on the 'Golden City.'

Looking at that same web site about ferries, Julia read; *"There were a number of boats built right in the city along the water front south of where the Bay Bridge is now. The 'Golden City' was one of those vessels; a classic double ender with a coal fired steam engine, side paddle wheels, with a large 'walking I beam' transferring power to the wheels via a huge single piston."*

"Let's get a metal detector!" She said, out of the blue. "We could scan the bottom for the gold and just pick it up!"

"Metal detectors just detect metal. It doesn't matter what kind," objected Matthew. "It would be a nightmare trying to tell gold from all the scraps of iron! Besides, what part of the wreck would we start looking in?"

"There must be a way…All those gold hunters are always using them."

"Yeah, and I bet they come home with a load of trash, too!"

"Well, it's better than feeling around under the water! It's going to be tough to see in the murky water unless we can get a camera real close."

"Lots of people have underwater video cameras, but we need one that shows what the camera is looking at when we are still in the boat," said Matthew.

Julia immediately grabbed the phone book and started to flip through the yellow pages. "There was a man working at the library who was really into treasure hunting and he said he had a great video unit." Let's see...'*Treasure hunting*'... No... *Underwater...Underwater salvage*...Here it is! I bet they know what works best."

After she made a few inquiries, Julia was directed to a dive shop down on Front Street and they went the next day. The owner was very helpful when he learned they were looking for submerged wrecks.

"Yeah," he said, "the best way to find wrecks in water like the bay is with sonar, but if you already know where it is an' you can get really close, video is the way to go...way less expensive, too! Basically, the more resolution the camera, the better the picture. But you won't be able to detect things from very far away...Can you get close to the wreck?" Matthew and Julia looked at each other and nodded. "Good. Then this is just the ticket!" The shop owner brought out a pamphlet from behind the counter. "I don't sell this stuff, not enough call for it, but you can find it on the 'net."

Back at Julia's, it wasn't long before they found a relatively inexpensive underwater video camera with a twenty-five-foot cord connected to a dedicated screen. The site claimed a high resolution of 200 dpi was possible, and it could be powered by a direct current battery.

Matthew paid for it on line with a credit card. "There. Now we just have to wait for it to be shipped. We're going to have to get a boat and some fishing gear too."

"What?!" Julia was confused.

"We can get a small boat and some fishing gear, tie up to the wreck and search for the gold in plain sight without being suspected!"

"I love you! You're a genius! Have I told you that before?"

"You never told me I was a genius before, but I'll never get tired of being loved by you."

They hugged, and Matthew took Julia's hand and waltzed around the room.

But there was still the 'needle in the haystack' problem. They still didn't know what part of the boat's remains to look in, how much gold there was, or even *if* there was any! But the plan was already set in motion.

Matthew knew that the railroad museum in Sacramento had plans and technical drawings for many of the ferry boats that Southern Pacific Railroad owned. He ordered a set of plans for a boat that was of a similar vintage as the 'Golden City' and poured over them one night with Julia.

"If you were going to hide a bar of gold on this boat," Mathew began, where would you put it?"

Julia thought for a second. "Some place easy to get to but where no one would think to look?"

"Exactly! So, look at these drawings. There are lots of small rooms and spaces for storage, but the only place that is accessible yet not meant for people to get into is the coal bunker!"

Julia's eyes lit up like she just hit the jackpot at Harrah's. "You're right! That's got to be it! That's the only place possible!"

"See this. The coal bunker is right here, next to the boilers and the fire box. And there's a hatch that's opened from the deck." Matthew put his finger down on the paper with the conviction of a gambler with a straight flush. "The gold *must* be here!"

A friend of Matthew's had a boat he could use for their little fishing expedition; a fifteen-footer with a thirty-horse motor. It wasn't very big but Matthew didn't want to rent something that might cause suspicion. He also had fishing gear Matthew begged off him. His excuse was that he promised to take an old friend fishing up around Suisun Bay for Stripers.

Matthew printed out tide tables from the 'net and looked up the best high tide for the month. Looking over his shoulder, Julia said, "Why are you looking for the *highest* tide? Wouldn't it be better if we had a *low* tide?"

"Low is better for picking up the gold, but high is best for *finding* it because we won't be causing suspicion, tied up to the wreck and fishing in eight feet of water!"

"Right again!" said Julia gleefully, "But if…I mean when we find it, we had better be doing it at low tide and some time when there won't be anyone around."

"Let's worry about that after we find it!"

Finally, the conditions were right. Matthew had the boat and trailer hooked up to the car with all the video gear stowed safely out of sight.

It was another fine spring day, unusually warm- earthquake weather. They crossed the Carquinez Bridge and went over to the Ninth Street boat launch in Benicia, upstream and on the opposite bank from the remains of the 'Golden City'.

After getting the boat in the water, they headed up the shore line because the current of the Sacramento River was sure to pull them back toward the bay. Upstream, Matthew could just make out the rotting pilings, that was the very spot that the ferry boat 'Solano' took entire passenger trains over to continue their trip to Oakland in the early 1900's.

Turning into the current, they were quickly swept downstream, but Matthew kept the boat facing upstream in a diagonal direction toward the south shore. They made their way down the shoreline until they came to the pier at Eckley. There were three fishermen on the pier and Julia waved as they slowly came around to the ferry boat's resting place.

Matthew circled the wreck, sizing up the orientation of the boilers and the spot where the coal bunker must have been. He tied up to the paddle wheel's shaft, upstream from the search site, to help conceal their real intentions.

Julia got the fishing rod out and made a cast toward the open water and slowly began to retrieve the lure.

"Hey! I got a bite!" Julia was so excited about her good luck that she didn't realize she had hooked a piece of vegetation and as she reeled it in and lifted it into the boat, the men on the pier let out a good-natured laugh.

"Keep at it, but leave some for us!" one elderly man yelled.

Meanwhile, Matthew slowly lowered his camera over the side of the boat and into the water, viewing the monitor while deftly maneuvering it toward the spot. As he viewed the screen, he could see the skeleton of the vessel with its ribs and the backbone of the hull. The wood had long since rotted or burned away and the iron was in an advanced state of rust but some structures were easy to make out. The boilers stuck out well above the water but the long, low bin that held the coal looked like a shallow funnel and was completely submerged. It was honeycombed with holes, so it was probable that it was fully under water at the time of the fire, and if the gold was there, it could still be intact. Moving the camera to the left and right, Matthew slowly scanned the bottom.

The iron was a consistent half inch thick plate, littered with other long pieces. Scanning once again to the left, Matthew stopped at a short, thick piece of metal that did not have the characteristic rough surface of rusted iron. He moved around and looked at it from the side. This metal was smooth and much thicker than any other piece and seemed to have a lighter color than the iron. Then behind it was another…and another. Looking to the right, identical pieces- Matthew dared not think what they might be, littering the bottom. He counted five, six…ten…fifteen! Matthew's hand began to shake and he could not keep the camera steady. He turned to Julia dutifully casting toward the open water and reeling the lure back.

"Julia." Matthew whispered almost inaudibly.

"Wait a second- I really think I got a bite!"

"Julia, I think…I—" Just then Julia pulled back on her rod and it responded, dipping toward the water.

"Oh, wow! I have a fish!" She reeled and the fish countered, stripping off line. She pumped the rod and gained some of the line back. "This is a good-sized fish! Honey, get the net!" She turned and saw that Matthew was not paying attention. "Mathew, get the net!" She could see he was shaking. "I thought *you* were the great fisherman! Get a hold of yourself!"

Matthew gathered his composure and held the net under the water. The fish was almost played out, lying in the water on its side, the shining silver and dark stripes revealed its species. Mathew led the net under the fish as it gave one last splash. Matthew flopped the fish into the boat and hit it on the head with a paddle, stunning it.

"Now it can't breathe. It won't feel anything now."

"Wow! That's a big fish!" exclaimed a breathless Julia.

"Yep. It's a keeper. Twenty-two inches, just big enough." Julia lifted her catch to the admiring shouts of the men on the pier.

The couple sat admiring Julia's trophy. In the excitement of the battle, Matthew had almost forgotten his find.

"Julia, what I was going to say was—"

"I know, you're so proud of me."

"No. I mean yes. But…" Matthew insisted, "I found something, I think it's the gold."

Julia jumped up and gave Matthew a big hug and a kiss, precariously rocking the boat

A man on the pier observed in amazement, "Must 'a been her first fish!"

When at last they calmed down, Matthew and Julia looked into each other's eyes and just smiled. "What now?"

"Let me show you." Matthew picked up the video monitor again and moved the camera back into position. There they were, as large as life on the screen. A small stack of bars in one spot and at least eight more spread out on the bottom. He turned over to the other bars and counted a half-dozen more. There was no doubt now. Nothing else could be submerged for this long and still be perfect. They were all there for the taking; after decades of travel to and from the city and just under foot as a fishing barge and dance hall, no one was ever the wiser… Ever since the fire destroyed what was left of the boat, they sat, waiting to make someone an instant multi-millionaire!

Matthew moved the boat directly over to the spot and dropped a lead weight with a line and a small orange bobber tied at the end.

"This is the spot." Matthew said calmly. "At the next low tide, we'll come out here and pick them up."

It was very hard to leave the area, knowing that anyone could wade out and start scooping up maybe millions of dollars' worth of gold, but they were the only ones with the knowledge...

Near the top of the railroad cut, concealed by some bushes, sat the mayor of Eckley.

Chapter 46

DREAMS AND NIGHTMARES

The video monitor had revealed at least twenty-two bars of gold. Matthew was already calculating; at $703.00 an ounce, 400 ounces each bar times twenty-two equals…$6,186,400.00 and in the eyes of a collector, maybe even more…

Julia looked up the next low tide and it would be in the middle of the night. The next one after that would be at 11:31 a.m. the next morning.

"We can't just leave work and take off looking for the gold. It'll be too suspicious," Matthew said. "No one knows. It's been sitting in the bowels of that boat for over a hundred years, another few days won't matter."

That night, Julia dreamed of homes in Hawaii and trips around the world but Matthew heard sounds in the night. It was the rushing of water- a flood that washed the gold into the bay and out of reach.

Matthew was distracted at work. He ordered the wrong type of waterproofing for resurfacing the deck of the 'Balclutha', but a co-worker caught it in time.

But Julia was on top of the world. She had floated through her day as if she didn't have a care.

That night, Matthew stayed at Julia's. They would soon go out one more time to retrieve the treasure they had worked so diligently to find. And then, they would complete a one-hundred-year-old quest in the making- one more night until they would possess the treasure that was waiting for them.

Sometime late in the night it started to rain. The gutter outside the window was filling with a steady rush. Suddenly Matthew bolted upright, frightening Julia out of her trip around the world. Matthew's heart was pounding out of his chest and he was sweating profusely.

"Matt! Honey! What's wrong?!" Matthew couldn't speak, his throat seemed swollen closed. Finally, he let out a gasp as he fell to the floor.

"I think I'm having a heart attack!" He blurted out. Julia kept her head and called 911. In just a few minutes, an ambulance was there, administering first aid to Matthew and whisking him to the hospital. Julia followed in Matthew's car and sat in the waiting room in her robe. In about thirty minutes the emergency room doctor came out to give Julia the news.

"His heart is fine," reassured the doctor. "He's just had an anxiety attack. Has he had any problems or unusual pressure at work lately?"

Julia gave a sigh of relief. "Yes, he has. Can I see him?"

"Of course. He's in room 743."

"All he needs is some rest and he'll be as good as new." The doctor patted Julia on the shoulder and walked back down the hall.

Julia entered the room quietly, seeing that Matthew was sleeping. A passing nurse poked her head in the room and said, "We gave him something. He'll be sleeping till morning. Why don't you go home and get some rest yourself." Julia kissed him on the forehead and went home.

Early the next day, Julia went back to the hospital and found Matthew already dressing. "Are you sure you are OK to go?"

"Don't worry, they already checked me out and I'm good to go. Julia, I saw something last night. Something terrible. I saw what Matthew saw on that boat a hundred years ago. I saw blood on my hands. I really thought I was going to die!"

"Let's just take it easy for a while. We can wait 'till next week or next month!"

"No. I'm fine now." Matthew insisted, "We still have time to make the low tide."

When they got back to Matthew's, they had a good breakfast and packed up for the trip across the bay.

It was a gray, dreary sort of a day, but Matthew and Julia's spirits were high. Not only was it going to be a good low tide, it was also bad weather which meant that no one would be out fishing on the pier.

One of the problems Matthew hadn't counted on was the amount of gold they found meant that they were going to have over 500 pounds to carry in the small boat. That meant they would have to take two trips, back and forth, across the strait.

They took the same route with the boat as before- going up stream then crossing with the current to the pier. Matthew was right. There was no one around and since the whole area was part of the Carquinez Strait Regional Shoreline Park, there were no houses or traffic.

As they came up to the mass of twisted rusting iron, the water was only about two feet deep and the float was twisted around some metal. Matthew tied the boat up and eased himself into the water, being careful not to get himself caught on any jagged metal. He felt down the line to the lead weight and immediately touched something smooth.

Matthew paused. He was shaking, partly from the cold water and partly from the anticipation. He got his hand under the bar and tried to lift it but it was a little heavy, so he grabbed it with both hands. Bending down in the choppy water, he got wet up to his chest. As he righted himself, Matthew slowly lifted the bar to water level. Julia peered over the side and gasped.

"How could it still be so shiny after all these years?"

He didn't say a thing, but handed it to her and chuckled when it was obvious that she wasn't prepared for the weight of the small bar. She put it in a wooden box and waited for more.

It didn't take long for Matthew to find another and another and after ten bars were safely in the box, he said, "Ten times twenty-five pounds is two hundred-fifty pounds. The boat is riding a little low in the water. I think we should take this load over to the car. Besides, I'm getting pretty cold."

As Matthew pulled himself over the side of the boat, he caught his leg on a piece of rusty iron. "Damn!" It was a pretty nasty cut, with a red trickle soon mixing with the water in the bottom of the boat.

"Here," said Julia, "Let me put this cloth around your leg." She deftly applied pressure to the wound and tied the cloth around his calf muscle. "When was the last time you had a Tetanus shot?"

"I don't know, maybe ten years ago. I cannot *believe* I did that!"

The boat made slow headway up the strait and when Matthew turned to start crossing, it came close to swamping. Easy does it! Matthew said to himself.

When they finally got to shore, they had another problem. How to move the 250-pound box! Julia backed the car down as close as she could to the boat and they put the bars in the trunk one at a time, all the while stealing suspicious glances around the boat launch.

On the return trip, Matthew's leg started to throb. He knew he would not be able to go back in the water. By this time, the tide was starting to come back in.

As they approached the pier, Matthew said, "Julia, you're going to have to get the rest."

"I know." was her only response.

As they pulled into position, Matthew could not spot the bobber. Julia slid over the side and took a short breath. The cold water from the bay was advancing and already reached above Julia's waist. In order to reach the bars, she would have to put her head underwater, but she was game. On the first dunk, she groped for the line and bobber, but came up empty handed. She threw her black mane back as she surfaced and held the side of the boat.

"That's cold!" she exclaimed with a shiver in her voice.

"You better make it quick, then."

"I've got an idea. I'm going to search with my feet until I find the bars, then dive."

"OK." encouraged Matthew. "Just be careful. That metal's dangerous."

Julia took off her tennis shoes and gingerly put her feet back on the bottom.

She was on solid metal, but as she felt along, it suddenly dropped off about six inches to the mud and rocks. All of a sudden, she was touching something smooth.

"This must be it!" Julia dipped down and completely disappeared from Matthew's sight for a second. When she broke the surface, Julia let out a small "Woa!" She struggled to get the gleaming bar over the side. "I could see five or six right there!" Julia said as she spit a little water.

She took another plunge, this time with her shoes on and surfaced with another. By the time she reemerged with the twelfth one, Julia was shaking uncontrollably.

"We better quit," said Matthew, "This is more than we ever imagined!"

But Julia just leaned forward again and came up a few seconds later with one more.

"That's going to be a pretty good down payment on our house in Kauai!"

"Come on, Julia. This is it," but Julia returned, "I saw one more!"

Again, she disappeared, but this time, she didn't pop right back up. Matthew peered over the side. Then he reached into the water. About three feet under the surface, Matthew could feel Julia's back. His eyes widened. Matthew threw off his blanket and slid into the now frigid water. He could tell now that Julia's belt was caught on a jagged piece of metal and had gotten twisted. She was in a panic and he could tell she had taken in some water and was about to drown. He quickly unbuckled the belt and slid it off. Cradling Julia in his arms, Matthew pushed her slumping body to the surface and held her there as he administered mouth to mouth resuscitation. Nothing. He repeated. A second later Julia's lungs convulsed reflexively and out came some water as she gasped and then started coughing. He carried her to the shore and gently laid her down in some grass. In a few minutes, Julia was much better, but they were both very cold and wet.

"I'm going to get the boat and the blankets." Said Matthew, as he half wadded and swam out to the boat. The water was now almost up to his neck, but he managed to pull the boat in to shore. Matthew sat next to Julia and wrapped both of the blankets around them. Matthew's body heat soon helped quiet Julia's shivering and they looked once more into each other's eyes.

He parted Julia's wavy, dripping hair from her face and smiled. "What a mess we've gotten ourselves into."

"But we did it together, and there's one more down there."

"One more what?" Another shiver coursed through Matthew and Julia but it wasn't from the cold. The voice came from just above them on the railroad tracks. They apprehensively turned around to see the mayor of Eckley sitting on one of the rails with a pistol in his hand.

"One more what?" he repeated. "You were saying, miss?"

Julia had to think quickly. "One more box."

The mayor chuckled. "What would you want with a waterlogged box?! Besides, it would have been burned up in the fire!"

"It's not just any box," continued Julia, "I work for the San Francisco Library and I've done research on this for the last five years. Around the turn of the last century, Abe Ruef controlled almost everything that happened in San Francisco. He got his man, Eugene Schmitz elected mayor in 1902 to do his bidding.

"So what?"

"So," Julia continued, "almost everyone in the city who wanted to do business there had to pay off Ruef and he became very rich. He was too smart to let himself be caught with the cash, so he insisted on bearer bonds.

"What's that mean?" Eckley's mayor was more confused than ever.

"That means that no one could ever trace the bearer bonds back to him. But the real kicker is that because they can't be traced, they're also just like cash! Whoever holds the bonds, owns them!"

The mayor took off his grimy San Francisco Giants ball cap and rubbed his balding head in thought. "You mean there's papers that's the same as money in that box?"

"That's right, interjected Matthew. "And we'll let you have that box if we can go with the rest."

The mayor thought that he had heard of Ruef, and the story seemed plausible, but he continued, "My ol' man used to say, 'a bird in the hand's worth two in the bush.' I think I'll just take a look see at what you got already in that boat."

He waved his revolver in the direction of the boat and motioned for Matthew and Julia to lead the way. Matthew's cut was bleeding and he had a noticeable limp but the mayor gave Matthew a nudge in the back with the barrel of the gun to remind him he meant business. When they got to the boat, the old man peeked in and motioned for Julia to open the wooden box that was in the center of the boat.

"Let's see what kind 'a bait you've been using!"

Reluctantly, Julia opened the box revealing the gleaming cargo. The mayor's eyes widened and he took a step back.

"Damn...That looks like the San Francisco mint!" He slowly turned his gun, pointing it directly between Matthew's eyes. "I don't suppose you were going to tell me about this little detail! Looks like I caught you red-handed, robbing from the city of Eckley's treasury!"

At that very second, a sea gull swooped down toward the boat, looking for scraps of bait that fishermen often leave behind.

Matthew took advantage of the momentary distraction and lunged toward the mayor. A shot rang out as Matthew hit his assailant and they both fell to the ground. Julia screamed, fearing the worst. For a moment, neither men stirred, but Matthew finally struggled to his feet and staggered back toward her, holding his stomach.

"Oh, Matthew! Are you hit? Why did you try such a foolish thing?! I don't care about the gold! All I wanted was for us to be together!"

"Don't worry. He just poked that gun right in my gut!"

"But, but why aren't you...BLEEDING or something!?"

"It was a false start!" replied Matthew with a chuckle.

"What?!" She was actually getting a little annoyed at Matthew's impudence.

"He couldn't have hurt me. He had a starter's pistol used in track meets! When he pointed it right at my face, I could see the barrel was solid metal. No hole for a bullet to go through!"

The mayor was slow to get up, his age and years of living in poor conditions showing.

"I'm sorry," he said with a sniffle. "I don't know what came over me. I use that thing to keep those damn kids from bothering me and wrecking my place." He motioned to a broken-down shack on the other side of the tracks. "That's all I have in the world!" The man started to sob quietly.

Matthew and Julia sat down in relief to take stock of the situation. Finally, Julia whispered something in Matthew's ear. Matthew rose and approached the old man who cowered slightly in fear.

"What are you going to do with me?"

"Well," Matthew began in a serious tone, "since you are the mayor of this fair city and we are making off with a good bit of its assets, we thought it only right that we should pay tax on the withdrawal. See that orange bobber out there?" Matthew pointed to the small float rising and falling between the rusted pieces of iron. "On the bottom there's one more bar like these. Next low tide, should be no problem to wade out there."

The man's face was filled with anticipation as he looked toward the remains of the ferry boat. "I'm really not a bad man, just down on my luck, is all. You're not going to turn me in, are you?"

"No," replied Matthew. "Don't worry. Just do something good for yourself with the money. And don't mention anything about us. You promise?"

The mayor nodded enthusiastically.

As Julia and Matthew got their things together and pushed the boat off the bank, the man said, "I promise! But who can I thank for this?"

Matthew turned to the old man. "Just thank a young hand on the 'Golden City.'"

The mayor followed the boat's progress up stream as he walked out the fishing pier and waved until it became a small speck on the north shore.

Matthew's cut was hurting pretty bad by now, but they managed to crank the boat onto its trailer then get the rest of the gold loaded into the car. For a minute, the new millionaires just sat and stared blankly out the window.

Finally, Matthew said, "First stop, the emergency room back in the city. Don't want anyone around here getting curious."

"Do you think we did the right thing, leaving that gold for him?"

"Don't worry. He'll probably sit on that gold for a long while. I think he'll have a hard time changing his life...and his title as mayor of Eckley."

They kissed and Julia drove away as the setting sun peeked from under the low clouds.

Zurich, Switzerland and the Alps

Chapter 47

A EUROPEAN VACATION

bout a month later, Matthew's cut had healed pretty well. Julia came over for dinner and as Matthew opened the door, she handed him a copy of the Chronicle.

"Take a look at this article. Does this remind you of anyone?"

He scanned the columns as a smile came over his face. "Our friend, the mayor!" He continued reading, this time out loud. "*Mr. Richard Landon entered a Martinez bank yesterday morning, and walked up to a teller wanting to cash a 400 ounce bar of gold...The Contra Costa County Sheriff's Office was contacted and Mr. Landon was held for questioning...Mr. Landon said he found the bar, stamped with the name of a Nevada gold mine along the Carquinez Straits at a point where the ferry boat 'Solano' used to take railroad trains across before the bridge was built... Authorities from the San Francisco*

Mint indicated that this was part of a shipment of gold that never reached the mint around the time of the great earthquake in 1906... Officials in Sacramento have confiscated the bar and Mr. Landon, a transient, was given a finders reward of $10,000." He continued; "*The Nevada State Attorney General's Office has requested a hearing to determine the rightful ownership of the gold.*"

"Well, I'll be...He lied about where he found it! I wonder if he did that to protect us."

"I'd like to think so."

"In any case, you can tell what would happen if we surfaced with the rest of it! We'd be handing over $6 million dollars in trade for $10,000...and a lot of questions to answer!"

Matthew and Julia went to the basement and after moving the wine rack, he opened a half-sized door revealing a crawl space. Reaching behind the wall, Matthew pulled out one of the bars. They admired it like a sleeping new born baby as it lay on Julia's lap. On top was stamped the word 'Mohawk' and '400' along with the stamp of the Carson City assay office.

"How are we going to sell this gold without every government official in the West crawling out from under the woodwork?"

Matthew was already partway up the stairs, "Let's check the internet. There must be some foreign company that can keep this kind of thing quiet. You always hear about those works of art going to 'anonymous' buyers from 'anonymous' sellers."

After a few minutes of searching, they came across an auction house in Zurich, Switzerland; 'Biser's'. It claimed the utmost in discrete transactions dealing in 'exceptional' art and artifacts.

"They sound a little snobbish, don't you think?" said Julia.

"Yeah, but that's what it takes to keep things quiet sometimes. Look here. They have an office in LA. I think we should go down there and see what it's all about. Maybe get something in writing."

After a few phone calls, Matthew and Julia made an appointment to meet with the manager at the Los Angeles office. They took a short commuter plane hop the next Friday morning.

Matthew pulled out photos of their treasure and the manager said, "Yes, I see what you mean. This is quite unique. These mines-you say they were in Nevada?"

"That's right," said Matthew. "They were all out of business by 1915."

"I think these would do quite well in a private auction. There is much interest in the American West and anything gold."

"But what about the auction itself? How can we keep certain parties from finding out about it?" asked Julia.

"I'm assuming you came by this property legally..."

"Of course!" Julia replied, a bit defensively.

"I will need you to sign an affidavit to that effect which also holds the company harmless in any legal proceedings."

"Of course," returned Matthew. "What is your commission?"

"We retain ten per cent..."

"Ten per cent! That's at least six hundred thousand dollars!"

"Probably closer to a million," the manager said coolly. "But we cover all shipping and insurance costs plus setting up a numbered Swiss bank account for the transaction. What we need from you is an assurance that you actually have the merchandise in your possession."

Matthew and Julia huddled for a moment and finally agreed.

The next Wednesday, Matthew received an envelope via special courier containing the contract. They signed it along with an agreement to personally oversee the shipping of the gold. They would be traveling with it from San Francisco to Zurich, Switzerland, all paid by the auction company!

"Do you think Biser's will be able to attract enough interested parties to make it worthwhile?"

"Don't worry," replied Matthew. "It's in their interest to find the most discrete buyers for this gold. This isn't just gold, it's part of history. Remember, the manager in LA told us he had never heard of another find like this in his twenty-five years in the business."

The next week, a private security truck arrived at Matthew's door. Along with the guards, was the Los Angeles auction house manager himself.

The guards started loading the bars, two per box. The manager took a look at each bar and said, "This is bigger than I thought. We are both going to be very happy with the results of this auction."

He had Matthew and Julia sign a paper stating they had witnessed the loading of the twenty-three bars and then they followed the armored car to the airport. Matthew and Julia watched from the cargo loading area as the small boxes were transferred to one large crate and then loaded on the United Airlines jet bound for Zurich.

As the crate disappeared into the belly of the 747, Julia and Matthew boarded.

The jet banked over the bay, just about the spot the robbery had taken place. Gaining altitude, they crossed over the Sierra's between Yosemite and Lake Tahoe.

"Wow…" Matthew said softly as he perused a San Francisco Chronicle. He nudged Julia who had been craning her neck looking at the massive granite monoliths. "Listen to this…"

"Contra Costa County search and rescue personnel had their hands full on Saturday when two small motor boats collided in Carquinez Strait, putting five people in the cold, swift waters. There was a small armada of boats and divers scouring the area where it is believed a shipment of gold bullion may have been lost around the time of the great earthquake in 1906." He turned to the next page. *"All the commotion stemmed from the discovery of a 400-ounce gold bar found by Richard Landon, a transient. He said he found the bar at the site of the old pier for the railroad ferryboat 'Solano'. The Coast Guard was called in to keep the shipping lanes open and keep any more 'prospectors' out of harm's way…"*

Julia just grinned and shrugged her shoulders, "It's amazing what some people will do for a little gold."

Somewhere over the Atlantic, Julia napped and dreamed of white sand beaches and African adventures. Matthew didn't sleep but daydreamed about a home in the redwoods near the ocean.

When they landed in Zurich, Matthew and Julia were met by a representative of the auction house and once again witnessed the unloading of the gold. They then followed the armored car to Biser's in the old part of town. The auction house was well prepared for merchandise this valuable with their own safe and security.

"We have made preparations for you to stay at the Dolder Grand Hotel," the man said, pointing to a chauffeured Mercedes waiting at the street. "The auction will begin the day after tomorrow."

They headed out of town and up a winding road. Near the top of the hill, the hotel came into view, an amalgamation of Swiss chalet and ultra-modern minimalism with lots of glass and curves.

As Matthew and Julia approached the front desk, the concierge motioned for their luggage to be brought up to the desk.

"Ah, Mr. and Mrs. Franklin. I trust you had a pleasant flight." Julia blushed slightly. "We have reserved the Grand Suite for you. Right this way." They took an elevator to the top floor and followed the concierge to their room. "I hope you find the accommodations to your liking."

They entered what could only be called a living room as the bell boy continued to the bed room with the luggage. Julia turned around in a circle trying to take it all in. The rooms were very formal and proper with an air of Swiss precision but comfortable. Lit fireplaces in both rooms, took the chill off the late September day.

As Matthew searched his pockets for an appropriate tip for the bell boy, the concierge said, "No need. Everything has been taken care of. Let me know if I can be of any further assistance. We hope you enjoy your stay."

Matthew and Julia were speechless except for a "thanks a lot," Matthew finally managed to blurt out.

As the door shut, Matthew and Julia looked at each other and grinned. Julia jumped into Matthew's arms and wrapped her legs around his waist as he swung her around.

"This is incredible! What do you think this would cost a night?"

Julia followed a staircase leading to a door to a roof top terrace. Once there, Julia could look over Zurich and its namesake lake, shimmering in the late afternoon haze. Far beyond, lay the legendary Alps with a fresh dusting of autumn snow. Matthew came up behind her and wrapped his arms around her waist, slowly moving down to her hips.

"This is a fairy tale." She said, as Matthew rested his chin on her shoulder.

"And you are my princess."

After a wonderful dinner, they retired to their room and soaked in the whirlpool tub. Suddenly, Julia's eyes met Matthew's. "What would you be doing if you hadn't met me?"

"Oh, the same old thing- scraping barnacles off of hulls!" Julia snickered. "Finding all this out about our family's past has really changed my ideas about history. I can't think of anything more exciting than teaching now! Maybe I'll go back to school and teach history like my dad."

"What about you?"

"Well, I think I might like to be the manager of some historic hotel...maybe in London or Paris...or Zurich."

As they lay in bed, Matthew stared at the ceiling. Finally, he said, almost to himself, "We have 23 bars at 400 ounces each. That's 9,200 ounces. If it was just worth the weight of gold right now it would be about $6.9 million.

Julia rolled over on top of Matthew with a peeved look. "And what about 115 pounds? What's *that* worth to you?"

Matthew rolled her back over, gazing down into her soul. "Everything."

Changing back to his calculations, Matthew continued, touching his nose to hers, "But I think it will go higher. Whenever you get rich people bidding against each other…" he sat up on the edge of the bed now, looking out the window, "it turns into an ego thing. We may double that."

Julia wrapped her arms around Matthew's chest and pressed her body against his. "Whatever becomes of this, we have gained so much in so many ways."

As they shared an intimacy only two in love could, there still seemed something lacking, a commitment that Matthew knew for him, only comes from marriage. He had been planning this for a long time, and yet he still felt a little awkward.

He abruptly got out of bed and went around to Julia's side. He got on one knee and before he could speak, she propped herself on her elbows and gasped, "Oh my! This is really it, isn't it?"

"Yes, it is. Julia, we have gone through so much just to find each other and together we have done so much more. I want to keep on as long as you will have me. Will you be my wife?"

"Oh, yes! Yes." Tears were welling up in Julia's eyes.

With that, Matthew pulled out a stunning platinum ring set with a huge aquamarine with small diamonds down the sides. "This ring was always meant for you, Julia."

He gently brushed the hair from her breast and turned to meet Julia's smiling lips. "I love everything about you."

Chapter 48

TOURISTS

⌘

The next day dawned clear and crisp. After breakfast, Matthew and Julia decided to be tourists. Michael, the concierge, was at his desk as they entered the lobby.

"Shall I call a driver?"

"Yes, thank you."

"May I suggest a few places you may enjoy?"

Matthew took out his pocket watch to check the time. "That would be nice."

"I notice you have a fine watch."

"Yes. It belonged to my great, great grandfather. He worked on a ferryboat on Lake Tahoe."

"Oh, yes," the concierge replied, "I have heard of this lake. It is similar to some of our lakes."

"But much deeper and much clearer." volunteered Matthew.

"Ah, yes…If you enjoy fine timepieces, you must see the 'Beyer Museum of Time'. It is down stairs in the basement at number thirty-one Bahnhofstrasse. Also, visit the Fraumünster Church. It has some exquisite stained-glass windows by Marc Chagal."

"Thank you very much," said Matthew, as they headed toward the door.

The cab took them back down the winding road and across the Munsterbrucke to the center of the city right in front of Fraumünster Church. It was not the imposing edifice they were prepared for. Its rather plain stone work, almost in a modern style, belied its more than seven-hundred-year age. The tower had golden clock faces on all sides topped by a tall, slender spire with a blue-green patina. Once inside, they couldn't help but notice the church's imposing pipe organ which dominated one end.

"That's just incredible!" marveled Julia. "There must be hundreds of pipes!" Above it was a beautiful rosette stained-glass window, but opposite them, five narrow, towering windows bathed the interior of the church with almost surreal light. The blue, green and yellow windows revealed stories from the bible with characters seeming to float, dreamlike in the glass.

They continued, arm in arm down Stadthausquai, strolling along the waterfront. One thing about Zurich that stood out because of its absence was that the city was incredibly free of litter and trash compared to cities in the U.S. Most of the buildings in this part of the city were large, long structures of grey or brown stone work, four or five stories tall, with businesses on the ground floor and apartments inhabiting the upper floors. Pleasure boats leisurely made their way up the Limmat River toward the lake.

Matthew stopped a businessman on the street and inquired about Biser's. It was only after the man had answered in perfect English that Matthew realized how spoiled and presumptuous Americans could be. His one semester of German in high school left him able to say only the most basic of phrases.

Turning up Borsenstrasse then Fraumünsterstrasse along the sidewalk cafes, Matthew and Julia finally came upon the auction house where the gold bars would be auctioned off the next day. Its brown stone archway was guarded by wrought iron gates with only the name 'Biser' mirroring the arch hinting at the business within. There was a small sign attached to the gate which announced the auction date and time, not mentioning what was to be sold. Matthew and Julia looked at each other and smiled.

The rest of the day, they wandered the exclusive shops; Cartier, Tiffany, Gucci and joked that they would actually be able to afford whatever they wanted tomorrow.

Not paying attention to their ramblings, they found themselves on Bahnhofstrasse and Julia said, "Why don't we look for that clock museum? It's on the first block, I think the concierge said number thirty-something."

"OK." Matthew took out his watch, silently ticking past three o'clock.

The street numbers in Zurich were a little different than in the states. One, two, three and so on are on the first block and Julia and Matthew soon realized they would have to go up Bahnhofstrasse three more blocks to get to the museum.

"This is definitely high end!" Julia remarked as they passed Tiffany & Co. then Prada. Further on, across the street was Sprüngli. Julia had heard about the fabulous chocolates they made so they had to try some.

After strolling up the street a few more blocks window shopping, Julia said, "Here it is! Beyer, Chronometrie." The store was more like a very modern Swiss home than a clock shop. A living room-like space had a couch and chairs and along one side, a counter with a bowl of fresh fruit. There were stations with comfortable chairs and brilliantly back-lit surfaces to show the watches. They inquired about the museum and were led to the basement level.

The museum was incredible with every type of time piece imaginable from rudimentary sun dials up to the very latest most accurate watches in the world. Julia's favorite was a gold Griffin with silver wings rearing up against a clock, perched upon a finely crafted wood base.

As the four o'clock hour approached, Julia motioned to Matthew. "Let's see if it chimes on the hour!" They both leaned over the glass case to listen.

Suddenly, a bell started to chime as the Griffin flapped its wings and stuck out its red tongue. They jumped back in laughter. Then almost in unison, chimes, bells and even chirps blended into a cacophony that drowned out any other sound.

Back up on the main level, Matthew checked his watch against one for sale.

"That's a very nice watch you have," commented one of the sales people, "Where did you get it?"

"It belonged to my great-great grandfather.

"Very nice. May I take a look at it?"

"OK." Matthew sat down at one of the personal stations. "It's from Tiffany's"

"The watch may say Tiffany and Company, but this is a Patek and Philippe." The man said as he inspected it.

"How can you tell?"

"Tiffany did not make their own watches back then. Take a look inside…" The man opened the back case and showed Matthew. "See this?" Engraved on the workings was the name Patek Philippe & Co. Geneva, Switzerland.

"Wow! What else can you tell me?"

"This is a 'minute repeater'. That means you can slide this lever on the side and it will chime the hour and minute without having to look at the watch. Very handy in the dark."

"So that's what it's for! I never messed with it because I was afraid I would break it." The man slid the lever and the watch dutifully chimed 4:08.

"You have a very fine watch. It would easily sell for $10,000 US dollars."

"Really!? I think I will hang on to it for a while more. It's kind of special to me. It was a gift."

The man smiled and responded, "The company has a saying-'You never actually own a Patek Philippe. You merely take care of it for the next generation.'"

He thanked the man for his help and as they walked back toward Biser's, Matthew commented, "That 'minute repeater' thing would have come in real handy on a dark night on a ferry,"

That evening, Matthew and Julia dined in the Dolder Garden restaurant. It had a modern elegant feel with sheer white curtains separating each table. As they looked through the menu, Mathew thought back to his high school German class and his teacher

Fraulein Weller, wishing he had paid more attention.

When the waiter came to take the order, he said, "Was wurde Sie, Herr mogen?" Matthew glanced up, fumbling with his salad fork.

Julia replied in passable German, "Wolfsbarsch mit Safran-fenchel, bitte." Tactfully turning to Julia, he continued, "Und Sie, fraulein?"

"Lummruckn ratatouille, danke."

The waiter bowed and as he turned to go, Matthew whispered, "Where did you learn to speak like that?"

"We had a foreign exchange student living with us three years ago. She was from Munich."

After the meal, Matthew and Julia enjoyed a full body massage and spa treatment.

Chapter 49

THE PAYOFF

⸻⸻⸻◦◦◦◦⸻⸻⸻

A nother beautiful early fall day met Mathew and Julia with bracing temperatures and a bright blue sky. Still lying in bed, Julia raised her left hand and slowly moved her fingers, letting the sun's rays scatter blue splashes of light from her ring onto the wall. After a light breakfast, they hurried to a waiting limousine.

"This is the day we've been waiting for." said Matthew as he leaned back in the plush seat.

"This is just the first of all the days." Julia stared out the window to the distant snowcapped peaks.

Biser's looked very quiet. There were a few cars parked on the opposite side of the narrow street, but little else to reveal that a multimillion-dollar sale was about to start. Matthew and Julia walked hand in hand through the gates toward carved walnut double doors. A man in a finely tailored suit checked their passports, nodded and opened the doors.

The room was reminiscent of a funeral parlor Matthew had been to when his uncle Jim had died. There were rows of comfortable leather chairs all pointing toward an elevated stage with red curtains. A handful of patrons sat quietly, some exchanging whispers.

On the left, was a lectern, with a gooseneck reading light. Above and to the right of the lectern was the Biser's coat of arms with fanciful stags supporting a shield and a motto in Latin. Below it, a white board with the words: 'Early 20th Century Gold Bullion, The State of Nevada, United States of America'

As Matthew and Julia took their seats in the rear, the curtains opened to reveal a bank of seven phones manned by well-dressed men. In the center, was a table covered in green velvet. A man walked to the lectern and introduced himself and the lots which were about to go under the gavel. There was polite applause and a murmur from the guests as another man entered from the rear with a stand that held a shiny gold ingot. As he set it on the table, a large flat screen monitor showed the gold bar close up. Matthew leaned forward, trying to read the markings that identified the gold from over a hundred years ago.

The auctioneer rapped his gavel three times and announced; "The first lot is gold bullion dated 1905 and marked 'Desert Queen'. This mine was in the western part of the state of Nevada, United States of America, and operated from 1902 to 1908. It is 99.96% pure gold at a weight of 400.32 troy ounces."

He continued; "Zurich gold at the close of the day yesterday was set at $749.56 per ounce, U.S. Therefore, bidding will start at three hundred thousand dollars, U.S. Do I hear three hundred?"

An older lady with a mink stole draped over her shoulder raised a paddle with a number on it.

"Thank you, Madame. I have three hundred. Do I hear four?" The men at the phones were talking in low voices and one of them nodded. "I have four, do I hear five?" Almost before the five left his mouth, another man, phone to his ear raised his hand. "Six, seven, eight!"

The price was skyrocketing with two men on the phones signaling back and forth one after the other bidding for their clients. Finally, the price slowed and at one million two hundred thousand dollars, one man relented.

"One million two, I have one million two. Do I hear one million three, sir? The man shook his head. "I have one million two going once, going twice...SOLD! to buyer number 253, for one million two hundred thousand dollars, U.S."

The gavel came down on the first lot and Matthew and Julia

smiled, squeezing each other's hand. No one knew who the phone bidders were and no one would. The bar was carried off and another was set in its place.

"Lot number two," the auctioneer continued, "is gold bullion dated 1906…" The next hour passed by in a blur. None of the people in attendance were winners of any bidding. After one or two bids, the phone representatives took over and eventually won every lot. One representative won six bars for his boss, another, eight. Most won two or three. By the end, the total for all 23 bars was $26,982,000. Matthew and Julia just sat there for a minute stunned as the small crowd filed out of the room.

Matthew was right. Someone out there wanted to have those bars more than the others and a vicious bidding war ensued around every bar of gold.

After the auctioneer thanked all participants and everyone had dispersed, a man appeared from a side door and introduced himself.

"Hello. I am Herr Schwitler. Please follow me."

They went into an office where Matthew and Julia signed papers confirming the total and authorizing transfer of the amount, less the ten percent the auction house took. The money would go to a private bank, 'The Swiss Enterprise Bank of Zurich'. Their account showed $24,283,800. And all Matthew and Julia had to do was show their private code to withdraw any amount they wanted. The only stipulation was that both Matthew and Julia agree on and sign for any transaction.

Leaving the auction house was a little like coming out of a movie matinee. The sun was still out and Matthew and Julia had to squint after hours in the darkened room. As they rode back to the hotel, Matthew was doing more calculating in his head.

"If we take just five million and put that in a secure bond and get just *two percent* return, we should realize at least $100,000 every year, without touching the principal! Just think what we could make with *all* of it invested!"

"Let's just take out that five million," interrupted Julia. "I don't like what's going on with the market these days. Everyone is making a killing and they're doing it by betting that everything will fall apart!"

"Where did you hear that?" said Matthew, dubious of Julia's newly disclosed financial acumen.

She just coyly responded, "someone has to take care of the purse strings!"

He just leaned back and smiled a contented smile, day dreaming about a certain ceremony he had been planning.

The next day, Matthew and Julia said goodbye to their luxury hotel and went straight to the bank. With credit cards in hand, they were directed to a local automobile dealer. An hour later, they pulled out of the Porsche dealership headed for the Alps.

Chapter 50

THE NOTE

⚬⚬⚬

t was a beautiful spring day in the bay area. But it was unusually warm for April, and Julia was making the most of it out in her flower garden. She noticed a truck pull up in front of her house and came around to find out what the man wanted.

"Letter for Miss Julia Bartlett." The uniformed man had a letter and a clip board and pen.

"That's me." She signed and the man tipped his hat and turned to go. The envelope was just labeled; 'For Julia'

She took it inside and reached for her letter opener. It was an antique with a raised depiction of very ornate buildings and a small jewel on the top of the highest one. Over the top the words 'Panama Pacific International Exposition' were almost worn away.

Julia sliced open the envelope, reached in and pulled out a piece of paper with the Palace Hotel letter head. The note, hand written read:

Dearest Julia,

Meet me at Lotta's Fountain at 10 a.m. tomorrow.
Wear your red hat, the one with the Ostrich feather. I will wear my bowler.
We will be married at the Palace Hotel and spend our first night together there.

Love forever, Matthew

Julia smiled and walked to the window overlooking downtown. She could see Market Street stretching out toward the bay and could almost make out where the Palace Hotel should be. She held the letter to her heart and thought about a day over a hundred years ago and a feeling and spirit that would not die after all this time.

The wedding had been planned for months and all the arrangements had been made. The only thing that stopped the wedding of those two star-crossed lovers from long ago was a... Julia abruptly halted her train of thought. "Nothing is going to stop this wedding!" she proclaimed out loud.

Palace Hotel

Chapter 51

THE GIFT

M atthew strolled along Market Street, stopping at a flower
vendor's kiosk.

"How much are those daises?"

The vendor, a young man with long stringy hair responded.
"For you," he scanned Matthew's clothes, a turn of the last century
suit with a vest and gold watch fob topped off with a black bowler.
"For you," he continued again, "Five dollars." Matthew smiled at
the exorbitant price but he didn't care.

"Perfect." He put the flower in the button hole of his lapel and as
he turned to continue, he flipped the vendor a coin. "That should
cover it!"

The man looked in astonishment at the coin, a gold five-dollar piece with an eagle on one side and the profile of Lady Liberty on the other.

As he walked along 'south of the slot' Matthew turned his attention to a woman at Lotta's fountain. She had long, jet-black hair flowing over her white dress and a fancy red hat with an ostrich feather. She turned her head, glancing across the wide street meeting Matthew's eyes. Her steely-blue eyes sparkled and a broad smile dominated her face. Matthew stepped out into the street, fixated on her eyes, paying no attention to the oncoming traffic. Cars and busses stopped in their tracks as they gawked at the man in the hundred-year-old suit.

When he finally reached the other side, he held out his hand and said, "I've been waiting for this day for a long time."

Julia responded, "We better do this before something catastrophic happens!"

Matthew took Julia's gloved hand and they stepped out once more into the street. Almost as if in a dream, the buildings were transformed and the traffic seemed to slow. Matthew thought he heard the clip-clop of hooves on brick and the faint smell of leather. Advertisements for cigars and photography plastered the brick businesses. Billiards and clothiers shared the street with the Examiner and Call buildings. He looked up at the Chronicle building clock as its hands just moved to ten o'clock.

They ran, hand in hand toward the entrance of the Palace Hotel. As they entered the Garden Court, Matthew and Julia were met with cheers and applause from all the guests dressed in period costumes. On the right, was a table holding the guest book and an antique photograph of two young lovers. Below them in the background was the Cliff House, with the Pacific Ocean, stretching out to the horizon. Julia turned in a slow circle as she scanned the crystal chandeliers suspended from the domed glass ceiling. Elegant columns hid behind graceful palms and a red carpet stretched toward the waiting wedding party.

Matthew went first and took his place next to his best man as a pianist played a Chopin nocturne. Then a string quintet began while the bride's maids entered.

Finally, the bridal music began and the flower girl, keeping time with the music, threw rose petals from a beautiful antique woven basket as she walked. Julia took her uncle's hand and proceeded confidently toward her destiny.

The ceremony was a blur with Matthew not remembering if he actually said anything. He must have done the right thing though, because he soon found himself pulling Julia toward him for their first kiss as husband and wife. A loud cheer erupted and the happy couple turned and waved.

The reception began immediately with Matthew passing out five-dollar gold coins to all their relatives on the receiving line. There were stories of ancestors from both sides as aunts and uncles, cousins and grandparents filed past. The first dance was a Straus Waltz, with a lilting, springtime feel.

After hours of revelry, the time had come for the newlyweds to retire to their honeymoon suite, a fifth-floor room facing Geary Street. He led his bride to the elevator and whisked Julia off her feet. They turned to more cheers and applause and Julia threw her bouquet as the doors slowly closed.

Matthew carried Julia across the threshold of their room and gently laid her on the bed and whispered, "we have come so far."

"And we have so much to look forward to. It was a gift."

As he knelt over her, Matthew saw, in the depths of Julia's soul, a wisdom and acceptance that they were always meant to be together. Finally, after all this time, two spirits were united as one, forever.

THE END

PHOTO CREDITS

Front Cover
Market St. at Post St., San Francisco, CA
Credit: R.J. Waters, Library of Congress,
Print and Photography Division

Chapter 1—Looking Back
Ferryboat on San Francisco Bay
Credit: Courtesy of the California History Room
California State Library, Sacramento, CA

Chapter 3—Tahoe
'Tahoe' Ferryboat with train on pier
Credit: Anthony Colbutn, personal collection

Chapter 5—Friends
Washoe Indian and baskets, Lake Tahoe
Credit: UNRS-P1984-22-09 Special Collections,
University Archives Department, University of Nevada, Reno

Chapter 7—The Bay and the Ferries
Ferryboats leaving Oakland Mole
Credit: Library of Congress, Prints and Photograph Division

Chapter 8—Market Street
View of Market St. from Ferry Building
Credit: SAN FRANCISCO HISTORY CENTER,
SAN FRANCISCO PUBLIC LIBRARY
www.sfpl.org/sfphotos

Chapter 9—Julia
Palace Hotel and Lotta's Fountain
Credit: Library of Congress, Prints and Photographs Division

Chapter 15—A Free Afternoon
Drum Bridge, Japanese Tea Garden
Credit: Anthony Colburn, personal collection

Chapter 16—A Proposal
The Cliff House from the Sutro Heights
Credit: Gary Stark, personal collection

Chapter 17—A Valuable Cargo
Virginia & Truckee Locomotive, #12, 'Genoa'
Credit: UNRS-P1533-07 Special Collections,
University Archives Department, University of Nevada, Reno

Chapter 22—Carmen & Caruso
Palace Hotel Balcony
Credit: Library of Congress, Prints and Photographs Division

Chapter 23—The Nightmare
Fire Spreading Through Downtown
Credit: Library of Congress, Prints and Photographs Division

Chapter 24—The Music Store
Crowd Watching the Fire
Credit: Library of Congress, Arnold Genthe Collection,
Prints and Photographs Division

Chapter 26—The Aftermath
City Hall
Credit: Library of Congress, Prints and Photographs Division

Chapter 30—A Different Direction
Hetch Hetchey Valley
Credit: Yosemite Research Library, National Park Service

Chapter 31—Making Preparations
Construction of Panama Pacific Exposition Buildings
Credit: Library of Congress, Prints and Photographs Divisions

Chapter 33—PPIE
South Gardens & Fountains
Credit: Anthony Colburn, private collection

Chapter 34—Building on Shaky Ground
Palace of Fine Arts
Credit: Library of Congress, Prints and Photographs Division

Chapter 38—Loma Prieta
Fire Fighters at the Marina District
(Palace of Fine Arts in the distance)
Credit: SAN FRANCISCO HISTORY CENTER,
SAN FRANCISCO PUBLIC LIBRARY
www.sfpl.org/sfphotos

Chapter 43—Portals of the Past
Columns at Lloyd Lake, Golden Gate Park
Credit: Anthony Colburn, personal collection

Chapter 44—The Puzzle
Ferryboat Wreck, Carquinez Strait
Credit: Larry Myhre, private collection

Chapter 47—A European Vacation
Zurich, Switzerland and Alps
Credit: Road Warrior Photography/Shutterstock

Chapter 51—The Gift
Interior of the Palace Hotel
Credit: The John B. Lovelace Collection of California Photographs,
Carol M. Highsmith's America Project,
Library of Congress, Prints and Photographs Division

Made in the USA
Las Vegas, NV
16 August 2021

28270279R00182